YOU SHALL LEAVE YOUR LAND

First published by Charco Press 2023

Charco Press Ltd., Office 59, 44-46 Morningside Road, Edinburgh EH10 4BF

ISBN: 9781913867300

e-book: 9781913867294

www.charcopress.com

Edited by Robin Myers

Cover designed by Pablo Font

Typeset by Laura Jones

Proofread by Fiona Mackintosh

Renato Cisneros

YOU SHALL LEAVE YOUR LAND

Translated by
Fionn Petch

CHARCO PRESS

For Natalia and Julieta, my family

In the beginning, a family's energy usually springs from misery. And this misery often produces a family member's drive to escape to a better life; and sometimes he paves the way for other members to follow. So you have a family on the rise, motivated and industrious. And within a generation this industriousness can produce wealth. And with wealth can come status, even nobility. And with nobility comes pride, and often arrogance. Arrogance is usually an element that leads to decline, and in time back to misery.

Gay Talese, *Unto the Sons,* 168

I have lived a hundred years without knowing these things: allow an old man to throw into disorder what has been written down, with what he knows.

Enrique Prochazka, *The Swineherd*

Now the Lord had said to Abram:
'Get out of your country,
From your family
And from your father's house,
To a land that I will show you.'

Genesis 12:1

Who has not, at one point or another, played with thoughts of his ancestors, with the prehistory of his flesh and blood?

Jorge Luis Borges, *I, a Jew*

PART ONE

CHAPTER 1

Lima, 2013

We went to the cemetery that day, resolved to confirm once and for all the truth of the story that great-great-grandmother Nicolasa was buried alongside Gregorio the priest. It was noon. The sun warmed the gravestones and dazzled the stray dogs, sending them off in search of shade. Little by little the silence of the Presbítero Maestro was broken, first with our breathing, then with the weary footsteps of the occasional people who came to commune with their dead at this time of day.

The sunlight did little to disperse the gloom of the labyrinthine pavilions that seemed to form whole districts of buildings with bricked-up windows, withered flowers in planters, and gravestones painted with elongated black crosses like teardrops. Decrepit, ravaged edifices stuffed with cadavers whose spectres surely waited for nightfall to roam abroad, sharing forgotten things, their mysteries and their sorrows.

Passing before the rusting gates placed at regular intervals, connecting the cemetery with the realm of the living, we noticed that the wardens had left their posts to get their lunch, or hadn't turned up yet, or perhaps there weren't even any wardens to occupy these faded booths that from afar resembled empty sarcophagi.

With no one to ask, it took us an hour to locate the San Job quarter, not before making false starts in the San Estanislao, San Joaquín and San Calixto sectors, where we amused ourselves with the afflicted expressions of the stone angels crowning the crypts and mausoleums of certain heroes of the Republic.

Once we'd identified San Job, guided by a new-found intuition, Uncle Gustavo strode with conviction towards the stones in the C sector and began a visual inspection, repeating three digits out loud.

> Two, five, three.
> Two, five, three.
> Two, five, three.

He looked like a sleepwalker uttering the magic words that would wake him up.

In no time at all he had identified the tomb we were searching for. Beneath encrusted dirt and ragged cobwebs, the lettering cut into the marble could still be read clearly:

> Here lies Doña Nicolasa Cisneros
> Born 10 September, 1800
> Died 3 January, 1867

Beneath that, an inscription in Latin:

> *Adveniat Regnum Tuum*
> 'Thy Kingdom Come'

At the bottom, less an epitaph than an injunction:

'Her children will love her always'

I touched my forearm and felt goosepimples. I knew that there was nothing inside but a pile of bones, eaten away by worms, perhaps wrapped in a bundle of frayed rags that was once a burial gown. I knew this, but for a minute wanted to believe that something of the spirit of the woman who had been my great-great-grandmother, a presence still so close to our world, could seep through a crack in the mortar and express itself clearly, whether to endorse our visit or chase us away.

Uncle Gustavo set out to clean the glass of the tomb with a cloth. He worked at first with delicacy and care, as if washing the hair of a dying man, and then with uncontained vehemence. Some force in him desired to crush or penetrate the mortar and profane that deposit, gathering up, however briefly, the debris of the woman who had left us her surname two centuries ago, and acknowledging in this detritus the material from which we too were made. Then he stopped abruptly, noticing the bas-relief sculpture in the middle of the stone. It showed the outline of a woman cradling a child in her arms.

'Take a good look,' he said, 'it's a mother and her child, alone – no father.' I wrote down his observation in my notebook and continued to examine the details of the carving, attentive to anything that might suggest a hidden meaning.

As I gazed at it, my eyes were drawn to the name on the adjacent tomb. Number 255. The surface was covered by wind-blown earth, which I brushed away.

'Look who's here,' I interrupted Uncle Gustavo's thoughts.

Some of the letters had been worn off, but the words could be made out perfectly. When he turned around and read them, his eyes widened dramatically in surprise or fright.

'You see! It was true!' he exclaimed, referring to the papers we'd discovered just a few days earlier in the archiepiscopal archives, which gave us the idea – or the hope – that Nicolasa and Gregorio, in a final act of justice, had purchased adjacent tombs in order to share for eternity the closeness that had been denied them in life. Uncle Gustavo, his glasses perched on his head, peered closely at the slab to make certain of it:

8 December, 1865
Here lies Dr. Gregorio Cartagena
Priest of Huácar

There was no need to see his face to know what was happening inside him. Far from unravelling, I felt that at his eighty years of age he was coming back to life. As if this discovery suddenly made sense of his decades-long excavation. Or as if someone had finally answered the question that as a child he had asked his father in the days of their Buenos Aires exile, a question the latter had always avoided: 'Dad, who was your grandfather?' Or as if he found himself once more in the body of the fifteen-year-old boy he'd been, recently arrived in Lima, who on a morning like this one, led by the hand of Agripina, his only aunt who didn't keep secrets, came to this same cemetery – lusher and less gloomy then – and heard tell of these graves for the first time. 'The tombs of the lovers,' Agripina whispered, saying nothing more but planting in him a question that would grow and grow until it became unbearable, transforming into a memory that would remain buried for years.

'I've been here before,' stammered Uncle Gustavo, glancing around, as if he'd just had a revelation and recognised his surroundings. Contemplating it now, his entire life – toughened by the loss of his first wife, the departure of several of his children, his countless affairs, the money he'd enjoyed to the full, his subsequent bankruptcy – seemed suddenly justified before the wall of the dead.

With our necrological expedition concluded, we departed in silence, leaving behind us the rancid aromas of the cemetery. We walked several long blocks parallel to the main avenue before climbing into a taxi to head for a Miraflores restaurant Uncle Gustavo said he knew. After a few minutes I realised he was still profoundly disoriented and struggling to identify the right route. Three times the driver complained at his erroneous directions, and was on the point of kicking us out of the cab.

Halfway to our supposed destination, as if to certify what we'd found and remove it from the realm of fiction, Gustavo turned to me and said: 'You see? I told you. Grandma and the priest were buried together.'

In the rear-view mirror, the driver's face darkened.

We finally made it to the restaurant in Tarapacá, and took a table by a window with an expansive view over Arequipa avenue. From the other side of the glass came the ceaseless rumble of the street: the bustle of the small stores, the pedestrians clustered at the corners waiting for buses, flocks of metallic-hued birds fleeing from the car horns or the electric fences. The habitual bewilderment of the city. After the first of the many whiskies we would drink that afternoon, I placed my voice recorder on the table, set it running and asked Uncle Gustavo to repeat in detail the story he'd told me so many times, and that for several years now we'd been reconstructing together: he with scrupulous rigour, I with unruly obsession.

'I'm ready to write about it now,' I told him from behind my glass.

His expression showed both satisfaction and caution: the look of someone who has resigned himself to abdicating and passing on his most prized endeavour, a project that deserves to survive and be appreciated by someone else, one that has inexplicably remained hidden and now lies in other hands.

'If you don't tell this story, no one else will,' he ordained, not without sorrow.

He soon began his tale, familiar to me yet new every time, of what happened in Huánuco two centuries back, when those men and women, who performed actions and took decisions without any awareness that they would become our ancestors, were still alive; men and women both spirited and fearful, of whose turbulent paths through the world only shards remain.

CHAPTER 2

Huánuco, 1828

On the evening of Saturday, the twenty-ninth of March, after descending from the final pass, Nicolasa Cisneros and Dominga Prieto were skirting the flanks of the mountain, hoping to run into some traveller who could tell them where they were. There was no one. They spent almost an hour on tenterhooks, and just when the horses were beginning to flag, nickering and chafing at their commands, and just as the women began to wonder if death would meet them here on this rocky slope that darkness was beginning to devour, they made out a building in the distance and first hoped and then deduced it must be the Andaymayo hacienda.

Four days earlier, on Tuesday the twenty-fifth, seeing that Nicolasa's swelling belly could no longer be concealed, Gregorio Cartagena persuaded her to go to stay for a time in Huacaybamba, a tiny village in the Peruvian sierra, in the high puna region, three hundred kilometres north of Huánuco on the misty frontier with Ancash, where he owned a hacienda. There, he assured her, far from the civilisation of the provinces and above all far from the gossip and scandal that would surely arise, she would find an ideal place to give birth. Nicolasa accepted without thinking twice and left on horseback two days later, on Thursday at dawn, accompanied by Dominga Prieto, the black servant whose loyalty and discretion would be rewarded many years later.

The packhorse trail to Huacaybamba was steep and winding, crossing mountain passes almost four thousand metres high, and so rough in parts that they were forced to lead the horses on foot. Whenever Nicolasa faltered and begged for them to halt, numb with exhaustion, Dominga Prieto would pass her a moistened handkerchief and say, 'We can't stop, child, Father Gregorio forbade it, you remember. Do it for the little one.' And she rubbed her swollen belly. As the hours went by they grew accustomed to taking a rest to eat, judging the hour from the position of the sun, or to sleep a little in a spot of shade in the wood where the lichen hung from the trees, or for Nicolasa to curl up in the undergrowth to recover from the continual fevers, shivering and nausea that afflicted her. Each time they paused, Dominga Prieto would withdraw a few yards, murmuring Ave Marias and prayers of protection to St Christopher or St Turibius, and once she'd taken a seat on any suitable rock or rise, she would take off her shoes, which were too tight, burst her blisters, and gather her strength with a swig of aguardiente from the hip flask she hid in the same pocket of her pinafore where she kept her prayer cards.

Three days and three nights it took them to complete this seemingly endless journey. Three days suffering the humid, ruthless heat that filled the air with swirling steam, and at night a dense fog that rose from the depths of the ravines. Three days at the mercy of the cutting late-summer wind, that turbulent summer of 1828, with the first great floods and mudslides caused by savage rains that fell like knives and made a quagmire of the path. Three days and three nights fearing the precipices and gullies, the poisonous fruits, the nests of snakes, the caves of bats, the soaked rats scuttling among the undergrowth, and attacks by pumas or skunks whose eyes glittered in the dark grottoes. Three moonless nights, guiding themselves by the succession of the mountains – the foothills of the cordillera proper – and by the thick, erect shadows of the acacias, the periodic migrations of the black-feathered hawks, and the sound carried up from the Marañón river, that dim roar like a wounded animal clattering in its cage.

At the entrance to the hacienda they were hurriedly received by a slim, sunken-eyed woman of mixed black and criollo ancestry who could neither speak nor hear, but who quickly set down the trays and jugs she was carrying and led them to the most secluded room in the building. Only once she had helped them get settled did she light the fire, round up the fowl that had been disturbed by the visitors, and lay out fodder for the famished horses, before untangling their manes, brushing their hooves and pulling ticks from their ears. The woman, whose face, arms and belly were disfigured by chicken pox scars, was Isidora Zabala, the only servant Gregorio Cartagena ever had, and with her rudimentary sign language and guttural sounds she was able to keep him apprised of everything that happened in that region where nothing ever happened.

After a week in this dungeon-like, windowless room, on the threadbare sheets of the iron bed, flanked by tin buckets filled with hot water, a collapsed mahogany wardrobe, two oil lamps, and Dominga Prieto as her midwife, and following twelve hours of labour, Nicolasa's son was born. She was left so worn-out and weak that she sighed deeply and fell into a faint, and Isidora Zabala – who had stood by her bedside throughout the entire birth – began to moan in fright, and poked her shoulder to see if she was dead.

'Leave her alone, she's only fainted!' objected Dominga Prieto.

Isidora Zabala managed to read her lips, nodded in obedience, and mumbled something.

Cartagena arrived at the hacienda hours later, leaping from his horse and heading straight for the bedroom, where he found Nicolasa sleeping in a nightgown still drenched with sweat and the baby swaddled in a blanket, shivering in the soft arms of Dominga Prieto. The priest tiptoed forward to keep the floorboards from creaking, stood before his son, and scrutinised him without coming too close, controlling himself as if to practise the nervous distance that would later prove decisive. In that fragile, peaceful face still blank of defining features, he sought himself, and stayed there for several minutes studying the veined forehead, the tiny nose, the doll-like chin. Dominga Prieto held the baby out to him as if offering a candy, but he startled and shrank back, beating down the rush of emotion that had welled up inside him. His backwards step caused the wooden floor to creak, and the baby opened his eyes. 'Is all well, Father?' Dominga asked. Gregorio waved his hands, fumbled to open the door and muttered something about the work to be done in the hacienda before fading into the night like a restless ghost.

★ ★ ★

Two months later, on the eve of his return to his centre of operations in Huácar, Cartagena told Nicolasa what had troubled him since before the child's birth.

'Very soon, it'll be time for him to be baptised and his birth registered in the church records.'

Nicolasa nodded.

'Care must be taken when it comes to recording the legal particulars,' Gregorio observed, insinuating the awkwardness of his surname appearing on any such document.

Before Nicolasa's widening eyes, he laid out his proposal to alter the papers.

'You don't want to appear as the father, do you?' she challenged him.

'I can't. You know that.'

'Whose name are we going to put, then?' Nicolasa said, fretful. Her voice was tremulous.

'It will have to be another man's name.'

'Another man's name?'

'Yes. It's a question of inventing one,' Gregorio said, boldly.

So this was the mission, the grievous mission delegated to Nicolasa: the invention of a father for the child. A legal, yet fictitious father. A fantasy father who would free the newborn from being treated as what he was, at bottom, and would always be: a bastard. The bastard son of a priest who could not or would not or dared not recognise him as his own before the eyes of God and of men. The first of the seven bastard children that he, the Reverend Don José Gregorio de Cartagena y Meneses, would have with Doña Nicolasa Cisneros La Torre, whose illegitimate relationship lasted almost half a century.

In her fright, or rather panic, Nicolasa would have preferred to refuse, but she unhesitatingly accepted the assignment, with the resolve that already defined her character at the age of twenty-eight. Over the following days, as she walked with Dominga Prieto through the monotonous fields of rice and other crops grown at the Andaymayo hacienda, she dedicated herself to fleshing out the identity of her son's imaginary father, her brand-new ghostly husband. She weighed up first names, rejected common surnames, considered the sound of the two conjoined names, seeking something both agreeable to the ear and wholly unusual. She repeated them aloud, savouring them on the tongue, until she was left with just one. Dominga Prieto listened in silence, asking herself if Nicolasa's ideas were real or just ravings.

This was the origin of Don Roberto Benjamín. A man enigmatic to all, whom no one had heard of because he never existed. Roberto Benjamín was a fiction, an artifice, a hasty lie that nonetheless endured. A being imagined into life by a woman whose joy at becoming a mother sparred with the inevitable bitterness of living out her maternity banished to the shadows.

A few months later, as was stipulated, the child received the holy sacrament in the church of La Merced in Huánuco, at an ordinary mass baptism not attended by Cartagena, and which concluded with attendees tossing abundant handfuls of flour in the air as a show of joy. When the time came to state the name of her son, Nicolasa called him Juan and asked the registrar to record on the certificate that Juan Benjamín Cisneros was the 'legitimate son of Don Roberto Benjamín and Doña Nicolasa Cisneros'.

Only Dominga Prieto accompanied her on that sunless day and stayed by her side, stiff but serene, with the same composure and companionable spirit she maintained at the christenings of the other children born successively between 1828 and 1837, all receiving the same well-intended yet fraudulent surname: Benjamín. The children would grow up asking after Don Roberto, their putative father, who was always away on business as a metals trader in indistinct far-off countries, from which he was always 'about to return'. They would also grow used to seeing the priest, Gregorio, their biological father, as an affectionate godparent, a stole-wearing relative who was often around the house to act as tutor, correct their mistakes, and sometimes, if they behaved, slip them unconsecrated communion wafers that melted like snow on the tongue.

Shortly before Juan's birth, in February 1828, Gregorio Cartagena, already the parish priest of Huácar, had founded a school he called the College of Virtue. In April, having served for a year as elected deputy for the province of Junín, he joined the Congress that would promulgate Peru's third constitution. He had recently turned forty and, despite this relative youth, he was already a parish priest, school director, member of the National Assembly, father of the fatherland, lover of a woman and progenitor of a secret child.

For her part, Nicolasa had not found motherhood to be overly taxing thanks to the know-how she'd earned growing up. Her parents – two Spaniards who arrived in Peru in the late 1700s and settled in Huánuco hoping to get rich from the mountains of gold they eventually tired of seeking – had died of tuberculosis when she was seventeen. As a result, under the watchful eye of Dominga Prieto, she had to take care of her six younger siblings: Antonio, Pedro, Pablo, Gerónimo, Armenio and Rosita. In acquiring these maternal traits early, Nicolasa had gained household expertise, and by the time she was twenty she was conscientious, self-sufficient and resolute in the face of the slightest setback. So much so that, years later, none of her siblings questioned the clandestine nature of her pregnancy nor of her mysterious marriage, and instead received news of their first nephew Juan with joy.

Their care not to discomfort their older sister with untoward questions didn't mean they weren't curious about the origins of this elusive Roberto Benjamín, this fellow of euphonic name, honourable no doubt, who had married Nicolasa overnight and become their brother-in-law without any of them having met or even seen him in those parts. The siblings were intrigued but not nosy, and only behind closed doors and in low voices did they give free rein to their speculations and hopes to soon meet this Roberto, to fête him and officially welcome him to the family. An occasion that, naturally, would never arrive.

* * *

Gregorio Cartagena had caught sight of Nicolasa for the first time at eleven o'clock in the morning on Friday the fifteenth of December, 1820. Though the heat was rising, a fine rain fell on Huánuco's central square. One week earlier, learning of the recent auspicious victory of the patriotic army over the Spanish royalist forces, the citizens had unanimously declared themselves in favour of independence at an open meeting. And so, on that Friday in December, at eleven on the dot, embodying the will of the local people, Nicolás de Herrera – the delegate of General Álvarez de Arenales, right-hand man of the general leading the liberation forces, the Argentinian José de San Martín – climbed onto a makeshift stage of four tables adorned with an embroidered cloth, and from this perch, surrounded by the men, women and children who had come from the nearby villages of Huamalíes, Huallanca and Ambo, all wearing rather impromptu festive attire and expressions of some puzzlement at what they were witnessing, and with the muddy landscape as a backdrop, took a deep breath to proclaim:

'Huanuqueños, do you swear by God and the cross to be free of the crown and rule of the King of Spain, and to be faithful to the homeland?'

The *Yes, I swear!* of the assembled population echoed across the valley.

There followed multiple cries of *Viva!* accompanied by a haphazard pealing of bells, the general din of an improvised street party, the intoning of *Te Deums* and *Misereres* in the town's seventeen churches, and the incessant popping of homemade rockets and fireworks that sent out brief explosions of light. Alcohol was soon passing from hand to hand and gradually the celebration spiralled out of control. The fiesta meant for one night lasted two days and in some households carried on for three.

In those initial minutes of joy and confusion among the throng, young Nicolasa stepped among the streamers and strings of oil lights newly hung around the square. A few yards away, Gregorio Cartagena – who had taken part in the open meeting – watched as the revellers broke up into tight bunches, shaking their rattles, taking leaps and turns, feeling the first symptoms of freedom in their very blood. As he slowly raised his head, he caught sight of Nicolasa. It was immediate. He stood motionless for several seconds, unable to take his eyes off her. When it seemed to him that she had finally noticed his presence, he flashed an automatic and effusive grin, as if his facial muscles and his brain had not previously agreed upon the necessity or propriety of this smile, so easily misinterpreted by someone – by the nearby member of the town council, for example, who was already turning to him with a frown. Feeling exposed, Gregorio rearranged his expression into something more appropriate, turned on his heel and hurried off. He hadn't gone far before he was overwhelmed by the temptation to look back. Nicolasa was still there. Again he was shaken by the energy she radiated, the sensuality of her movements, the grace and dexterity with which she handled the flaming torch that only men were supposed to carry. All this was enough for him to conjecture that she must have grown up accustomed to overcoming hardship, and dissimulating her need for protection. He stood there a while longer, prudently observing her from afar, dazzled by her eyes, the most voracious and exalted eyes he had ever seen. Gregorio had no way to foresee that by his side, as a result of his actions, those same eyes would become a sad depository of affliction.

Nevertheless, they wouldn't meet each other properly until four years later, in the first days of 1824.

On Friday, 19 December, 1823, the Venezuelan military leader Simón Bolívar, known as the Liberator, arrived in Huánuco on his march to Cerro de Pasco. He had already spent three months in Peru, leading an expedition that sought to put an end to the last bastions of the Spanish viceroyalty and consolidate the independence declared by San Martín in 1821. Mounted on Palomo – the mythical white horse with high tail and well-greased hoofs that had accompanied him since Panama; no one else was permitted to attach the bit shank, stroke his nose or spur him on – Bolívar disguised his short, skinny frame with the uniform of the Grenadiers: high-necked dress coat, tails as far as the back of the knee, embroidered epaulettes, tricoloured sash, tight breeches over blue trousers, knee-high leather gaiters, steel spurs, elegant cape and a dashing plumed bicorne hat.

That Friday, Bolívar decided to spend the night in Huácar. He needed to bolster the ranks of his regiment and gather supplies and cattle for his men, and so he judged it fit to approach whoever was in charge there. The residents offered him only one name, because they couldn't think of anyone but Gregorio Cartagena. Who better than the parish priest, they reckoned, to help him secure rations and attract volunteers to join the liberating army. Bolívar sent for him. Once he had been introduced and they had exchanged brief opinions on this and that, the military leader determined the priest to be a trust-worthy man, and made him a key liaison in the central sierra. Over the following weeks and months, whenever he found himself in the vicinity of Huánuco, he would seek out the priest for news of his progress.

From the outset, Gregorio was a sincere supporter of Bolívar's project, unaware of his dictatorial ambitions and the disdain with which he referred to Peruvians in private. At first he limited himself to conveying the latest goings-on in the area, but later, anxious not to awaken ill-intentioned suspicions or to be seen as a tattletale or informer, he asked to be put in charge of recruitment in Huácar. His request granted, Cartagena began to organise the weekly call-ups in the town square, announcing them after officiating holy mass at noon and reading the parish news. Dozens of men and women, retired soldiers, young folk without trades, pensioners and even precocious children attended these recruiting sessions, all inflamed with patriotic fervour, fully committed to the cause of freedom, and anxious to be part of a story that was still unfinished; indeed, that for many was just beginning to be written.

Unlike provinces where conscription was brutal and indiscriminate, proceedings in the town of Huácar were civil thanks to the intervention of Gregorio, who weeded out the volunteers according to his own criteria, without paying much attention to those stipulated by Bolívar: 'Remember that I have no use for cowards ready to desert, nor good-for-nothings who question orders, nor wimps who fall ill from lack of sleep.'

It was at one such session, on a Sunday in January, that Nicolasa Cisneros appeared alongside her brother Pedro, the third-born and the closest to her in character, a twenty-year-old soldier with sideburns who, like, many others, had stood down from the ranks of the Spanish forces and was now enlisting to fight them instead. Gregorio Cartagena recognised her straight away. As he stretched out a hand of welcome, he observed her unmistakable prominent cheekbones, the red bud of her mouth, and finally her eyes, whose elongated and opaque colour he would come to associate, many years later, with eucalyptus leaves.

In a matter of seconds, without ignoring Pedro – who was seeking to impress him by embarking on an ardent speech of patriotic love – Gregorio recalled the sequence of events that December four years earlier: the drizzle in Huánuco, the words spoken by Nicolás de Herrera, the peals of bells, the rockets, the flaming torches. He then realised he had never forgotten this woman of angular beauty who, on that morning in 1820, amid the crowd congregated in the Plaza de Armas, had joined in with the euphoric shouts of *Viva!*, sung along with the multitude and embraced her fellows after the town's declaration of independence.

Since that day, Cartagena had thought of her so often that now he had her in front of him for a second time, now that she was no longer an ideal or a mirage or a memory, now that he knew her name, he didn't hesitate in treating the reencounter as a gift of fate, an opportunity granted him by some divine agency that would allow him to explore the single realm where his desires were still a turbulent sea.

* * *

Gregorio had advanced in his priestly vocation without missing out on any of the ranks he aspired to hold or tasks he sought to perform. It was far from easy. His career in the Church only really gathered steam once he had weathered the consequences of the licentious behaviour he had displayed in his early days in Lima, when he was studying for ordination as sub-deacon.

The very day he was ordained, on Tuesday, 14 March 1815, just hours after the ceremony in the cathedral, a citizen by the name of Juan Antonio Monserrat approached the Vicariate to denounce him. 'I have come to bear witness before this ecclesiastical office to the inappropriate behaviour and moral insolvency of a young priest by the name of Cartagena,' Monserrat declared. He went on to explain that 'he is known to be engaged in an amorous liaison, and to have insulted honourable individuals under the influence of drink.'

Around about that time, Gregorio was often to be seen at the fiestas held by Josefa Posadas, a woman of overflowing bosom and slim hips who had 'a gift for singing, playing guitar and telling tales' before an audience of her neighbours in the Lima district of Los Huérfanos. Every evening, Josefa would receive dozens of guests and entertain them into the early hours, much to the displeasure of the man who was still her husband at that time, a doltish and bad-tempered fellow by the name of Ramón Heredia, who spent his time spying on her and refusing to accept the definitive separation Josefa had proposed, fed up with his idleness and neglect. Of all the visitors she hosted, the one who aroused most jealousy in Ramón Heredia was the young Cartagena, whose status as a priest seemed to present no impediment when he chose, at any hour of the day and in the middle of the street, to deploy a daring repertoire of winks, flattery and compliments in Josefa's direction, which she would receive with sly glances, and which Ramón qualified as outrageous and sacrilegious, given who they came from. Over the course of two months, Heredia and the priest had 'quarrels and differences of opinion that concluded without harm done', but on the day of Cartagena's ordination, they overstepped the boundary they had unwittingly traced.

That Tuesday, passing by the cathedral as he did every morning, Ramón Heredia crossed himself in relief to see Gregorio join the line of newly minted sub-deacons, thinking that the twenty-seven-year-old, at last taking his religious calling to heart, would now leave Josefa alone, allowing him to restore the peace with his wife. Ramón approached the church door and, just as the sub-deacons knelt before the altar, he glanced at the sky and was struck by the symmetrical outlines of two clouds suggesting the entwined forms of a man and a woman. He smiled inwardly, convinced that this must be a sign from above, a clear declaration that there was still hope for his marriage. He left, serene, but when he returned home unannounced three hours later, he found Josefa Posadas together with Cartagena, 'drinking liquor in excess and in an attitude of imminent intimacy'. His ingenuous premonitions shattered, he began to yell like a man possessed. Overcome by fury, he propelled the priest out of the building and challenged him to 'settle it there in the street, like men'.

Once they were outside, the two of them squared up, ready to throw punches, hissing threats, staring at each other with a distaste that verged on disgust, unflinching before the gaze of the men and women who crept closer until they formed a whispering circle around them. Josefa Posadas alternated entreaties with coarse shrieks. Gregorio rolled up the sleeves of his habit and took up a fighting stance, while Ramón Heredia hiked up his trousers, eyes fixed on his enemy.

'You can't hide from me anymore, Cartagena!'

'One who is at peace with himself has no need to hide.'

Ramón's jaw trembled with rage, but the self-control of the tipsy priest was a thing to see.

'Degenerate! That's what you are!'

The men and women murmured in surprise.

'Watch your tongue, Ramón, you don't want these fine people to think that jealousy is clouding your brain.'

The two moved in circles, sizing each other up.

'And you watch your faith, if you have any that is!'

'Bravo, Heredia!' a voice called from the crowd. Other male voices echoed the exhortation.

'Don't be ridiculous, Ramón. The best thing you can do is leave.'

'The one who should leave is you. There's no room for hypocrites in this neighbourhood.'

The crowd's applause in support of his opponent made Gregorio hesitate for the first time. He looked for Josefa Posadas, but couldn't find her.

'Not even going to open your trap to beg an apology, are you?'

'I was unaware I had offended you.'

'Oh, and now you deny it...'

'Does anyone have the slightest idea what this man is talking about?' Gregorio asked the onlookers.

'Confess, you liar!' growled Heredia.

'I have nothing to say to anyone. Least of all to you.'

'You're chancing your luck, but it'll run out sooner or later.'

'The only thing that's running out is my patience, Ramón.'

The audience, tired of them beating about the bush, began to jeer.

'Why don't you tell everyone what you were doing with my wife just now?'

The growing rumble of voices obliged Gregorio to abandon his calm tone.

'Wife? Do you mean the woman who kicked you out onto the street two months ago for being a wastrel and a bawd?'

Male laughter rose from the assembled throng. Gregorio looked at them more closely. Among the faces he recognised a few regulars from Josefa's soirées.

'The only bawd here is yourself!' yelled Heredia.

Emboldened by the rising tumult from the crowd, they took a step closer, raising their fists and circling each other more rapidly.

'What are you after, Ramón?' Cartagena riled him. 'If you're in need of a blessing, I'll give you one. Go on! You may leave in peace.'

The mirth spread.

'Your insolence means nothing to me, little priestling.'

'I promise to pray for your sins.'

Gregorio saw two old ladies cross themselves and felt he had the crowd on his side.

'Sins, schmins! Enough of this blethering!'

'Come on then, if your legs have stopped trembling, that is.'

'My fist is all I need to put you in your place, Gregorio!'

'My place is with God.'

'Blasphemer!'

'Better a blasphemer than a cuckold!'

'Better a cuckold than a wretch!'

Ramón Heredia spat to quell his nerves, stepped forward, closed his eyes, and let fly his right arm with all the strength of his rage, expecting it to connect with Gregorio's face, but instead encountering only the sour afternoon air. The surprise intervention of two young ladies prevented the row becoming a worse scandal. They dragged Cartagena away by his arms, reminding him how that very morning he had entered the sacred rite as sub-deacon, read whole paragraphs of the catechism before the cathedral altar, swore to be a 'vigilant sentinel of the celestial militia', and promised to maintain 'moderation and tolerance'. No one knew for certain where these women had come from, though in his denunciation before the vicariate, Juan Antonio Monserrat described them as 'two streetwalking whores, of no greater virtue than Josefa Posadas'.

★ ★ ★

In addition to the public denunciation, this episode led to Gregorio's swift transfer from Lima to Huácar. Withdrawn to that province, his spiritual advisors believed, he would find greater peace. However, while the Church supported him – for political convenience more than anything else, since the Cartagena family had made available to the diocesans a two-storey building with shops and orchards of physalis bushes on one corner of the main square of Huánuco – and while the influential priest Toribio Rodríguez de Mendoza had signed a favourable certificate of discipline, the ordinary people in both Lima and Huánuco would long associate Gregorio's name with the broadsides uttered that morning he walked drunk into the neighbourhood of Los Huérfanos and wound up causing havoc alongside 'women of dubious virtue'.

Once the gossip reached Huácar, Gregorio weathered months of embarrassing accusations and mockery in the street. He only had to come to the sacristy door of the town's main church – its only church – for the local women to point him out, and turn their gossiping to 'the perverted priest'. Some even claimed, with great confidence, that 'the new padre is continually breaking his vow of celibacy'; others that 'a pagan such as he dishonours the clergy', and a few, the most venomous – first kissing the tips of their thumbs and raising them to the sky – swore that 'this reprobate' suffered from 'fits of masturbation' and had 'lice and fleas in his crotch'.

Cartagena heard these calumnies and felt like a fraud, an obstacle, an interference between God and the faithful. Throughout the duration of this harassment, not a night passed without him doubting his vocation or fearing for his future. Only with the forgetfulness brought by the passage of time, but above all thanks to his seeing the error of his ways, did the people of Huácar begin to forgo their complaints and mistrust.

They saw how Gregorio took money from the pouch hanging under his tunic to pay for repairs to the churches and chapels, damaged by the heavy snows, and how he personally set to work underpinning and renovating shrines dating back centuries that storms had left half-buried in mud. They saw how he spent countless hours in the sacristy, reading manuscripts and volumes from ancient treatises that not only served to instruct the illiterate but to predict the seasons and to publicly refute certain supposedly universal laws that the viceregal authorities invoked to exploit people's superstitious beliefs. They saw how he contrived to act as a bell ringer for the main church, and several observed his dedication, ringing the hour every day at noon, announcing births, communicating deaths, notifying marriages and warning of natural disasters without repeating the same peal of the bells. They saw that he didn't mind disobeying his superiors or defying the protocols in order to bring swift remedy to the hardships and sufferings of the faithful. And they saw with particular appreciation that he was ready to leave the church at any hour of day or night in response to people's urgent needs, including the mothers and fathers who called for him in terror, crying that their adolescent firstborns were twisting and turning in their beds, possessed by the devil or some malignant spirit, while a greenish bile spilled from their mouths. On these occasions, Gregorio carried out the same operation without even changing out of his pyjamas: he draped his stole around his neck, threw a few jars into a case and rushed to the site of the emergency. He would quickly discern in the apparently possessed youth the pestilential breath and spasms of drunkenness, and would clean up their vomit, clear their heads with two smart slaps, force a purgative of parsley down their throats to ease the nausea of the hangover, and in order to conceal their real condition from their parents, who continued weeping and crossing themselves, would sprinkle holy water on their foreheads and pretend to exorcise them, improvising spells in Latin. The same insubordinate character that made Cartagena a pain in the neck for the most recalcitrant priors and Spanish governors sent by the Crown, transformed him for the men and women of Huácar into an ever-more valued priest, to the point that he became a model of courage in those anxious years before independence.

Within himself, however, Gregorio was no longer a full man. He felt incomplete, diminished, as if pained by an arm or leg he didn't even realise was missing. Even though every Sunday he continued to declare himself from the pulpit a 'fervent soldier of God' and tried to renounce the acts that had won him fame as profane and libertine, he felt the stirring of hopes that threatened the vows of chastity, feelings neither identified nor named but that, once enlivened by his reunion with Nicolasa Cisneros, would never again be appeased.

CHAPTER 3

Lima, 2013

I first heard mention of great-great-grandmother Nicolasa on 22 November, 1992, at a family reunion held by Uncle Gustavo to commemorate yet another anniversary of the birth of his father, my grandfather, the poet and journalist Fernán Cisneros Bustamante. At the time my father, the military man, former Minister of War, known as the Gaucho, still lived. I was still trying half-heartedly to pass my university entrance exams, and family history was of little interest. Very little, even. Or none at all. Those were the years that I felt furthest removed from what it meant to be a Cisneros, if it even meant anything. I was sixteen years old and only wanted to scorn my academic context, read and write poetry, watch films on television, fall in love, masturbate, squeeze spots, make grainy Betamax copies of Argentinian and German football matches, and hang out with friends from the neighbourhood who didn't care much about the future either.

At this reunion we grandchildren were asked, as was customary, to recite poems by Fernán: those same musical, consonant poems I'd loved reading as a child – and later would come to love again – but which at that moment, when all I was interested in was striking a pose as an idle, iconoclastic poet, found corny and affected. The grandchildren were grouped by clan to take our turn at the front of the room: the Cisneros Bermejo, the Cisneros Razzeto, the Cisneros Hilman, the Cisneros Zaldívar, the Cisneros Mendiola, the Cisneros Ferreira, the Cisneros Ramos. From hand to hand was passed an old anthology by our grandfather entitled *All is Love*: third edition, published in Buenos Aires in 1933, red leather cover, 185 pages, aroma of mothballs.

Most recited his romantic poems: 'Woman of Lima', 'Grandson', 'Born to Die', 'Poetry My Betrothed', 'How I Love You'. When my turn came, I set the book aside, pulled a sheaf of crumpled papers from my pocket, and read a poem I'd written that same morning. A rambling, unrhymed poem about a man who never grew old, who raved deliriously and burped grotesquely as he walked naked around the deck of a rusty, empty ocean liner. Was that man me? Was the ocean liner my family? I remember some weak applause greeting this gauche or arrogant intervention that today only makes sense to me as an embarrassing show of unhappiness. I didn't want to be a part of all that, but I didn't know what I wanted to be a part of instead. I felt fond of my uncles, aunts and cousins, some more than others – some I only really knew by name or face – but there was something about all of them, or rather, about what happened when they all came together, that bothered me, that seemed overacted or outright false. They always recalled the family's past with a petit bourgeois haughtiness I found over-the-top. They went on about how special we were, how privileged we should feel to belong to such a lineage, even though no one really seemed to know much about it.

They evoked grandfather Fernán and great-grandfather Luis Benjamín in the same terms as the encyclopaedia did. Of course, they emphasised attributes omitted from the official accounts, but at bottom they simply regurgitated a list of high-flown biographical passages, famous sayings, lines and songs, expecting us to follow our duty and learn them by heart. The worst thing was, it worked. We memorised all this information administered to us and repeated it like a doctrine, at school or social events, with a pride that merely imitated the pride of our parents. We grandchildren were taught to boast about our ancestry, but we were never told – or at least I wasn't – who Luis Benjamín and Fernán Cisneros really were. Not the poets, but the men of flesh and blood. We knew they had been prominent figures in the world of letters, but we knew nothing about their real and private lives, their feelings, their sorrows, the setbacks that had led them to pursue this solitary calling that earned, so many years later, our reverence. None of the older cousins, perhaps not even the uncles and aunts could have persuasively explained why, over and above the political roles, journalistic activities or daily lives of Luis Benjamín and Fernán, poetry had been a kind of ferment or bacteria that consumed and ruined them. Nor why, when they wrote it, they so willingly crossed the border where radiance turns to fever or tragedy. Nor why their lines made them sound so defeated, so idealistic, or so ceremoniously mournful. No one could answer that. But no one asked these questions, either. We lived in total darkness, though the shadows were elegant. For this reason, I learned both to love and to resist the Cisneros clan. Because they said things by halves, because they spent their lives talking superficially about our dead ancestors at literary soirées that felt like joyful funerals, or rather the same funeral being reprised over the decades. I saw them celebrate a worn-out, ossified, long-lost nobility, but even so I let them beguile me with their overweening vanity, their artistic pretence, their pedantry. For there was something enchanting, something truly irresistible and delightful about these eternal refrains by which my uncles and aunts and my own father so earnestly bragged about our 'pedigree', as they called it, about the fervour they showed towards a family memory they hadn't actually dared to explore, and about these songs of praise to Luis Benjamín and Fernán that descended into drunken revelries that were at first charming and melancholy but soon became overwhelming and unbearable. I resented my participation in their deceit by the mere fact of my presence, for having been born and raised in this clan or troupe, for having treated their stories as my inheritance, and I knew, or rather sensed, that one day, out of inertia as well as pride, I would have to mark a distance, leave it all behind and betray the blood pact with my paternal family in order to form my own dynasty instead of being just another tormented link in the chain that tethered me to my origins to which I would, nevertheless, remain irremediably bound.

* * *

My questions about the family only increased in number over the years. Not only about my grandfather and great-grandfather, but about all the uncles who had died early deaths, my father's brothers I'd seen only in faded photographs. Smiling men with slicked-back hair in spotless shirts, socks and shoes. Absent men who seemed almost unreal, but had clearly existed and gone about with a specific name, weight, and dimension, and shared an epoch and a way of exploring the world.

I didn't know, for example, what had really happened with Uncle Roque, who was run over by a train. Were all my cousins aware that Roque had been born with a mental disability after his mother Esperanza fell during her pregnancy? Did we all know that she had tumbled down the stairs while chasing after Fernán in an argument? Roque's physical development didn't keep pace with his age. When he was fourteen he looked nine. When he was twenty he looked fourteen. He received private tuition because he was unable to keep up with the regular school curriculum. They say he was the child hit hardest by his father's death because Fernán had protected him and done his best to alleviate his disability and make him a part of the world. Did we all know that one night Uncle Roque disappeared from the house?

When he returned home three hours later, he said nothing about where he'd been. The following night the same thing happened and so on, for an entire month. His siblings thought he was visiting the Matute sisters, who offered free photography classes for local amateurs, or perhaps he was sneaking into the Barranco cinema to watch Mexican films. One such night, someone noticed Roque heading out the front door, taking a gentle amble around the block, and tiptoeing back indoors via the garage, where he headed straight for the servant's quarters and opened the door to the room of Jacoba, the maid.

Roque slipped into Jacoba's bed so many times that he ended up falling in love with her, not knowing that all of his brothers had previously undergone their sexual initiation with the same woman. Within a month, Roque was wandering the corridors declaring that he loved Jacoba even more than actress Gloria Marín, the fiancée of Jorge Negrete, photographs of whom adorned the walls of his bedroom. It seemed like a joke on his part, but one night in 1956, the same night Uncle Gustavo chose to announce to the family he was getting engaged for the first time, Roque – the twenty-two year old uncle, the mentally impaired uncle – appeared in his pyjamas in the middle of the living room and announced he was getting married to the maid. Everyone clapped, following his lead, with the exception of Jacoba, who, overhearing everything from the kitchen, packed her bags and left the house forever.

The accident happened a week later. Roque fell onto the rails in Barranco and the wheels of four carriages passed over his legs. 'I didn't mean to fall, I swear' he cried when his brothers arrived in the emergency room. His femurs were crushed, the tibias exposed, the muscle torn like frayed elastic, his ankles bent backwards. The doctors recommended amputation to prevent gangrene. My father – who had rushed from his barracks – sent a platoon of soldiers to donate blood to his younger brother, but Roque didn't survive the night. Ever since, the family's official version has been that he slipped from the train. The other, whispered version – the one I believe – is that, disconsolate at the death of his father, guilty at Jacoba's flight, he found no more reason to continue living and threw himself onto the tracks.

Of Uncle Sarino I knew little either, other than the fact he had died of a heart attack. I was unaware of his hardened tobacco addiction, sucking on Inca or Nacional Presidente brand cigarettes like a chimney from five in the morning until he went to bed, trailing ash wherever he went; that he even took his bath with a cigarette in his mouth, taking care not to get it wet, or that a brown stain spread across the ceiling above his bed from where he exhaled his foul breath. Before the age of fifty Sarino had dry eyes, yellow teeth, a palate carpeted in pustules, nails bronzed by nicotine and a legendary cough that announced his arrival wherever he went. The morning of his death, he entered intensive care with infected bronchial tubes and blocked lungs. They didn't even manage to operate. The family claimed he was killed by an adverse reaction to the anaesthetic, but there was little doubt that his damaged smoker's brain – by this point a mass of grey matter – blew out as soon as he entered the operating room. Having believed that tobacco was an addiction exclusive to my father, I found Sarino to be a forerunner who revealed a pattern of family anxiety, the cause of which was waiting to be discovered.

It was the same with Uncle Fortunato. All we knew about him was that he was the handsome one, the heart-throb, athlete, dancer. He won fame in San Isidro and Miraflores for his conquest of the Gallardo twins, a pair of haughty girls whose fake aristocratic airs induced pity, and who allowed Fortunato to have his way with them while claiming to reject all suitors. 'I'm not made for marriage,' he would proclaim – until, that is, he met the voluptuous Cuchita Bermejo, an older red-haired beauty who loved to party. They wedded within months, but didn't make it to the end of the year, since Fortunato discovered Cuchita going behind his back with a commander from the Republican Guards. They say he went mad with rage. This madness, combined with his indolence at work, was his downfall. Fortunato was laid back or faint-hearted or simply lazy. His brother Sarino, the smoker, wangled him a position at a company dealing in heavy machinery. He didn't last a month. He was caught taking cash out of the till and fired on the spot. It seems it wasn't the first time, because when Sarino heard about the theft he punched the wall in anger, yelling 'This time I'm not lifting a finger for him!' And he didn't. Fortunato was unemployed for years and spent his days and nights drinking, migrating from bar to liquor store to grubby dance hall. What really sent him over the edge wasn't the lack of work or alcoholism, but Cuchita Bermejo's infidelity. They say he died from a heart attack, but some whisper that one night in November he locked himself up in the room he rented in Barrios Altos, switched off the sole light, and put a bullet through his skull. There are even some who claim to have seen the cadaver: still gripping the pistol, the head perforated, a pool of blood, a cloud of flies.

★ ★ ★

At that family reunion in 1992, one wall of the room was covered by a diagram made in coloured pen. It was a drawing of our tangled family tree. There, right at the top, was the name of Nicolasa Cisneros. Some uncle or other briefly mentioned her without alluding, of course, to her relationship with the priest Gregorio Cartagena. Nor was anything said about 'Roberto Benjamín'. They spoke about her descendants in the most offhanded way, as if the woman had had children spontaneously, as if she had fallen pregnant from the Andean breeze, a miraculous bird that emerged from the Huallaga river, or the intervention of some Huanuqueño archangel. No one asked about Nicolasa's husband, the father of her children. Nor did I. The little that was said about my great-great-grandmother went in one ear and out the other, without making a stopover in my brain. That day only one thing came clear: if our surname was Cisneros, it was thanks to her. And for the first time, I asked myself a very faint, very vague question deep inside: why?

My reaction was different in July 2007, at a lunch that brought together hundreds of Cisneros at an estate on the outskirts of Lima. My father had been dead twelve years. I'd just turned thirty and for some time now had been delving into the sentimental archives of my ancestors. It was an afternoon of sun and beer and mosquito repellent. My Uncle Gustavo, once again the host, had pinned up some large sheets of paper by the entrance with an updated version of the increasingly intricate family tree. On the trunk, like a kind of founding stone, was Nicolasa. It was the first image of her we had ever seen. Most of us couldn't identify her.

'That's Nicolasa, right?' I asked a snow-haired relative.

'Correct. The mother of Luis Benjamín, your great-grandfather.'

'And who was his father?' I wondered.

'What's that?' he said with a suspicious glance, feigning deafness.

'Who was Luis Benjamín's father?'

He took a sip from his glass. 'How d'ya mean? You don't know?'

'No. Do you?'

'I did know, but I've forgotten,' he said, and turned his back.

That white-haired man was one of the few relatives to know who Gregorio Cartagena had been and who did their best to ensure that his name was never spoken. It was absurd, but also revealing: 170 years after this priest burst into the life of my great-great-grand-mother, the mere mention of him still caused panic. Even Uncle Juvenal, the one I felt closest to and was the most comfortable around, avoided speaking about these gaps in the past. Twice I went to his house to discuss this specific issue, and twice he evaded me. So I wasn't surprised when Uncle Gustavo told me years later that Juvenal discouraged family research and treated it with disinterest, as if it were unseemly.

That image of Nicolasa, the only one there is, is a reproduction of an anonymous painting. The eighty-six-by-sixty-five-centimetre original was among the assets of the Banco Industrial. After that bank was sold off, it wound up in the basement of the Banco de la Nación following a decision by the National Institute of Culture. The technical description reads: 'Half-length portrait of a seated old woman.'

Today that old woman hangs in the meeting room of the Business Department of the Banco de la Nación, on the seventh floor of a building located at the corner of Aramburú and República de Panamá. From there she distracts bankers with her humourless grin, sharp nose, stiff lips, and hair as black as pitch. Her black dress is adorned with a mother-of-pearl cameo and on her left index finger glimmers a worn sapphire ring. Her head is covered with a lace mantilla identical to the one used in certain portraits by Goya. Her right hand holds a half-open missal. She barely has eyebrows. Her white cuffs contrast with the cerulean upholstery of her chair.

The day I went to see the painting I asked someone working at the bank if anyone on the seventh floor knew who the woman was. 'We've no idea,' he replied, 'but she looks so much like the mother of Pietro Malfitano, one of the department heads, that here we've taken to calling her "Malfitano's mum".'

CHAPTER 4

Huánuco, 1824

Pedro and Nicolasa signed up with the liberation army and agreed to meet Gregorio Cartagena every Friday of the summer of 1824 for details of their new tasks. The pair took the road to Huácar each week to receive the priest's advice, earn his friendship, and learn how he'd dealt with the weariness and disillusionment among the people of the city, who felt that emancipation from Spain, even though won on paper, was failing to manifest itself in everyday life. Many found the encouragement they needed at Cartagena's Sunday masses, where his pious yet energetic homilies induced shame at the mere thought of abandoning the struggle.

Gradually Gregorio took the Cisneros siblings into his circle of trusted companions, treating them differently from the other volunteers. One fine day, following patient behind-the-scenes efforts, he took them to meet the high command of the liberation army, and even arranged for them to share a meal with Simón Bolívar himself at Conchamarca, on the outskirts of Huácar. At that lunch – seated at the corner of a table laden with salads, succulent goat stews with chillies, chupes, pepianes, and glasses of red Burgundy – it occurred to Nicolasa to tell the story of meeting General José de San Martín after the declaration of independence in Lima in July 1821, and readily described him as a 'wise leader' and 'a gentleman of great courtesy', remarks that triggered a coughing fit in Bolívar, who from Venezuela had sought to sabotage and destabilise the government of the Argentinian, placing spies in his entourage. Beside her, Pedro was horrified by his sister's loose tongue and impertinence, praising San Martín in Bolívar's presence when the great liberators' mutual resentment was notorious. They had been rivals since they met in July 1822 in Guayaquil, where it took them forty-eight hours to study each other, weigh their conflicting styles, and lament the many discrepancies and discordances between their respective military visions. Like so many young patriots in uniform, Pedro worshiped Bolívar, seeing him as the grandest guide to the future of the continent, more astute than San Martín and the only leader capable of emancipating the people of South America once and for all. For this reason he barely opened his mouth at that lavish dinner, and avoided saying anything that might annoy the Venezuelan. Nicolasa, by contrast, thought that Bolívar sought personal glory before the wellbeing of Peruvians; she considered him a brave man, but morally inferior to San Martín and in no way worthy of greater tribute than the civilian national heroes who had already set the country on the course that one day would make it the Republic of Peru. Cartagena, meanwhile, was disarmed by this subtle expression of disrespect, perhaps because it recalled his own youthful rebellions, and his interest in the young Nicolasa deepened.

Uncomfortable as it was for Bolívar, Nicolasa's story wasn't far from the truth. In December 1820, following the swearing of allegiance to the independence struggle in Huánuco, she swiftly travelled to Lima, where a similar event was planned on a larger scale. Nicolasa had been born in the capital during one of the brief periods her parents lived there, and spent a good part of her childhood in the centre of Lima. As a result, she still had friends in the city, who received her insurgency-inspired visits with enthusiasm. When she reached Lima ahead of San Martín, she found conservative sectors of the population still defending the royalists: much of the Church, certain newspapers, the criollo elite for whom the Spanish were family. So she helped the patriots to spread the message of the Argentinian general, hoping that it would reach the uninformed majority who would hesitate until the very end about whether or not to join the struggle 'for this thing they call independence'.

At that time, Lima comprised some 200 city blocks and had a population of no more than 70,000. It was suffering food shortages due to the royalist troops razing the crops in the highlands; above all, though, it was suffering from fear. On the one side were those who feared the supposed pillaging that would result from the patriotic uprising, and who hid in their homes behind the gilded balustrades of the balconies, or locked themselves in churches, cloisters and convents, or took shelter behind the massive walls of the Callao castle. On the other side were those fearful of the position taken up on the outskirts of the capital by the troops of the Spanish General José de Canterac: they remained in the orchards, shops and yards, awaiting the next assault by the royalist leader. This atmosphere of discord and belligerence ended with the entry of San Martín into the city, and the oath sworn in four different plazas on Saturday, 28 July, 1821. The royalists, forewarned, marched towards Cusco, leaving Lima in a state of watchful calm.

Around about this time Nicolasa – following the example of other ladies from various parts – requested an audience with San Martín, in order to greet him on behalf of the people of Huánuco and offer her services to the new regime. The Argentinian general received her, listened to her attentively and rewarded her with an invitation to the weekly parties that began to be held in the Government Palace: receptions – decorated with Argentinian ornaments, furniture and crockery provided by wealthy locals – that began at ten in the morning each Friday and, enlivened by hot punch and the music of the River Plate Grenadiers, lasted until well past noon the next day.

Nicolasa attended at least three of these festivities, always finding them excessive, and although she didn't dance with San Martín she did watch him moving around the room, noting his skills with the waltz, his competence with the sajuriana, and his inexperience with the quadrille and the zamacueca. Rather than seek the company of the anonymous guests, the Argentinian Protector preferred to dance with the marchionesses decorated with the Order of the Sun, the most sought-after being Mariana Echevarría de Santiago y Ulloa, wife of the unfortunate Marquis of Torre Tagle, who watched from the edge of the room, punch in hand, as his wife beamed in the general's arms.

Once her brother Pedro left to join the liberation army camped near Cerro de Pasco – the unit that would later fight in the decisive battles of Junín and Ayacucho – the friendship between Nicolasa and the priest Cartagena grew warmer. Initially they met only on Fridays, but soon they were seeing each other up to three times a week, always in the little stone building that served as the parish house for the main church of Huácar, where Gregorio carried out his duties each day at a table laden with papers, listening to the confessions of contrite believers seeking the balm of penance. But later – so as not to encourage the gossip of those same Christians, who raised an eyebrow whenever they saw Miss Cisneros appear in the parish, and observed the poorly concealed eagerness with which the priest received her – the two agreed to continue their 'sessions of independent instruction', as Gregorio called them, in Nicolasa's home, the residence that had belonged to her parents, close to the main square.

With her parents deceased, and almost all her siblings working in other districts, such as Conchucos, Corongo and Yungay, the only ones left at home were Pedro and Nicolasa. But now that Pedro had joined the unified army, Nicolasa lived alone with Dominga Prieto, the plump servant of mixed African and indigenous ancestry who had worked there for more years than anyone could remember, alternating as confidante, maid, cook, housekeeper, seamstress, governess and midwife. Indeed, she was the only one to witness Gregorio Cartagena slipping in and out of the wrought-iron gate at the rear of the house, greeting him with an offhand respect and no sign of affection, as if she could smell the real intentions hidden beneath his pastoral disguise. Yet after a few months without any outburst or unusual behaviour that would have been unworthy of his investiture, Dominga Prieto felt her suspicions had been misplaced and began to treat the clergyman more courteously, asking for his blessing when he left, and offering him her maize porridge with squash, her corn pudding, her stuffed limes, her star fruit jams, her calming teas made from annatto, rosemary and abuta, balsamic herbs that, she said, prevented anaemia, were good for rheumatism, cured asthma and protected the kidneys from premature damage.

Yet one night, before retiring to her own room,

framed in the half-closed side door to the rear courtyard, not meaning to spy but spying nonetheless, Dominga observed the exact moment that Cartagena, perched on a maroon sofa, took Nicolasa's hand, imprisoning it like a canary and conveying it slowly towards his mouth to kiss once, twice, thrice and more, with eager kisses that soon reached the wrist, the arm, the bony shoulder, the chaste neck, the earlobe. Gripped by sudden alarm, Dominga put her hand to her mouth, stuck a finger between her square white teeth and – so as not to cry out – bit it so hard that a small crescent-shaped bruise would always remain beneath the nail. Before removing herself from the scene she put an ear to the wall, but hearing nothing cast another glance towards the room in case the mirages of drowsiness were deceiving her. The scene was so vivid shone it: her girl, Nicolasa, was now lying on the chest of the holy man and had begun responding to his attentions. Dominga leapt backwards, shaking her head. She ran to her room, at the back of the house on the ground floor, where she crossed herself three times, breathing hard behind the door, before crumpling the St Turibius prayer card she carried in her apron pocket and slapping herself hard for putting her nose where she should not.

* * *

The early absence of her parents had forced Nicolasa to grow up fast. As the eldest daughter, she had little choice but to dedicate her adolescence and youth not only to the care and education of her younger siblings but also to managing the inherited properties. This didn't prevent her from acquiring knowledge of the public and political affairs that had interested her since childhood. She remembered, for example, that at the age of twelve, when her parents had not yet contracted the disease that would ultimately kill them, she had seen and heard, with fear and delight, the chaotic events surrounding the Huánuco rebellion of February 1812.

In the course of those skirmishes, a mob of malnourished indigenous people and irate peasant farmers took to the streets to protest against the representatives and vassals of the King of Spain, Ferdinand VII, against whom they had multiple grievances: for tolerating the abuses of the peninsular oligarchs, for endorsing the imposition of villainous taxes, for hoarding the harvest, for arbitrary distribution of mules, for prohibiting the cultivation of tobacco, and for encouraging the eradication of their own staple crops. The rebels – almost all indigenous, some of mixed race and a few rude criollos – were not fighting for independence per se, but for the restoration of a fairer monarchical regime. At least, that's the impression Nicolasa formed hearing their ambivalent and contradictory proclamations, which bitterly vituperated against the king, yet continued to call for his long life; or the huzzas that resounded in the name of Ferdinand VII, only to become threats that the 'return of a new Inca' was imminent. This supposed vengeful Inca would be none other than Julián Castelli, an Argentinian adventurer who had arrived in Peruvian territory a year earlier and was urging the malcontent indigenous people to rise up and claim what 'was rightly theirs'. For four days, under the rallying cry 'death to the chapetones' – as the Spaniards were known – there were riots, fires, pillaging and all kinds of outrages in the streets, homesteads, farms, ranches and plazas of Huánuco. Not even the churches were safe from bearing the brunt of the rebellion. Many of the agitators – inflamed yet armed with little more than slingshots, cudgels, knives and rocks – were struck down by the Spanish bullets and ended up floating like swollen sacks in the Huallaga river, or bouncing down the steep cliffs. It took an informal procession out of the church, bearing aloft the rotund image of the Virgin of Dolores, to put an end to the barbarity, but the rebellion was only fully quelled by the mediation efforts of a governing council of notable criollos together with a committee of friars and deacons who walked the streets in their mitres and ornamented chasubles, crosiers held high, to cool the vitriolic mood. From her hiding place in the attic, since her parents had prohibited her from opening the lace curtains, Nicolasa perched alongside the startled Dominga Prieto – whose nails were buried in her forearm throughout – and observed this cruel spectacle without truly understanding its cause, yet was fascinated by the earth-shaking stampede of the insurgents, with whom she had begun to identify as they showed signs of winning power.

Given this experience, it is no surprise that the adult Nicolasa closely followed the events of the patriotic campaign for independence, nor that she should commit herself to it so fervently that she donated her jewels to finance individual uprisings, or made her house available to shelter opponents of the crown, who gathered there in morose subversive discussions that never made it beyond simple frustrated conspiracies. It was amid this family and political routine, determined to look out for the safety of her siblings and for the future of Huánuco, never allowing herself recreation nor distraction, that Nicolasa decided to enrol as a volunteer together with her brother Pedro in the liberation army, and take a more active role in the resistance. That is where she met Gregorio Cartagena, who engulfed her life like a wave of peace, wisdom and redemption.

Although at first she awaited him with no great expectation, like a good student and no more, it wasn't long before she started to count the hours before their next meeting. She believed she felt nothing but admiration for the clergyman until one night, the first in which he was delayed without having sent word, Nicolasa felt a tingling in her stomach, eating her up. It was not annoyance but eagerness, impatience. Something changed from that moment on. One afternoon, she caught herself preening before his arrival: gathering her hair in a bow adorned with false plaits, adjusting the lace of her English gown, and draping herself in perfumed shawls that had belonged to her mother. Though she had once boasted there was no man alive who could daunt her, now she began to yield to Gregorio's insistent gaze and musical words: she could no longer resist them without lowering her head or blushing. Their ever-more lingering farewell embraces squeezed the breath from her in a manner she had never felt before and, on retiring to her room she noted, bewildered and astonished, that her racing heartbeat hadn't slowed.

The day that Gregorio Cartagena touched Nicolasa's mouth with his lips for the first time, perched on the edge of that maroon sofa, she was less aware of the trembling kiss than of the sudden rigidity of her warm nipples; and the day she allowed him to slip a hand along the inside of her thigh, she felt a brief, swift gushing sensation beneath her petticoat, together with an avalanche of unfamiliar guilt. This guilt was redoubled the night that Gregorio tenderly undid the laces of her dress, skilfully unbuttoned her bodice, freed her from the ridiculous scaffold of her underwear, batted away the last traces of her pretended shame and laid her on the bed before delicately opening her legs, kissing her luxuriant pubis and introducing himself into her body, allowing her to feel the vigour of his sex little by little, procuring tremors that shook gasps and moans from her, an alarming discovery when she had no idea she was capable of panting like an animal.

Returning from the vertigo of orgasm, still in a trance, amid the wild palpitations of her heart, Nicolasa found herself desperately clinging to Gregorio, without care for modesty, when she noticed a red trickle from between her legs, and fled to the far side of the bed, wrapping the white sheets around her however she could, and begged Cartagena to leave her alone. Only then did she look around her and, failing to fully recognise the walls and ceiling of her own room, suddenly felt trapped in a limbo.

Since that night, a voice hammered in her head, reminding her of her mortal sin, unworthy of atonement.

For Nicolasa it was as if the voice of God had taken over her mind and so, to shake off her sense of indecency and persecution, and to silence her doubts and regrets, she began to stay up late counting the beads of the rosary made with Jordan wood she found in the chest containing her dead parents' last possessions. Yet even praying with conviction, and pausing to utter the Creed before the small reliquaries and osculatories she had arranged on the windowsill, and commending herself to the Christ of the Agonies to banish temptations, and mortifying herself with fasts, and lacerating herself by beating her breast and tying spiked belts around her thighs once a week, even with all this, she couldn't shake the sense of subjugation and, moreover, of captivation by this man twelve years her senior who promised not to abandon her, who illuminated her with his ecumenical knowledge, who evangelised her with his liturgy of simple phrases, proverbs and charismatic songs, and who seemed to know everything about the unremembered past and the unknown future.

Consenting to Cartagena's love meant that Nicolasa denied a part of herself. She was not blinded by infatuation; in fact, she was perfectly aware of the state of things. She knew that this man married to the Church was prohibited to her, but when it came to choosing between passion and conscience, when there was no other way out, she opted for passion, defending it with the same determination that she had defended her siblings as children, or fought for the emancipation of her people. She desired liberty for herself and for everyone else. But, she asked herself, what purpose did the sovereignty of others serve if she herself did not feel free in her heart, and on the contrary, what purpose would that serve if her country remained under the yoke? Nicolasa couldn't see it, but for a long time she had been caught in the spell of everything that happened around her. Or perhaps she did see it, which is why she took a final decision: though the world she knew were to turn its back on her, though the prayers of the holier-than-thou, sanctimonious townspeople should seek to deprive her of the promise of salvation and condemn her soul to infernal fire, and though all of God's reprisals should come one by one, she, Nicolasa Cisneros would not renounce her decision: until the end, until her very last day, she would love the priest Gregorio Cartagena and be his lover, with this stubborn and doomed love that gushed in a torrent from the depths of her body.

★ ★ ★

In their day-to-day lives, not much changed at first. Nicolasa was punctual in attending the billet tents where women carried out the many tasks demanded by the independence effort: collecting victuals, cooking, serving out portions; sewing calico uniforms for the troops; storing ammunition, supplies and provisions; looking after the mules and horses; healing soldiers who returned mutilated and unconscious from the front; gathering orphans and housing widows, giving priority to young mothers with newborns; and making inventories of medicines, camp beds, swords, bayonets and all kinds of other armaments. Some of these women, the ones with greatest powers of attraction and guile, disguised or dressed up in tunics and shawls, risked their skins delivering letters between patriots, weaving a web of espionage and propaganda to boost the Montonera guerrillas in the mountains who collaborated with the liberation army.

One day, Nicolasa saw a recruit dragging himself towards the encampment and, hurrying to assist him, found him to be bleeding heavily. He was a boy not even twenty years old. She saw in him such a likeness to her brother Pedro that she took great pains in his care, and after two weeks of healing unguents, iodine compresses, mistletoe infusions and compassionate caresses that helped to restore his vitality, the solider declared his love. His name was Darío Lechuga and he had a birthmark that darkened half of his face, close-set eyes around an arched nose, prominent ears and a thick tufted beard reminiscent of a sea anemone.

'What is it – am I too young or don't I take your fancy?' the convalescent asked of Nicolasa when she insisted he dispense with his silly avowals.

'What I don't like, Darío, is that you won't take no for an answer,' she complained as she removed the last bandages from his leg.

'That's what your head says, but your heart speaks differently.'

'What my heart speaks is my business and one else's.'

'Perhaps you intend to die a virgin, Nicolasa?' the soldier reproached her, blinking rapidly as was his wont.

'Yes! And what of it!' she replied in anger.

They remained silent for some minutes. Then, as Darío was hobbling out of the tent, he turned to her again.

'Spurning me won't get you into heaven, you know.'

'I assure you, Darío, that in heaven there is no place for women like me,' Nicolasa decreed without raising her eyes.

★ ★ ★

Gregorio Cartagena, meanwhile, travelled back and forth between Huácar and Pasco on Christian missions, distributing mercies and penances, taking the time to teach classes in maths and science at forgotten schools in nameless villages, and thus he interspersed religious and academic service with the civic obligations that his new role as a Bolivarian agent entailed, among them, reporting the latest news to the political elite of Lima, so dependent on Simón Bolívar.

Despite the general unrest and their many distractions, the heat of love did not fade but rather expanded, steady as a tide. Their encounters at Nicolasa's house remained cautious and nocturnal, but they could now rely on the silent complicity of Dominga Prieto, who lowered her eyes in resignation whenever Gregorio announced himself from the other side of the fence, with a whistle that only the three of them recognised as a password.

In that house they celebrated together the victories of Junín and Ayacucho – which sealed independence at the end of 1824 – as well as the triumphant return of Pedro, who as soon as he was back in Huánuco asked Cartagena for an urgent favour: to officiate his wedding with Trinidad Rubín, whom he had secretly asked to marry a year earlier.

This was done.

Some of the Cisneros siblings who lived in distant provinces arrived in time to attend the ceremony, held on the second day of January in the Church of San Cristóbal. There they met Gregorio for the first time in person, having heard so much about the priest from Nicolasa and Pedro's periodic letters.

On the night of the wedding it was Trinidad's mother who walked her down the aisle. Their faces were funereal. The father, Colonel Joaquín Rubín, a bastion of the Royalist army, had been killed just weeks earlier in the Battle of Ayacucho. He died unaware that his daughter was secretly engaged to Pedro Cisneros, his enemy like all the patriots. If he had survived, he would have resolutely opposed the union.

The day of the battle, the previous 9 December, Colonel Rubín and his 2000 men were waiting for the independence army to appear on the slopes of Kunturkunka, or more precisely on the open plain of the Pampa de la Quina. As soon as they appeared on the horizon the forces advanced. The clash was bloody from the off, and soon descended into hand-to-hand fighting. The colonel was about to give an order to a man in his regiment when he heard the whistle of a bullet close by. It had already hit him: he let out a sharp exhalation and, with no great fuss, fell to the ground. Feeling for the wound in his abdomen, he found a deep hole gushing with blood and his entrails protruding: he knew that his hour had come. The cold sweat and spasms only confirmed it. Making one last effort before expiring, he peered around and identified his assassin. The pistol still raised, and barely regaining his balance amid the smoke and the din of explosions and death cries, Pedro refocused his wild eyes and realised that the astonished face of the dying man he had just hit, whose unfathomable gaze he would never forget, was none other than the father of his betrothed.

It took fifteen months for him to confess this to his new bride, with disastrous consequences. He swore it had been unintentional, but it was no use. She not only left off speaking to him or sharing his bed, but began to have nightmares in which the Colonel, his cheekbones visible and stomach ruptured, manifested himself to curse her. Tormented by these visions and devastated by the irreversible fact of being married to her father's assassin, Trinidad could not sleep again. One night, after weeping until she felt her corneas might burst, she shut herself in the kitchen and hacked off uneven tufts of her hair with the same knife she then used to open her wrists with two vertical slashes. To make absolutely sure she would pass to the next life, she unstoppered one of the little bottles Pedro kept in the drawer of products for disinfecting the stables, took a fistful of its grainy content and swallowed without looking. It was black arsenic crystal. Trinidad took less than twenty-five minutes to perish. When Pedro found her on the floor, bent double in a pool of blood, vomit and phlegm that he remembered as reeking of garlic, she resembled a youthful mummy: the cracked mouth, frozen in a cry no one heard, the desiccated arms pressed against the belly in a final retch, the lustrous blond hair now a clump of yellow wires.

★ ★ ★

The years that followed were years of authoritarian government by Simón Bolívar in Peru, a dictatorship that relied on the blessing of many servile oligarchs, leading most to believe that the independence struggle had been in vain and the oft-proclaimed liberty would never arrive, or would prove worthless if it ever did.

After three years of concentrating power in his own hands, oppressing dissenters, failing to listen to indigenous leaders, putting the slavery issue on the backburner and engaging in illicit manoeuvres to have himself named

51

president for life, Bolívar departed for Gran Colombia, never to return.

This period would be followed by a spate of internal uprisings, the establishment of the Congress, and in 1827 the election of Marshal de la Mar as first president of the new republic.

* * *

Given the trials she had suffered giving birth to Juan in Huacaybamba, Nicolasa refused to repeat the treacherous journey to the Andaymayo hacienda when she discovered she was pregnant for a second time in September 1829. She had already decided by then that, were she to have more children, they would be born either in Huánuco or Lima. Cartagena acceded to her demands, confident that Dominga Prieto and the deaf-mute Isidora Zabala would attend this and subsequent deliveries with the same patience, austerity and reserve as on the first occasion.

And so it proved. Manuel, Francisca and Luciano were born in the mansion at Huánuco; Feliciano, Catalina and Luis arrived in Lima, in a Barrios Altos property Nicolasa had acquired in order to be closer to Gregorio, whose political activities obliged him to spend long periods in the capital. That is how they lived for years, dividing their time between the two cities.

This house in Barrios Altos, located on the street known as Peña Horadada – named after the oddly-shaped boulder with a hole in it someone had placed on the corner centuries earlier and that, the legends of the older residents said, was pierced by the devil himself to escape a saint's procession – was big enough for all seven children to play inside, in a kind of whimsical captivity. While the children were small it was easy to control them and keep them hidden, but each year, as they grew and the sounds from outside pricked their curiosity, the challenges of confinement intensified. 'If you go outside the devil will gobble you up!' Dominga Prieto threatened them, and told them about the cursed stone. These were the instructions of Nicolasa and Gregorio, who preferred to use lies to conceal them than expose them to neighbourhood gossip.

It was not unusual for priests to hide their children at the time. There are entire archives from the period with lists of clerics' progeny, unacknowledged children who grew up inside mansions and monasteries and only discovered the outside world after a certain age, learning how to get around out there while knowing nothing of their biological fathers. That is, if they succeeded in being born at all, as most of the women impregnated by priests – society ladies, domestic servants, reformatory inmates and cloistered nuns – were forced to abort and maintain a sepulchral silence about the event, living with permanent trauma.

Those in charge of making the foetuses disappear were a group of macabre nuns that first strangled them and then buried them in tunnels and catacombs. In Huánuco, in the mid-twentieth century, following the demolition of the Santa Isabel, San Teodoro and San Miguel monasteries, it became commonplace to uncover piles of miniature cadavers, skeletons of aborted babies, the skin and bones of children torn from their mothers and murdered in these filthy holes on the orders of infanticidal priests.

What was not at all frequent – indeed vanishingly rare – was for priests to fall in love as Gregorio Cartagena had fallen in love. The clergyman of Huácar, my great-great-grandfather, managed to skew his spiritual predicament to such a degree that he no longer saw his romance with Nicolasa Cisneros as an obstacle but as an incentive.

While she felt hapless at her fate and tortured herself for failing God with her weaknesses, Cartagena thanked that same deity every morning for placing such a generous and bountiful woman in his path.

'Only the divinity of our Lord may conceive of so purifying a love,' he pronounced to Nicolasa in his episcopal, far-sighted tone, attempting to alleviate her sorrows on those vertiginous nights of summary encounter. How many times did he swear to her that their feelings 'had the blessing of Christ and of Mother Mary'; that their kisses 'pleased the saints, who were human too'; that their caresses 'undermined no commandment, for they were mystical and not sinful'; that spending the night together 'was not incompatible with the mandates of Scripture'; and that their souls 'would not be judged for the offence of their actions but for the purity of their intentions'.

This was how he spoke to her.

It was not that Cartagena was ignorant of the grave repercussions his attitude might entail: he knew all too well that, if revealed, he would be denounced before the archbishop and expelled from the Church 'for conduct contrary to the exercise of the ministry', or alternatively obliged to declare himself apostate. Yet this is not what first came to mind when Nicolasa stood before him, gazing at him with eyes that always reminded him in their colour and shape of eucalyptus leaves.

The priest's devotion to Nicolasa was as true as it was shameless. He loved her without moderation and without discretion. Irremediably. The proof was the seven children they had together. Seven children that Gregorio educated and supported, without ever granting them his surname.

What neither ever considered was that this alliance born of silence and fated to secrecy could bring them harm.

Perhaps not to all of the children, but to some.

Or at least to one.

That son, the one who bore the brunt of their illicit, errant and shadowy love; the one who spent his life trying to explain why he was hounded by a sadness that lay beyond his reach, why his own love was so inchoate, and why these ulcers grew inside him that no one showed him how to cure, was the final child.

The seventh bastard. My great-grandfather.

He was born in 1837.

They called him Luis, his name recorded in a Lima church as Luis Benjamín Cisneros, '*legitimate* son of Don Roberto Benjamín and Nicolasa Cisneros'.

He would be the main heir to his parents' buried shame.

CHAPTER 5

Lima, 2013

Huácar is a hamlet of little washed-out streets tumbled together at the foot of a line of hills covered by sparse vegetation. To get there, you have to take the road for Oyón from the gateway marking the entrance to Huánuco. The inhabitants are shy and unsociable, but not distrustful. The houses are made of adobe and their doors are always open for the dogs to come and go as they please.

Uncle Gustavo and I reached Huácar in 2012, on the trail of Nicolasa and Gregorio. We wanted, or at least I wanted, to get to the root of the story. Even if I still lacked the courage to commit it to paper, I was obsessed with knowing the truth.

We stayed in the province of Ambo, in the residence of the Trelles family, a 200-year-old stone-built house with a garden of ancient orange and avocado trees, and a pond inhabited by toads that croaked in the evenings while keeping themselves hidden.

In the mornings breakfast was corn tamales, black cherry juice and scorching-hot coffee with cinnamon, before we began our rounds of interviews in the village. When we returned each evening, we would share our progress with our hosts, drinking a pisco and cranberry cocktail under the pergola, or in a creaking wood-lined lounge we would listen to waltzes on a pianola whose keys moved by themselves as if a docile ghost were playing from the beyond.

There is a veritable army of Cisneros in the depths of Huácar. On the first exploration alone we met Seragio Cisneros, Alcides Cisneros, Didiosa Cisneros, Austrajilda Cisneros, Constancia Cisneros, Epifania Cisneros, Casilda Cisneros, Eleuteria Cisneros, Apolinaria Cisneros, Asunta Cisneros, Pascual and Pascuala Cisneros. Then there was Teodoro Cisneros Ponce, son of Cirilo Cisneros Baldeón, grandson of Vinicio Cisneros Puente, half-brother of the Cisneros Melgarejo, the Cisneros Estela, the Cisneros Martell, and grandson of Pío Cisneros Zevallos, who was father of Leo and Sabina Cisneros Martínez, grandchildren of Isaac Cisneros Reynoso and Eutimia Cisneros Lavalle. We also came across a one-armed man with a glass eye who presented himself as Colonel Próspero Cisneros, 'Chieftain of Yanahuanca', and a Damiana Cisneros, just like the character from *Pedro Páramo*, a small, rosy-cheeked woman who had a habit of biting her tongue and didn't know whether to laugh or cry when she learned that her name appeared in a novel where dead souls spoke with the living.

The homes of these families were all alike: narrow rooms with worm-eaten roofs and mud walls permeated with damp. Images of indeterminate Virgins hung from pins alongside folk art imagery and obsolete calendars. There was nothing to show the time of day nor anyone who needed to know it. The sole family bedroom could be glimpsed behind a curtain: a humble space with an earth floor, bunk beds, piles of clothes and assorted odds and ends. In place of electric lamps were countless candles that came and went in improvised candelabra made from soda bottles. No sooner had we entered than we were invited to sit down on the benches, boxes and tubs that comprised the lounge suite, and then, without even having explained the reason for our visit, a table appeared before us laden with boiled corn, slabs of cheese, sweet humitas, thick broths, greasy pork rind and Pepsi bottles filled with home-brewed chicha de jora. Uncle Gustavo signalled to me to keep eating, as lack of appetite might be taken for a slight.

These Cisneros together formed a fabulous crowd of siblings, cousins, brothers- and sisters-in-law, uncles and aunts, nephews and nieces, and stepchildren who had grown up with the tradition of marrying among themselves in a disorderly, promiscuous manner, without anyone being scandalised by these incestuous relationships or unusual matrimonies. Colonel Próspero – father of three women, Zelmira, Eufemia and Sufrida Cisneros, all three married to one man, Plácido, who also happened to be their half-brother – claimed that the nearby hamlets of Chicopata and Viroy were even more infested with men, women and children of the same surname. 'They're all Cisneros there, even the pigs in the sties, the hens in their tin-roofed houses, the monkeys in the sapote trees,' he swore, laughing with all his rotted teeth, his glass eye staring and clapping with his one hand.

It cannot be discounted that many of the Cisneros in these parts are descendants of dour Juan, the first-born son of Nicolasa and Gregorio Cartagena, who spent many years in Huánuco before seeking isolation in the heights of Pasco, where he had numerous children and scuttled ever further into the depths of the jungle, as if rejecting his suspicious origins, writing only a few anguished letters that repeatedly mentioned his mother and siblings but never the priest Gregorio, his real father, nor Roberto Benjamín, the traveller, the invented father.

Yet each time we asked about Cartagena, providing exact references about the place and time the priest had lived and worked here, the Cisneros of Huácar looked at each other and shrugged their shoulders.

* * *

The church of San Miguel Arcángel stands over Huácar's plaza, the first centre of Christian evangelisation in the region. Its rusty yellow bell tower is the highest point in the whole valley. From afar, the church gives the impression of a basilica; from up close, a rustic little box like the retablo scenes made by the local artisans. This is the same church where Cartagena offered mass for so many years, and that later, crumbling from storm damage, had to be rebuilt and reinforced. In this tower, Gregorio would alert the populace to the village events by sounding the bell clapper, but would also hide children from mistreatment by their alcoholic fathers, as well as young men fleeing a thrashing from some cuckolded husband.

That morning we were received by the parish priest Víctor Fabián, a short, round and chatty man draped in a vast tunic that hid his feet, making him look like a ghost gliding over the floor tiles.

'Father, we're looking for some baptismal records,' I explained as soon as we had said good morning.

'Whose?' he asked, flicking through some papers on his desk.

'The first children of Nicolasa Cisneros,' replied Uncle Gustavo.

'What years are we talking about?' He suddenly took an interest.

'Between 1828 and 1837,' I said. 'Is there any chance they could be in the church archives?'

'Impossible,' he answered. 'All the parish's papers were burned in 1945, when Father Anatolio Trujillo was here.'

'What happened?' Uncle Gustavo inquired.

'It was a Sunday. The official report says that lightning struck the church, but the old folk here suspected Father Anatolio, because that day he finished mass early, requisitioned the alms, threw out the parishioners and barred the doors. An hour later, after stealing the crowns from the Virgin and the jewels from Saint Michael, he set fire to the church. But that didn't come out until much later. At first, everyone believed it had been an accident.'

'How did they realise that the fire was deliberate?'

'An altar boy was burned to death. They found his little body wrapped around a column. A pile of blackened bones. When Father Anatolio heard, he couldn't bear the guilt and confessed all.'

'Was there anything left?'

'The church building survived, but not the archive. It was reduced to ashes.'

* * *

Huácar's plaza also contains a bust of Simón Bolívar and a rusty plaque commemorating his passage through the village in 1823, the year he met Gregorio Cartagena and called on him to join the independence army.

The parish priest Víctor Fabián notes that people make money even today with the story of the Liberator's visit. 'The travel agencies have turned all that into a business,' he complained. In his version, the tourist guides charge foreigners a fortune just to show them a little room beside the church and a bed with a canopy and bronze columns they claim Bolívar slept in.

'The gringos believe it and take photos, but it's just a tale to get money out of them,' he told us.

'Whose bed is it, in that case?' asked Uncle Gustavo.

'A bishop from Ambo donated it to the church thirty years ago. It belonged to his grandma, who died of mumps. No one wanted to keep the bed, and so he brought it here.'

Arrayed around the plaza and looking onto the church of San Miguel Arcángel, there is a poorly stocked pharmacy that opens twenty-four hours a day, a tailor-less tailor, a police station without any police officers, and a store called Wilder, after its owner, who attends clients without shifting from his hammock. The final ornament around the square is the most important secondary school in the area, sited opposite the church. Its name is the Gregorio Cartagena Public Educational Institution. On the façade, beside an olive-green coat of arms, the precepts upheld by the school may be read:

Discipline. Honour. Responsibility.

That August morning in 2012, the school principal had called in sick and his office was closed. In any case we were allowed to wander the three pavilions of the building, and we fruitlessly sought out a portrait of Cartagena. I found it impossible to credit that neither teachers nor pupils – almost all sons of mule drivers and farmers from the hamlets of Acobamba – had ever seen an image of the figure who gave his name to their place of work and study, and about whom they would offer clashing and self-evidently nonsensical stories. At first they seemed bashful and unwilling to cooperate, gripped by a watchful silence, but it was enough for one to open his mouth for the rest to follow.

Some said that Gregorio had been a munificent Spanish healer or seer who suffered from hallucinations, who spoke of the transmigration of souls and worked occasional miracles thanks to his psychic powers, and they described the 'famous case' of the woman blind from birth who lived in Pachitea, her pupils red as plums, whose vision Cartagena restored by rubbing her eyelids with water from a stream and drying them with a replica of the Turin Shroud. Others declared that he had been a blue-eyed riverboat captain, tall yet hunchbacked, who lived for years among the reeds along the banks of the Huallaga river and who came to be – no one quite knew how – the first and last commander of the city of Huánuco. There was even a teacher, the school's head librarian, who claimed with great conviction that Cartagena had been a famous Caribbean soldier from a good family, a backer of Bolívar's campaign, who as an old man had headed into the jungle in pursuit of a silver-haired albino woman, daughter of the first Austrian colonists in a fertile area known as Codo de Pozuzo, and that he remained there until his death from the poisonous bite of an indeterminate animal.

I left Huácar with the impression that I was leaving behind a chapter in my family history that had remained bound and closed for centuries. Except for Uncle Gustavo, no one had ever mentioned this place. Exploring its narrow streets, sensing the breath of its people, the jumble of its constructions, the bulk of the surrounding peaks that felt like waiting deities, I felt I was pulling aside an immemorial veil, crossing a frontier and entering a territory where the living and the dead could coexist amicably, a cast of flickering presences like dying light bulbs.

That morning, I wrote in my notebook:

This is where Nicolasa and Gregorio met. Here they learned to love and to conceal their love. The very air is thick with the fear that oppressed them. How much Nicolasa must have suffered in her silence. How much she must have wept. It is no coincidence that this is the very meaning of the name Huácar in Quechua: *to weep.*

★ ★ ★

One Saturday we went to look for Virgilio Luzuriaga, a doctor and historian whose memory is considered the black box of Huánuco. Luzuriaga is a rotund man with white hair and very dark eyes, magnified by thick glasses that give him the appearance of a hunting salamander. He spent his primary school years in a classroom with the name of my great-grandfather, Luis Benjamín Cisneros, written over the blackboard, and ever since he has wanted to find out who the man was.

He received us in his gloomy consulting room in a small clinic three streets from the main plaza. Seated behind his desk, with his back to a glass case laden with empty jars, fragmentary skulls, well-thumbed medical books, false teeth, stopped hourglasses and countless other dusty objects, Virgilio Luzuriaga launched into a hypothesis about Gregorio Cartagena that we found disconcerting, adding to the pile of wacky theories we'd heard in Huácar – although this one seemed to have something going for it.

'Cartagena was Colombian,' he claimed. 'It's even said he was a fifth columnist for Simón Bolívar, who sent him to Peru as a spy and saboteur.' For emphasis, he placed both hands on the table and opened wide his amphibious gaze to scrutinise us. This wasn't the most interesting thing he said that morning, however. What cut me the deepest was his account of the remark made by a well-known historian twenty years earlier, when Virgilio was trying to discover if Cartagena had any connection with the Cisneros family, as was already whispered at the time. The historian deterred him, saying: 'Don't get into all that, Virgilio, these things need to be wrapped in a veil of silence or very respectable people could be hurt. I cordially invite you to forget it.'

Veil of silence. Hurt. Forget.

I jotted these words down in my notebook just like that: together but separate, linked by full stops, a sort of minimalist or unfinished poem, the keys to a still-mysterious history. The historian's exhortation to Virgilio Luzuriaga revealed a custom that in Peru – or in certain sectors of Peruvian society – has the weight of ritual tradition: silence as protection. Or rather, a belief in the protection afforded by silence. In my family, like in many – perhaps all – there are people who tend to keep quiet, who don't speak up, who don't say 'more than is necessary', who opt for prudence so as 'not to hurt anyone', who force forgetting so that certain episodes never see the light of day. God forbid they should be the ones to ruin everything.

After some frustrating back-and-forth in search of documents in the cellars of the bishop's office, we headed for the Leoncio Prado school, also founded by Gregorio. No photograph or portrait was to be found there either. Some of the locals had heard of him, but no one knew if he was tall or short, large or small, pale or ruddy, rough or smooth. His appearance remained an enigma.

Facing the Leoncio Prado school building, by the church of San Francisco, there is a small park that also bears Cartagena's name. It consists of six benches bolted to concrete blocks, three street lamps and patches of greenery without any particularly showy flowers, where the tree trunks are limewashed to protect them from insects. Sitting on one of these benches, I had the feeling that Gregorio was everywhere and nowhere, that he was a vaporous presence, as if he hadn't died altogether and was perhaps not outside but inside of me, not in any tangible sense but not in a merely spiritual one either. We like to think that ghosts inhabit old houses and dark corners, but we too in our body and soul become these very things: an old house, a dark corner, a storehouse for the memories of the people who preceded us and whose rest we eventually decided to disturb.

Since I was there, my plan was to travel to Huacaybamba to explore the remains of the hacienda complex where Cartagena sent Nicolasa so that the birth of their first child would go unnoticed. In fact, I wanted to follow the same precipitous trail that Gregorio rode when he made his inspection tours of the Huamalíes province – where the remote churches were in a deplorable state – but it proved impossible to complete either of the two routes, which involved extreme temperatures and arduous, exhausting distances on horseback. All I saw was one half-collapsed diminutive church with a battered door that displayed an undated sign that suggested an unrepeatable event: 'Don Gregorio Cartagena, enlightened and illustrious priest, passed this way.' A hellish stink wafted from inside. A man appeared who confessed that it had been a long time since the church had functioned as a place of worship, and that, although the original façade remained, the locals had found themselves obliged to use the premises for other purposes. Firstly, as a jail to lock up the bandits and thieves no one wanted to deal with; then as a clandestine brothel attended by gaunt young whores who were prohibited from falling in love with their clients; and most recently as a public latrine or, to quote him literally, 'communal shithouse'. The sign alluding to Cartagena, however, remained untouched.

Upon my return to Lima, while I sought new information to resolve the riddle that had been my great-great-grandfather, I mulled over these opposing theories about his origins. Was he Peruvian or Spanish, Venezuelan or Colombian? The uncertainty was cleared up the morning that Uncle Gustavo and I found his baptismal certificate on the penultimate shelf of the furthest corridor of the archive in the Archbishop's residence.

> In this Holy Parish of Huánuco, on the twenty-fourth day of April 1788, I exorcised, baptised with holy ointment and chrism José Gregorio, one day of age, legitimate son of Don Francisco Cartagena and Doña María Soledad de Meneses Aparragué. The godfather was Don José Florencio de Savala. Witnessed by Captain Don Cleto de Laura and Maestre de Campo Don José González. In witness whereof, signed by Father Pedro Gallegos.

My great-great-grandfather, there could no longer be any doubt, was Peruvian. His parents were Spaniards just as Nicolasa's were, and they likewise sailed to Peru in search of mythical treasures they never saw.

The documents also included some notes in the hand of Colonel Antonio Echegoyen, for several years the mayor of Huánuco. At a time when women and wine threatened to be the undoing of the rebellious sub-deacon Cartagena, Echegoyen resolutely defended him from the religious authorities of Lima, with whom he was closely connected. In one note he described Gregorio as 'a young man of good character and education'. Perhaps the Colonel sincerely liked him, or maybe he wanted to help because the mansion adorned with screens and crosses from Huamantanga that he rented in the centre of the city at a very good price belonged to one Don Francisco Cartagena.

I also came across a report dating from 1829, submitted by Melitón de Herrera to the ecclesiastical council of the Archbishop's seat in Lima, alleging the following:

> The priest and curate of Huácar, José Gregorio Cartagena, rarely makes any contribution to doctrine, as he is always too busy as rector of the College of Sciences. He never plans ahead. He even has two secretaries when he only requires one and, as if that were not enough, as far as the people of Huácar are concerned, his moral comportment is far from exemplary.

Apart from this imputation, which may be an indirect allusion to his relationship with Nicolasa (by 1829 his first son Juan had arrived), I found nothing else referring to his hidden romance or illegitimate children.

On one occasion, Gregorio was asked to provide his superiors with an opinion on the case of Father Anacleto Landaeta, a turbulent priest from the hamlet of Lauricocha in his parish jurisdiction. According to the allegations made by some highly disgruntled ladies, Anacleto Landaeta was living in 'scandalous concubinage' with a woman who worked in the sacristy, and with whom he walked abroad in the old quarter 'in full sight and trying the patience' of the populace. 'Not satisfied with this,' the letter continued, 'the incontinent curate has seduced as many as five more parishioners, with whom he has carnal relations in the confessional, availing of the intimacy of the penitence.'

The ladies demanded that either the canonical laws were obeyed and Father Anacleto excommunicated for the crimes of 'solicitation and fornication' – they also insinuated that he had fathered the most recent daughter of the wife of Orestes Murillo, the village sawbones, 'who looks just like him' – or that he be subjected to one of the public tortures that the Spanish Inquisition saved for 'infidels' and that were still practised there, such as red-hot tongs used to tear and burn the penis, castration, extirpation of the member or amputation of the entire genital triad 'before he turns Lauricocha into Sodom'.

When Cartagena received the denunciation containing these demands, whether out of identification or solidarity – or perhaps in response to the views expressed by other locals who found the conduct of Father Anacleto Landaeta perfectly natural and demanded he be allowed to stay in his post – he wrote a note absolving his colleague of the charges and saving him from castration.

While accusations built up against him, Gregorio held a professorship at San Marcos University, where he enjoyed the backing of the academic community. His political activities also kept him occupied. After his first experience as an elected deputy for the province of Junín in 1827, he was elected deputy and then senator in representation of other parts of the Sierra. His highest appointment came in December 1841, when he was made a member of the Council of State, a body then formed of ten parliamentarians who took over the president's powers in the event of his absence or illness. As part of the Council, Cartagena signed the declaration of war on Bolivia after that country's army – under orders from the villainous southern tyrant José Ballivián – killed the Peruvian President Agustín Gamarra in the Battle of Ingavi and occupied the territories of Moquegau, Puno and Tarapacá.

At the request of the Council, Cartagena not only signed the declaration, but also wrote the communiqué, passed out as handbills in streets and plazas across the country, that announced the war.

Peruvians: your Council of State, heeding the voice of the nation and satisfying its obligations, has resolved to declare war on Bolivia, the capital enemy of Peru, and on the treacherous ingrate Ballivián. In authorising this harsh but necessary measure, we demanded no other sacrifice of Bolivia than to provide Peru with assurances that its tyrant would not attack our tranquillity and independence, and that our homeland would never again fall prey to his perfidious machinations, nor the theatre of ferocious massacres with which he commenced his usurpation. Yet it appears that providence desires to test our fortitude, leading the army responsible for such a noble and selfless mission to endure a setback just when it anticipated victory, and Generalissimo President Gamarra and his chiefs and officers to perish barbarously and ignominiously at the hands of that people, slaughtered by order of the baneful Ballivián, whom they had favoured in his wretchedness and reconciled with his motherland. Citizens! Since these unprecedented atrocities became known, a cry of indignation and fury has resounded incessantly throughout our Republic, and the Council, as faithful interpreter of public sentiment, hastened to fortify the Government so as to avenge the outrages inflicted on our national honour by an enemy that boasts of trampling over the rights of war and of humanity itself. The prayers addressed to us by our compatriots in their dying breaths, summoning us to arms, are echoed by all the fathers and all the mothers whose sons, husbands and brothers have paid their debt to nature and to the motherland. In the transport of their suffering they demand revenge, and they will obtain it without any offense to morality, for such horrendous crimes should not go unpunished. What! Can our enemy, just because an unforeseen reversal has destroyed a part of our Army, flatter themselves into believing they can dispose of our territory at the whim of their ambition and impose the law on us, or reduce us to accepting a shameful peace? No! The nation, abundantly confident in its Government, which is the palladium of its independence and security, will find in the patriotism of its children sufficient reserves to reject such foolish pretensions; and if fate should aggravate their misfortunes to the point that they can no longer be withstood, then we shall all sacrifice ourselves together, rather than consent to our humiliation and disgrace. Peruvians: saving the Republic by banishing the horrors of war; preventing our brothers in the south from burning, looting and murder; this is and shall be the vote of the Council. Peru needs peace, and wants it; but honourably; and it is resolved to secure it by employing all the ardour and ferocity that was deployed by its enemies after the battle.

Lima, 7 December 1841

Even though Cartagena speaks here in the name of Peru and invokes idealistic motives, it occurs to me now that at times, in certain passages, this letter reads like the fervent missive he would have liked to send to his biological children, imploring them to defend the honour of their mother if the truth ever came to light.

Perhaps this was the only way Gregorio found in his lifetime to express, on paper, everything he longed to say in private, employing the symbolism of war and patriotic metaphor to ennoble Nicolasa and attempt to reach the hearts of his children – who didn't yet know they were denied by him, who continued to see him as a relative, while awaiting the ever-more improbable arrival of their father, 'Roberto Benjamín'.

CHAPTER 6

Huánuco, 1844

Pedro Cisneros, the soldier with the sideburns and the axe-hewn mouth, the brother closest to Nicolasa, the widower of Trinidad Rubín, had been grateful to Cartagena since the day the priest, as part of the Council of State, backed a decree to grant pensions and welfare funds to soldiers who, like he, had joined the liberation army and fought with valour at the battles of Junín and Ayacucho. This gesture deepened his long-standing admiration for the curate into real fondness. While before he saw him as an occasional friend, he now treated him as one of the family.

It was thanks to this fondness that he spent many years ignoring the persistent rumours on the streets of Huánuco about his sister's involvement with the clergyman. Pedro felt that these stories and imaginings were born of malice and envy, and in order to refute them, he thought it fitting to organise a reception with Gregorio, the parish priest, and Roberto Benjamín, his brother-in-law, Nicolasa's husband, the father of his nephews and nieces, the invisible man who was always traveling. This, he believed, would put an end to the gossip once and for all.

Around this time, however, the conflict with Bolivia broke out and Pedro was driven away from domestic life, just as had occurred during the independence struggle. This time the battle at Ingavi turned out to be his worst nightmare: the Peruvian army was defeated, and President Gamarra – who was under his personal protection as first aide-de-campe – was killed. On top of that, he was taken prisoner and forced to walk to Palca Grande, in Cochabamba, where he was confined with hundreds of other officers, in a damp dungeon where he spent eight months with his wrists shackled to the bars.

That battle was the trigger, two weeks later, for Peru officially declaring war on Bolivia. As he composed the document, Gregorio Cartagena thought above all about Pedro, about the tortures he would be suffering as a hostage, and could only marvel at how much time had gone by, and the events that had marked their lives since that day in 1824 when the Cisneros siblings appeared before him, there in Huácar, determined to join the liberation army.

Over a year was to pass before Pedro could return and rejoin Nicolasa in the house in Huánuco. He did so as a general, and intimate friend of the new president-elect, Marshal Ramón Castilla, who had named him prefect of Arequipa and Tacna, and would later designate him Minister of War. Their friendship was forged in those months in the Cochabamba jail, from which they emerged together once the peace treaty was signed with the Bolivians.

The afternoon of his reunion with his sister, once they had run some errands around the main square and could finally sit down in the rear courtyard for a cup of tea, Pedro did not want to speak about the war and asked

Nicolasa to give him a rundown of what had happened in Huánuco during the year he was imprisoned. From her rocking chair, she proceeded to tell him the news of their neighbours. The Figueroas. The Pancorvos. The Sánchez Aizcorbes. Families they had grown up with, that they'd watched grow up. Listening to her, Pedro's attention was caught by his sister's children as they came and went around the corridors of the house and at one point were all gathered on the threshold of the back garden, and recalling the gossip that linked his sister with Cartagena it occurred to him to ask once more after Roberto Benjamín.

'Tell me something… what about your husband?' he interrupted her.

'What makes you ask like that, out of the blue?'

'I'm just wondering… Do you remember that before the war I wanted to organise a dinner with him and Gregorio? It's an idea I'd like to take up again. Where is he? I think it's about time we met him.'

Taken by surprise, Nicolasa trotted out the usual story.

'You know, travelling, on business.'

'Again?'

'Yes, yes, again!' she sighed. Then she picked up the teapot and fixed her gaze on the dark stream as it filled the cups.

'So… where is he at present?' Pedro insisted.

'In his most recent letter he wrote that he had disembarked in southern Spain.'

Nicolasa had prepared this answer.

'Southern Spain is a very large place. Where exactly?'

'He didn't go into detail.'

'And is that where he'll be staying?'

'He didn't tell me that, either.'

'And when will he return?'

'Not before December,' Nicolasa invented on the spot.

In her lap, her hands, entwined but restless, told another story.

'But it's barely February!'

'Maybe a little sooner.'

Pedro was not at all satisfied with these answers. He found them theatrical, evasive, inconsistent. Within himself, he refused to give credit to the old, malicious rumour about his sister's affair with the priest Gregorio, but he lacked any way to refute it, and at this point only the physical presence of Roberto Benjamín would be proof enough, or at the very least some other genuine evidence of his existence.

'Can you show me his most recent letter?' Pedro inquired, placing his cup on the table. 'At least that way I can know the handwriting of my brother-in-law.'

'How I would love to, Pedro, but I do not keep those letters. As soon as I've finished reading them, I burn them. You know better than anyone how I hate to feel nostalgic. I don't like the children seeing me like that.'

It wasn't Nicolasa's excuses but the false lack of concern with which she made them that incited Pedro to keep digging. What is Nicolasa hiding, and above all why? he asked himself. How long has she been keeping secrets from me? He had a sudden idea: the family's chaotic papers urgently needed putting in order, and he would need to gather different certificates from all the brothers and sisters.

'It's on the advice of Gibson, an expert in legal affairs. He is acting as my consultant, and he has recommended we get our papers in order. We need a family archive.'

'I agree entirely. What can I do to help?'

'I was thinking… since I'm here, we could begin with you. Do you have your marriage certificate?'

Nicolasa's eyes opened wide in fright. This was a

preposterous idea, without any foundation whatsoever.

'As I say, it's only to help resolve a legal matter,' Pedro explained, sitting back in his seat. 'I don't suppose you've burnt the certificate as well, have you?'

Nicolasa recognised the sarcasm in her brother's voice and identified his intentions. She stood up from the rocking chair and, turning her back on Pedro, declared that the certificate must be mixed up with other papers somewhere.

'Perhaps I can find it for you in a few days' time,' she stammered.

Her words were interspersed with the creaking of the chair, which was gradually rocking itself to a standstill, as if a soul in torment was suspended there.

'I want to see it *now*!' Pedro demanded, suddenly angry, certain that Nicolasa was just trying to win time.

'Don't torture me,' begged Nicolasa. 'What is all of this about? What are these legal matters? What do you want, Pedro?' She stood frozen to the spot in the middle of the courtyard, unblinking, rubbing her hands while she tried to plot a way out.

'Without that certificate your and the family's honour are in question, don't you realise?' Pedro exclaimed with a gesture of frustration, revealing his true fears at last.

'My honour is none of your business,' shot back Nicolasa, and walked towards the French window, in a futile attempt to get away from the conversation.

Pedro, blinded by rage, leapt up and advanced upon her, grabbing her by her forearm and shaking her.

'You're going to tell me what is going on right this minute!'

'Let go of me!'

She shook him off, only to deny once more what she had denied so many times, with a tenacity that was beginning to peel apart like a rotten onion.

'Roberto's not here. He's not! How can I make you understand?'

The explosion in her voice gave way to an agitation and then a murmur, a tremulous buzzing around her heart. Pedro continued to assail her with questions, no longer spitting in rage but with a tense disappointment in his eyes.

'Who is Robert Benjamín, Nicolasa? Why have we never met him all these years? Why not? Who is he hiding from? Is he in trouble with the law? If that's the case, then perhaps I could help him, I'm sure Gibson would know how,' he added slowly, with sterile optimism. Seeing that even this failed to draw his sister out, he sat back down, defeated.

After a few seconds of silence, adjusting her shawl which had slipped down in the tussle, glassy-eyed, shivering all over, and becoming aware again of her children, who were tripping around the garden picking flowers that issued luminous clouds of pollen, Nicolasa noticed the growing gloom of the evening – it was time to light the candles and close the curtains – and only then did she let fall her armour and open her lips to let out three cutting sentences that bore the force of the inexorable.

'We're too old now to keep secrets from each other. The piece of paper you are looking for doesn't exist. Nor does that man.'

Before her brother could react, while he was still in suspense, Nicolasa forced herself to look at him scornfully before bringing the conversation to a close.

'Now please be so kind as to go and leave me in peace.'

Pedro dropped his severe expression, closed his eyes and prayed in silence that the truths he had just heard were falsehoods, even though they hurt as if someone had suddenly brought down a crown of thorns on his head. Just when the cup of tea was about to slip from his hand, he raised it, drank the last drops to gather strength, stood, straightened his back, flexed his shoulder blades, clenched his jaw and smoothed out the jacket of his uniform before leaving without bidding farewell to anyone. He didn't even allow Dominga Prieto to open the door for him, and when she wished him good afternoon with a lowered gaze, he deciphered in that guilty gesture her cooperation in the whole deceit, and although she had been his nanny his whole life, although he had been raised loving her like a second mother, and even as a child suckled at her ample brown bosom, he didn't hesitate to stare at her in disgust and cut her down with a single phrase:

'Half-caste traitor!'

Mere hours later, seated in the poorly-lit study of the house where he lived in a widower's chaos, loading and unloading the chamber of the pistol that years earlier he had accidentally used to kill Colonel Joaquín Rubín and never aimed at anyone since, Pedro threaded together the facts implicit in Nicolasa's confession and gradually came to realise who was who in the story. Once he had deduced the role played by Gregorio Cartagena in his sister's life, his stomach clenched. His fury wasn't directed so much at her as at him, and he spent the following days and nights railing at him in silence, caressing his weapon, stroking the trigger with his index finger. He was disgusted to think of how many years he had been taken in by the priest, and how the latter had mocked his family by exploiting her siblings' absence to prowl around the family house and become intimate with Nicolasa. When his nieces and nephews came into his thoughts, Pedro felt his skin crawl. 'So, they are all children of that wretch,' he ruminated, tightening his fists as if he wanted to keep hold of his rage. It was then that he relinquished him forever. Days later, his sister wrote, imploring that he reconsider, that he not take reprisals against Gregorio, but it was already too late. In a general's code, Pedro retorted, an affront of this nature could not go unpunished.

One night, while he was planning his vengeance, rolling a steel bullet between his teeth, he realised that he hadn't felt such bitterness since Trinidad Rubín's suicide, and although this was a different kind of pain – one that lacerated his stomach, rather than eating away at his bones – it was enough to bring out his darkest side.

And so, one day in 1846, as cabinet chief to President Ramón Castilla, he sought his ear to update him on some potential complaints that had 'reached him' concerning a 'very troublesome, bitter and intractable' priest from Huánuco, who had to be taught a lesson. Now he was the one lying and swearing in vain. Without asking for any further incriminating evidence, oblivious to the fact that this was a matter of personal reprisal, President Castilla trustingly signed the paper that Pedro had prepared, ordering that 'the priest Don José Gregorio de Cartagena y Meneses' should be sent as chaplain to a military outpost located in the heights of Meseta de Bombón.

Impossible to imagine a more wretched place.

The Meseta in question was little more than a forlorn upland, a place to go and rot, forsaken by God and the Devil alike, where the bitter cold of the altiplano shattered the backbones of the few poor grunts who kept guard, lethargic yet stoical, clutching their frozen rifles; a cold that paralysed with macabre agonies the rare travellers who turned up there, disoriented by mountain sickness, their hands numb and their lips blistered; a cold that repelled even the toughest birds, the condors, which retreated beating their ice-covered wings, their ruffs taut and the skin of their necks cracked. That is what the cold did in Bombón.

When the notification of his new posting arrived, Gregorio set off for this dreadful place without protest, like someone walking to the gallows, and submitted to the penance resolved, certain that it was Pedro's doing. There he spent the most dreadful months of his life: eating insipid or rotten food, lacking news of the outside world because the military postal service didn't come so far, without sufficient blankets to sleep, and falling so ill that he spent the nights shaking, his teeth chattering, coughing like a terminal consumptive and spitting out the crystals of ice that formed in his intestines. In this wintry purgatory, unable even to fulfil the task assigned to him, as the barracks was nothing but a mouldy storeroom where no one ever came in search of service nor pardon, suffering from the heart palpitations typical of altitude sickness, and clutching his ribs which felt as if stalactites were growing beneath the skin, Cartagena restricted himself to daily but fruitless novenas of indulgence, mumbling litanies to Our Lady of Good Remedy, and enduring like a faithless martyr his condition as a piece of human waste.

★ ★ ★

Seven months later, thanks to some forceful letters of dissent from the Archbishop's office, Marshal Castilla learned of the plot in which he had been an unwitting participant. He reproved Pedro for his deceit, separated him from his responsibilities, and for a long time prevented him from entering army premises. Immediately afterwards, he countermanded the order, returning Cartagena to the parish where he'd worked before being confined to that icy hell from which no one believed he would return alive.

Hurt by the actions of the president, Pedro turned his back on him and began to declare his enmity wherever he went. 'This country is led by a shit-for-brains,' he muttered in bars, cafés and corridors, speaking with repulsion, his eyes resentful, well aware that the president's spies were listening. When he found out, Castilla responded with similar hostility, sending him intimidating messages via the few acquaintances they still shared, accusing him of being a 'wretch, liar and deserter'.

A whole decade passed in this way, exchanging verbal provocations and skirmishes, and just when it seemed like the matter would remain an unsettled account, the day arrived when they found themselves face to face.

It was at the Battle of La Plama, in Miraflores, one January afternoon in 1855. The conservative José Rufino Echenique was now president, and had been caught up in a blatant case of corruption and profligacy. The people were ready to defenestrate him and Marshal Castilla was the one leading the revolution.

The day of the battle, beneath a lowering sky, the Marshal saw General Pedro Cisneros, his former prime minister, his old friend, now his harshest adversary, in the front rank of the governmental cavalry. As soon as the bugle sounded, Pedro launched a surprise attack at a gallop that sought to throw one of Castilla's battalions into disarray, but his intrepidness backfired: he not only failed to outflank his opponents but quickly suffered a bad wound from the bayonet of one of the rebels in the Sacred Invincibles squadron – allies of the Marshal – which skewered his right thumb, amputating it with a jerk. His chestnut horse began to buck and reared so abruptly that Pedro lost control of the animal, slipped from the saddle and was deposited on a rise where the opposing army had stationed its artillery. There lay General Cisneros, on his back, defenceless, rolling around amid the commotion and the bullet cases, screaming curses at Ramón Castilla, staring in shock at the gush of blood from his missing finger. Just when he was struggling to his feet, a powerful explosion from a cannon surprised him from the rear, depriving him of his reflexes and shaking him so hard it dislocated his collarbone. It wasn't until a few seconds later, as the dense cloud of gunpowder dispersed, that Pedro, again on the ground, realised that his ears were blocked. A constant sharp buzzing sound filled his ear canal, as if a platoon of flies were circling endlessly inside the cylinder of his head. Despite the pain that followed, he was so disoriented that it took him several minutes to grasp that he had been left completely deaf. And that they'd lost the battle.

This double tragedy, which he refused to acknowledge as the upshot of his colossal miscalculation and would later describe as the result of 'an unforgiveable ambush', did not put an end to his military career – he still signed up as a reservist for the battle of 2 May 1866 against Spain, wearing a black glove on his injured hand – but it clearly marked a point of no return. He spent his final months archiving decrepit tomes in an old military library, whose cloistered silence helped him to temporarily forget the irreversible mishap of his deafness.

He never admitted to doctors, friends or relatives how humiliating he found his inability to hear. 'At least I won't have to be poisoned with the shitty gossip of this hypocritical town any longer,' he consoled himself the day he returned to Huánuco, his head bandaged, his hand blunted, his gaze baleful, lacking any further desire to interact with the people of this place where, as he would repeat misanthropically, he had come to await the end of the world.

* * *

The fate of Gregorio Cartagena in the years following his banishment to the Meseta de Bombón remains uncertain. Yet whether it was the physical and emotional after-effects of that ostracism, or due to some other unexpected journey, or simply because life made things turn out that way, the priest stayed physically apart from Nicolasa and their children.

What is known – because it appears in the accounting records of Virgilio Luzuriaga – is that at some point the curate began a voluntary pilgrimage through the lower slopes of the cordillera, and that one day, after much wandering, he reached some neglected hamlets where new families had recently settled. Gregorio joined them, helped them to get organised and dedicated his days to preaching aloud: blessing the work of the community, teaching the children the commandments and the beatitudes, and instructing the parents in the mysteries of the rosary, in seeking the cardinal virtues and fearing the symbols of the apocalypse. The townspeople were so primitive and superstitious that they began to see the increase of their crops not as the result of the abundant rains nor the fertility of the soil they tilled from dawn to dusk, but as a miracle arising from the sermons and blessings brought by the outsider, Cartagena. The same occurred when their grazing animals began to mate and multiply: they took it as a miracle he had wrought. And when, at the height of their esoteric naivety, they believed it was Gregorio who soothed the sickness of their children with his curative proverbs – when in fact the virus had simply taken its natural course – they raised a hermitage and began to idolatrise him. Within a few months, it began to concern the priest that he was treated as an infallible predictor of the future, and that the slightest boon due to the cycles of nature was ascribed to him, and so he decided to leave before the fearful drought arrived, the period of abundance ended and the cows and llamas began to die, for he knew that when this occurred the populace would demand his supernatural intercession in defiance of the heavens, as was their custom, and once their eyes were opened to the fruit-lessness of his efforts and the futility of his sorcery, they would likely turn on him and sacrifice him as a devil and, faced with widespread famine, offer him up as food for the mountain gods.

After riding a famished horse for weeks without measuring the passage of time and bearing no luggage but his precarious humanity, Gregorio Cartagena arrived in Lima with the last of his resolve, shut himself up as the sole guest in a hospice pertaining to his diocese, and there he remained, waiting for a divinity or providence to take pity on his soul. He couldn't be diagnosed with a specific disease, yet he seemed to be carrying the weight of all the world's epidemics on his shoulders. For weeks he sought a priest to whom he could confess his sins, but no one was ready to offer him absolution. If he didn't die alone, it was only due to the noble actions of Isidora Zabala, the deaf-mute servant who arrived from Huacaybamba and stayed by his side, unsleeping, watching over his high fever, taking his pulse, listening as he enumerated sins that made her whimper with shock, and sharpening the hours like long knives. There she remained until the night her gaunt master obediently closed his eyes and became a corpse in a heartbeat.

Days earlier, much weakened yet still alert, Gregorio had dictated his last will and testament, declaring himself a 'curate, vicar and ecclesiastical judge' before a notary. Although he swore he had 'no obligatory nor legal heirs', he distributed almost the entirety of his worldly possessions among the children he had with Nicolasa. Subtracting the 500 pesos he donated to each of the parish churches he had served, and the 300 he bequeathed to two hospitals in Huánuco, the rest was for the blood family he had denied:

'Fourteen thousand pesos to Nicolasa Cisneros, to be distributed among her seven children.'

Isidora Zavala received a pouch with 100 pesos, some pieces of worked silver, and his horse, a nag with cracked hooves that had long stopped whinnying.

He also ensured that the precise location where his remains would be deposited was put in writing: niche 255 in sector C of the San Job pavilion of the Presbítero Maestro cemetery in Lima.

Gregorio Cartagena died on 8 December 1865. He was buried following a high-cross ceremony in recognition of his place in the ecclesiastical hierarchy. During the mass, which was attended by two monsignors, four friars, a sacristan, a bell ringer, an organist and three out-of-tune cantors, Gregorio's body was exhibited on a sacred catafalque. The attendees – including Nicolasa, in the third row, unrecognisable, almost consumed by tuberculosis – took communion, prayed, inhaled the aromatic smoke from the censer and enlivened the vigil by emptying not a few jars of sweet wine.

According to the death certificate, Cartagena died of consumption.

Weakened and drained.

That is, he died of exhaustion.

He grew tired of being something he was not.

CHAPTER 7

Chorrillos, 1867

Nicolasa never resented the absence of the bonds of formal marriage, because she had never known them. Her own parents had never wed, meaning she had no model to follow. On one of the visits Uncle Gustavo and I made to the archives of the Santa Ana parish church in Lima, we came across her two baptismal records in a book dating from 1800. The scribe had initially written: '*legitimate* daughter of Pablo Cisneros de Puerta and Juana de la Torre'. Noting his error, he had crossed out the word *legitimate*. This erasure still leaps out today as a mark that must once have been bright blue ink. In the second record, the correction appears: '*natural* daughter'.

Nicolasa did not consider it a grave matter that her children were illegitimate. What made her most unhappy was the zealous need to guard them from the truth. She was never able to tell them that the priest Cartagena was their father, and Roberto Benjamín a convenient fantasy. And so she followed the same strategy as Gregorio, compensating for her cowardice by leaving her children a cluster of loose ends in her will that they would use one day to dismantle the fairy tale of their origins.

On 2 January, 1867, at six in the evening, in a room at her final residence, number 10, San Pedro de Chorrillos, very ill but conscious, Nicolasa received Don Custodio Palacios – the same notary who had taken Cartagena's will – and before him she professed to be sixty-six years of age, of Roman Catholic, Apostolic religion, 'under whose faith I live, have always lived and will die.' When the notary asked her about her marital status, she declared herself to be unwed. In a stroke, her purported marriage to the apocryphal Roberto Benjamín was suppressed, erased. Likewise, she stated that she owned two properties: a house located on Junín street – previously called Peña Horadada – and the Chorrillos ranch where she now lived, or rather died, which she left to her black servant Dominga Prieto in recompense for her perennial loyalty, but where the servant would never want to live out of fear that those walls had become infused with the misadventures that plagued the Cisneros clan until the end. Nicolasa also indicated that she held possession of the Andaymayo hacienda located in Huacaybamba, since the original owner, 'the doctor and parish priest Don Gregorio Cartagena', had put it in her name.

Why would the priest have ceded that property to her? Custodio Palacios wondered to himself while taking down the words that the dying woman strained to articulate, remembering Gregorio's statement two years earlier when dictating his own testament and which at the time had aroused his curiosity. Now he managed to connect the contents of both documents and arrived at conjectures that, out of professional ethics, he was obliged to keep private, but that same night he shared with his wife before going to sleep. 'Today I discovered that the priest Cartagena had an affair with Señora Cisneros,' the notary blurted out, without looking at her. He spoke quietly, having extinguished the bedside lamp, as if the darkness and his low voice made it less of an indiscretion to reveal others' secrets.

'Ach, you're always the last to find out about anything,' his wife grumbled, turning her back on him under the covers.

Nicolasa informed Custodio Palacios that she had no more than seven children, two already dead, Francisca and Feliciano, and as she named the latter she was saddened to remember his children, her two lost and distanced granddaughters, whom she hadn't seen for a long time. Feliciano, the fifth of the bastard children, had had one legal and one extramarital daughter, conceived almost at the same time. He acknowledged the illegitimate one when she was born, but refused to have anything to do with her, and purchased the mother's silence for a certain sum. Fate has its ways of doing justice, however, and it so happened that the two girls attended the same school, and not only that, but were assigned to the same class, and not only that, but the same desk: and so from the very first day of school they got along and became inseparable friends. The day of their first communion – which they had prepared for with three months of classes and rehearsals – just after renewing their baptismal vows and as they were singing a *Te Deum* in chorus to the full church, the friends swapped the devotionals and commemorative medals engraved with the names of their parents, and comparing them saw that their father's name was the same. Feliciano Benjamín Cisneros. Then the two girls stared at each other with all the innocence of their eleven years on earth and knew or felt that they were blood sisters, daughters of a man who had concealed the truth for so long. When they turned around to seek him out, they only found an empty spot on a pew. Confused and disappointed, for a long time they never mentioned the issue. They would speak about it once, in the future, and from that day on they always looked out for each other, but they never forgave their father, and as soon as they were married they kept their distance from him and his relatives in the Cisneros family. So they remained until they learned of Feliciano's death. Neither attended the funeral, but together they arranged to send a single bunch of flowers with a note that caused a flurry of gossip: 'May he rest in peace. If he can.'

★ ★ ★

When Nicolasa fell ill, her children had already long accepted that her marriage with Roberto Benjamín was a pretence. The enchantment of the early years had long since broken, though they hadn't said anything then or later.

As children they had firmly believed in the existence of this man, even without having ever seen him, persuaded by the authentic-sounding stories Nicolasa told about his travels 'through the Caribbean, Paris, Portugal, Spain, Africa and Peking', recounting outlandish sea voyages only possible in the geography of her imagination and that gave rise to endless questions from the children, not only about the whereabouts of their father but about the true dimensions of the globe.

The children also believed they saw Roberto in the clothing that Nicolasa carefully placed in distinct corners of the house with the assistance of Gregorio who, whether out of love or regret, organised charity collections of used clothing and other articles that provided the overcoats, scarves, hats, shoes, pipes, gloves, books, and razors used by the ethereal Roberto Benjamín, and even the washbowl where he supposedly shaved, together of course with the suitcases, pencils and notebooks that were his imaginary working materials. To the children's innocent minds, these were more than irrefutable proof of their father's existence, and his occasional presence in the house while they were sleeping. Some nights they slipped drowsily out of their rooms, grabbing one or the other of these purported paternal items and taking them to bed, resigned to this way of being close to the man they didn't need to see to hold in their hearts.

There were times that Nicolasa herself, endlessly handling these props, reserving for her 'husband' the place at the head of the table for breakfast, lunch and dinner, rumpling the other side of the bed where he supposedly slept, and writing so many letters for her children in his purported hand, came to imagine he could really acquire bodily form and perhaps appear one morning in that home where, despite her efforts and those of Dominga Prieto to do the best for the children, the lack of a flesh-and-blood man was so keenly felt.

The deception became so natural that one lunchtime she scolded Dominga in the kitchen for using a spoon to taste a soup, snatching it from her hands and shouting 'that's my husband's!' The children weren't even there to witness the scene. The black servant stared at her in alarm, thinking that this dogged fantasy about a ghost had begun to drive her around the bend.

During their adolescence, the children continued to believe in their 'father', but gradually came to accept what the neighbours whispered: that Roberto Benjamín had forgotten them, that he would never return, that he had 'another family' in one of those distant countries where he traded in precious metals. Nicolasa told them that these remarks were malicious, but they asked her not to tell them any more stories and decided to erase the name of 'that man' from their conversations for evermore.

One fine day, however, they realised that they were not abandoned children but rather children denied, and that their father was no traveller but the priest Gregorio Cartagena himself. No one told them. No one had to open their eyes for them. They simply stopped guessing at it, tied things together and began to feel it in their bones. It was a visceral certainty. Pure instinct. Overnight, the evidence became overwhelming, and all prior turbulence acquired the purest clarity. They understood all at once that the Roberto Benjamín of their baptismal certificates, the lead player in Nicolasa's inconsistent tales, was nothing but a myth inhabiting the mental darkness of their mother, and they grasped – this was the hardest part of all, a touchpaper for the rest – that they could only be children of the one man who had visited the house all these years, the priest Gregorio, who they heard deliver mass every Sunday at twelve, whom they greeted with the sign of the cross, from whom they received a kiss on the forehead when giving the sign of peace, and whose features, only now did they seem to realise, were scattered over each and every one of their faces.

Years later Nicolasa's will would only confirm the truth for them, but when they discovered it for themselves by following these premonitory hunches, they reacted with sharp disappointment. They saw themselves helpless, empty; as if they had sent their own solid centre spinning off its axis, ripping off the protective shell and turning upside down the world that their mother had forged with her fables.

Such was the shame they began to feel on the slightest reference to Cartagena and to the Church in general that, as soon as Nicolasa died, and despite having willingly received first communion, and been educated with the catechism in their hands, and learning the names of the prophets and certain verses of the Old Testament by heart, and despite the years they'd spent fasting during Lent and lighting Pentecostal candles, they came to implacably deplore all religious emblems, pitilessly destroying their filigree rosaries, tearing the crucifixes from their walls, burning to ashes their scapulars of the Immaculate Conception, and uprooting the life-size statues of the apostles they had grown up with, which they had always gazed upon with fear and respect as if they were severe relatives who had been turned to stone.

Gregorio had been dead two years, so they had no way of demanding explanations from him, though who knows if they would even have attempted to do so. They preferred to bury his memory, and so they never said a single word about the matter. They silenced the entire business about the priest with a smooth, metallic, subterranean, unbroken silence.

But it was never going to be that easy. Gregorio had been close to them, the man they sometimes called padrino, the one who would arrive early in the morning after stormy nights and show them how to repair leaks in the ancient roof. It happened dozens of times. They'd climb up onto the tiles together, scrape off the salty residue built up by the humidity, and repair the cracks with a mortar made of lime and brick dust. They could never shake off what they'd learned. For decades, however hard they tried, though they lowered their heads, closed their eyes and pressed their lips together, the sound of dripping water would always return the face and the name of the priest to their minds.

★ ★ ★

Nicolasa's last words, as immortalised in her will, were these:

I ask my children to forgive a debt to their uncle Pedro in consideration of the paternal affection that he has always professed for them and that, out of love for their mother, they preserve the most perpetual union and follow the good examples of Christian morality that I have instilled in them all my life.

The next day, she died of tuberculosis.

Neither in death nor in life was Nicolasa touched by the resentment her children felt on learning of their bastard status. The imposter, the priest, was the one who they determined to ignore, to snub, and ultimately to forget. She, on the other hand, was not the target of their criticism at all; in fact, she became the recipient of a veneration caused by a lopsided filial love: they praised her both for being the mother she was and for supplanting the father they never had. They never blamed her for keeping quiet about him or falsifying her papers or filling their heads with crazy tales. 'She must have had her reasons for lying to us,' the children said, forgiving her sacrifices, with no desire to rake through things that had already settled.

In reality, they had absolved her much earlier, since the day they decided to use Cisneros as their first surname, meaning that it would be the one to endure among their descendants, given their father's manifest absence. This was while Nicolasa was still alive, and when the children shared their decision with her, she asked them straight out what they would do with their 'legal' paternal surname, the one belonging to Roberto Benjamín. They vacillated until Manuel, the second-oldest, offered a decisive argument: 'We have never seen that man you always speak of, we have no contact with him, we don't even know where he lives or with whom – his surname does not represent us, we owe him nothing. We, like you, are Cisneros.' Feliciano, the fifth child, proposed not eliminating the paternal surname altogether, but relegating it to a middle name. The others went along with this, and even the girls accepted that their names would be Francisca Benjamín Cisneros and Catalina Benjamín Cisneros.

'What if someone asks after our second surname?' Francisca queried anxiously.

'You can say that it is Cisneros too,' Nicolasa decreed.

'What if we are accused of having no father?' Manuel wondered.

'You will tell the truth: that your father is travelling.'

'Does this man really exist, mother?' Feliciano asked. 'Or is it true what they say: that we are bastards?'

Nicolasa approached him and slapped him cleanly across the face without a second thought.

'No one has the right to use that word in this house!'

Thus, without official papers, by symbolic agreement, the children resolved to use two names from then on and only one surname: their mother's.

Unsurprisingly, the pact expired once they began to marry. As natural children of a single woman they feared social ostracisation and the impact on their family and professional prospects. The only way to put things 'in order' and achieve validation was by resuscitating the fantasy of the father. They filled out their marriage certificates with the twisted formula of their baptismal records – 'legitimate son of Roberto Benjamín and Nicolasa Cisneros' – and married before the Church and sang psalms and took the Eucharist even when recently, so very recently, they had spurned God forever as a way of inflicting revenge on Gregorio Cartagena.

Nicolasa's children soon formed Catholic homes, trying not to contaminate them with the frustrations of their orphanhood and, later, striving to exorcise the curse of the past, deactivate confusion, quell misunderstandings and banish disgrace, they baptised their children with the surname Cisneros, hoping they would never have to explain.

Only the youngest, Luis Benjamín, the man who would become my great-grandfather, refrained from marriage. At first, anyway.

Instead, he veered down the shadowy dead-end that experience screamed he should avoid. He became obsessed with another man's wife, and through her he came to know both love and distress.

It was in him. He had inherited it. No matter how hard he'd tried, he could never have tamed the impulses of his nature.

PART TWO

CHAPTER 8

Lima, 1854

The most illustrious teachers at the Colegio San Carlos, in Lima, made enthusiastic remarks about the poems that Luis Benjamín showed them during recess at the Convictorio. As a result they benevolently overlooked his ramblings in the classroom, and encouraged him to pick up his steel fountain pen and seek inspiration from the pool in the Patio de los Jazmines or the galleries of the Patio de los Naranjos, that he might write more of the sentimental ditties that even the school director, the legendary Bartolomé Herrera, read with his eyeglasses firmly affixed to his nose from the highest viewpoint of that vice-regal building.

One day, when his poems were already circulating from hand to hand among the classrooms, a fellow pupil in the final year, El Curcuncho Navarrete, bestowed a nickname on him before all the others: The Metaphorical Poet. Luis Benjamín transformed this pseudonym into his nom de plume and with a wooden-handled knife etched the initials TMP everywhere he could: a corner of his desk, on the side of certain tables in the non-boarders' Dining Hall, two columns in the Graduation Hall, four pews in the chapel of the General Hall and as many as seven of the wrought-iron grilles that separated the Huerta de Noviciados from the vacant lots where the students often stealthily gathered to watch the head-scarved women parade down Inambari street, leaving a nimbus of sensual unreality in their wake.

At home, together with his siblings, Luis Benjamín followed political life closely: these were the times of harsh confrontation between Marshal Castilla and President Echenique. Inspired by this struggle, and seeking to set himself apart from 'the cult of whimpering, melting-heart poets who appear to have invaded Lima's literary circles', as a critic had put it in a local paper, Luis Benjamín spent his first summer after high school writing a work of theatre entitled *The Peruvian Pavilion*. He was just seventeen years old.

The Poet let a few months go by before showing his progress to some of his former schoolteachers, who, as soon as they looked over the draft script, astonished at the prodigy, urged him to finish it and promised to support the staging of this 'openly patriotic allegory that contrasts with the juvenile and prissy tone of other compositions of his generation'.

Funded wholly with money from the teachers of San Carlos, the play premiered at the Principal theatre in Lima on 28 July 1855, a few days after Marshal Ramón Castilla had been sworn in as provisional President of the Republic, having defeated Echenique at the Battle of La Palma six months earlier, the same battle in which General Pedro Cisneros lost both a thumb and his hearing.

The performance of *The Peruvian Pavilion* was a re-sounding success. The standing ovation by the full house echoed around the theatre and out into the streets. Acclaimed by the audience, Luis Benjamín – wild curls, downy hair on his chin, and hands interlaced behind his back – emerged from behind the curtains to acknowledge their response. Minutes later, as he was returning backstage, still shaken by the intensity of the applause, a military guard intercepted him.

'The President wishes to congratulate you in person,' the official informed him, in an expressionless voice.

'The President is here? Where?' asked Luis Benjamín, suddenly overwhelmed by the idea of coming face to face with Marshal Castilla, the enemy of his family, the same man that his uncle Pedro had tried to kill in La Palma months earlier and to whom he had dedicated his most bitter curses and invectives ever since.

'Follow me,' said the laconic soldier.

When he arrived in the royal box – heaving with obese ministers, unctuous functionaries and miscellaneous arse-lickers – Castilla stood up and removed the glove from his right hand to shake that of the Poet. The young man returned the greeting, unable to take his eyes off the sinewy fingers, the neglected nails, and added a bow for good measure. After an introduction that exhibited the ungainliness and monotony of his oratory, Castilla smoothed his square-cut moustache and asked him with an inquisitive air if he happened to be related to 'the traitor Pedro Cisneros'. The marshal had the ability to instil fear in others just by laying his eyes on them, which is why Luis Benjamín, even though he loved and admired Pedro as the most stalwart of his uncles, felt vulnerable in this new territory and judged it inconvenient to acknowledge the connection.

'He is a distant relative,' he conceded, in a low voice.

'If that's the case, then today my delight for you is double,' Castilla replied mockingly, then issued a guffaw that revealed his irregular teeth. His guests echoed his laughter, among them El Mono Quintín, an uncouth, sinuous character who was the Marshal's personal aide and enforcer, following his orders to the letter, whether it was to deal the cards in the weekly games of rocambor that were Castilla's obsession at the central tables in the Quinta de Presa, or to 'straighten out' the government opponents who got in his way, whom he threatened like a thug, cracking against the floor the whip he carried around on his belt.

Luis Benjamín was disgusted at himself for having denied his mother's brother, but smiled at the president through his disgust, listening to his pompous, stuttering, interminable congratulations. The only thing that distracted him from the bad taste of disloyalty was the outline of a bejewelled women with thick black eyelashes who, seated beside Castilla, was cooling herself with a tortoiseshell fan draped with silk ribbons on each side, he noticed, and adorned with drawings of herons and chrysanthemums. The Poet couldn't take his eyes off her. 'We need' – continued the Marshal – 'to foster a new image of Peru, which is why a talent like yours must be placed at the service of the motherland. Our Foreign Minister, who is here with us tonight, hopes that tomorrow you will be joining his team.' The minister in question rose and confirmed the invitation: 'What do you say, Mr Cisneros?' Luis Benjamín accepted mechanically, and minutes later excused himself and left the box without having fully taken in what had just happened. He descended the steps of the galleries in the direction of the street, where the cast were awaiting him impatiently to celebrate the premiere in a little bar on Tagle; as he reached the last step he realised that those black eyelashes had printed themselves on his mind like a gentle brush-stroke of China ink.

The Poet arrived at the ministry offices the next day. His fame as 'the new protégé of the President' had preceded him, which may have contributed to the amiable reception he received from most of the civil servants, all bigger than he was both in age and physique. Despite the prevailing atmosphere of seriousness and his status as the snotty-nosed upstart, it didn't take Luis Benjamín long to find a place among these men: the sharpness and originality with which he analysed the country's foreign affairs was hardly typical of a recent high-school graduate. Likewise, the maturity of the political articles that he began to publish in newspapers and magazines did not go unnoticed and he received continual congratulations from the diplomatic commissioners. While his inoffensive appearance and self-conscious gait oozed juvenility, his attitude as he sat and debated was that of a man established in his position.

One morning, while waiting for someone at the door of the ministry, he overheard a pair of ushers talking about a woman they referred to disdainfully as 'that Colichón'. After a few minutes of eavesdropping he deduced that it must be the same carefree woman he had seen in the theatre box three weeks earlier. He set about gathering information on her and within a few days he had learned that her full name was Lucrecia Colichón Alegría; that she was the eldest daughter of a coachman of longstanding service at the Government Palace, and had been introduced to Castilla by Hilario Buenaventura, a pimp well-known in the corridors of the Palace for supplying lady companions to ministers and political leaders. According to the same source, not long after embarking on a relationship with the president, Lucrecia had borne him a son, the Marshal's third, who they called Agapito.

Castilla's first two sons – about whom he himself said

he'd have 'preferred not to have fathered' them – were born to different women. No one was certain whether they were brief love affairs or, as rumoured, victims of rape at a hacienda in Piura.

Paradoxically, his only wife, Francisca Diez Canseco, never became pregnant. On the day of their spectacular wedding in the countryside of Arequipa, before hundreds of witnesses at the foot of a flagstone altar, Castilla swore to Francisca lifelong fidelity, but 'lifelong' proved to be a mere three years; the time it took for the women selected by Hilario Buenaventura to start filing in through the false door of his office.

The fourth of these women was Lucrecia Colichón. From the first day he saw her, she became Castilla's favourite. He felt such a libidinous furore in her presence that she was pregnant within two months. Although Lucrecia told him she would abort so as not to cause him any trouble, the Marshal was dead set on her keeping the child, and told his wife as much. Lacking the courage to contradict him, she acquiesced with a benign grimace.

When Agapito was born, to ease the scandal of her husband's adultery and protect the blessed image of their Catholic home, Francisca Diez Canseco consented to passing the baby off as her own, raising it in her house on Divorciadas street, and even tolerating Castilla's unconcealed dalliance with Lucrecia, that captivating creature who the old aristocratic ladies denigrated, calling her 'trollop', 'strumpet', 'kept woman', while their husbands lusted after her with uncontrollable longing.

In the office, Luis Benjamín enjoyed his colleagues' descriptions of the ins and outs of these infidelities, and found it comical how Lucrecia seemed to dominate the president at will. At the same time he found it sad that Castilla scorned Francisca, whom, according to an account attributed to Mono Quintín, he used to harangue and even beat up when he returned drunk from losing his games of rocambor.

What the Poet didn't yet know, despite his ardent hunger since the night he first set eyes on Lucrecia Colichón in the theatre, was that he would soon become entangled with that woman and turn his own life into a maelstrom of unhappiness.

* * *

An older friend from school, Ricardo Palma, invited him to a literary soirée in the home of another young poet, Carlos Augusto Salaverry, who each month hosted companions, writers, novice poets and versifiers of doggerel, booksellers, opera fans and more than a few hacks and disenchanted bohemians. At this soirée, Luis Benjamín met a brotherhood of ashen-faced poets who spent their nights in the taverns of the city centre, paying for their drinks by declaiming satirical verses. They called themselves 'the Romantic Crows', sported thick, brush-like moustaches and dressed in English three-piece suits. They introduced themselves using only their paternal surnames: Corpancho, Márquez, Parra, Castillo, and García.

That night, the guests surrounded Ricardo Palma as soon as he began to relate his adventures aboard the *Rímac*, the first steamer in Latin America. Thanks to its propulsion system, the boat was so novel that when it reached the port of Paita on its maiden voyage, the populace, seeing the great column of steam emerging from the funnel, raised the alarm, believing it was on fire. The point of Palma's story was not this, however, but the details of the accident that was on everyone's lips in Lima at that time: the sinking of the *Rímac* at Punta de San

Juan, on Los Leones beach, where the craft collided with a rock formation known as the Elephant on a moonless night. The news of the survivors' odyssey travelled around the globe. The collision broke it in two and the passengers – including Palma – threw themselves into the sea in desperation, shouting for help and swimming, at least those who could swim, in different directions. Only sixty of the 400 unfortunates on board made it to shore, barely alive, vomiting seaweed and spume. The others perished, flung against the sharp reefs, or from cramp and hypothermia after swimming for hours until the point of exhaustion, fighting the waves, their flailing arms taking them nowhere. The survivors toiled for two days among the dunes and plains in search of any sign of civilisation, before fatigue, hunger and thirst carried off a further forty of them. Only nineteen lived to tell the tale. 'When we finally made it to the first town we had the countenance of ghosts,' Palma recalled, sucking on a cigar, while the others listened to his testimony in awe, gaping, their glasses of pisco forgotten in front of them.

Luis Benjamín listened attentively to Palma until a sudden vision distracted him from the story. Four young ladies appeared through the door and wove their way towards them, their folded parasols over their arms, passing beneath a clock on the wall marking eight on the dot. Outside, the night was as black as the mouth of a corpse.

Although Salaverry's soirées were usually attended only by men, the young ladies introduced themselves as 'friends of Juana Manuela Gorriti', an Argentinian writer whose house on Valladolid street street was well known for its writers' evenings and smart drinkers. Their claim of Gorriti's friendship was a good enough calling card.

Suddenly everyone's eyes were on the newcomers and the dazzling necklines of their French–style dresses

confected with imported fabrics. Beneath their crinolines their legs fell into rhythm as they crossed the floor
tiles and took refuge in a corner, from where they studied
the room with an air of disregard or petulance, while
a servant filled their glasses with a liquor that looked
like chirimoya brandy. A fop festooned with ostentatious and bizarre names, one Víctor Fulgencio Ramiro
Regalado de la Riva Agüero y Looz Corswarem, who
claimed to be the son of Princess Arnoldina Irene de
Looz Corswarem, nodded in their direction muttering
'here come the mazorqueras', which was the aristocrats'
contemptuous term for the wives and daughters of the
nouveau riche who had emerged in Lima a few years
earlier thanks to the global demand for guano and who,
gathered in a political party popularly known as the
'party of the corn cob', supported the government of the
fallen Rufino Echenique.

Of the four girls, one stood out for her voluptuous
figure and easy-going, frivolous air. It was Lucrecia
Colichón. As soon as he saw her, Luis Benjamín focused
all his attention on the contours of her face, and after
spending a while looking at her careless corkscrew curls,
he gauged her weight, inhaled the mixture of fragrances
that enveloped her – ambers, civets, benzoins, camphors
– approached her with a studied, afflicted air, and assailed
her without preamble, declaring urgently: 'I'm seventeen
years old and I've been in love with you all my life.'

Colichón laughed out loud, a laugh that travelled
across the room like a drifting cloud and echoed on
the far wall, cutting off Ricardo Palma, who was still
telling his tale of adventure on the high seas, to a waning
crowd of listeners who were beginning to show signs of
weariness.

Luis Benjamín had read somewhere – perhaps in the
book of Voltaire's anecdotes that he carried everywhere

— that 'a woman's laugh is a sensuous act', so he was not disheartened by the apparent mockery. In any case, something of his shameless confession must have penetrated Lucrecia's guise as an unattainable woman of Lima, because suddenly, as if putting on a show of not wanting to, with a poorly acted effort, she began to pay more attention to him than to the dolled-up girls with whom she had arrived minutes earlier. That was how, listening to him, Lucrecia discovered that her audacious and very young admirer was the author of the play that Marshal Castilla had liked so much and that she herself had applauded in fascination from the gallery of the theatre.

'Did you not use a fan with wooden lacework that evening?' Luis Benjamín inquired.

'Indeed I did. Do you always observe fans so closely?'

'It depends on who is using them.'

'Should I take that as a compliment?'

'Or a clumsy attempt at gallantry. In any case, I do not wish to vex you.'

'A gallant only vexes if he is impetuous.'

'You will understand that it is sometimes difficult to halt one's impetus.'

'Are you suggesting you don't have full control over yourself, Luis Benjamín?'

'Not in front of you.'

'This is when I feel the need for a fan.'

'You didn't bring it today?'

'I left it at home.'

'Do you regret that?'

'A little. I didn't know it would get so warm around here.'

Lucrecia uttered this last phrase looking at him with the expansive smugness of her twenty-one years, and in that instant Luis Benjamín knew that he had no escape.

What does it matter that she is older than me. That she is Castilla's lover. That she has had his child. That they call her a strumpet and a tart. What does it matter if it were true, he raved in silence, no longer governing the uncomfortable simmer of his ideas and his blood.

Encouraged by the host's piano, the Romantic Crows invited the mazorqueras to dance polkas, schottisches and mazurkas. The Poet took Lucrecia by the hand to lead her into the group, but just as he took the first turns of the dance and prepared to babble something in her ear, Ricardo Palma appeared by his side and, whether out of envy or friendship, proceeded to rescue his comrade from the danger of flirting with the President's woman.

'Excuse us, young lady,' he said, addressing Lucrecia. 'Another literary salon awaits us.'

'What are you doing?' muttered Luis Benjamín between his teeth.

'Saving your life, Poet.'

In the long run, Palma's impertinence would have no bearing on the outcome. The darts had been launched in one direction, and there was little anyone could do to alter the fate that from that night on slowly closed in around the Poet like thick treacle.

* * *

Within a matter of days, Luis Benjamín began to visit twice a week the imposing rustic house with stable, garden and two cherub-fed pools that Castilla had purchased as a safe place of encounter with Lucrecia Colichón.

The Poet would arrive at dawn and crouch behind some dense bushes opposite the house, waiting for the Marshal, like every morning, to leave for the Government Palace on business with his ministers. As soon as the coast was clear, he'd slip through the tall grasses that swayed in the morning breeze and quickly penetrate the domain. He had only to reach through the gate and lift the metal latch and, once inside, cross the first courtyard and continue straight down the passage with lanterns hanging from the walls that led to the main hall. The light at that hour was always grey and the night-time damp of the house was impregnated with the fresh smell of magnolias, bougainvillea, honeysuckle and jacarandas growing in the garden outside. Lucrecia would greet him on the tiled staircase with an outstretched hand, and he would let her guide him into the master bedroom, where – after bolting the door, shutting the curtains, and adjusting the blinds – he would ardently undress her, climbing on top of her, thrusting inside her and making love to her twice on the still-warm bed. They stayed there, their sticky bodies puffing side by side, inspecting the corners of the ceiling, lying like boats face up on the wet sand, so exhausted or ecstatic that it became routine to lose any sense of the passing hours.

On more than one occasion, the Poet – trousers and frock coat in hand – had to leap over the balustraded balconies of the terrace, climb down the ivy and take cover in the first possible hiding place before the imminent arrival of the president or one of the peons or gendarmes from his retinue of guards. If he didn't conceal himself in the yard with the chicken run, then he hid in the back of the stables or in the tiny servants' cloakroom, and in extreme cases, when taken by surprise, he secreted himself inside the mahogany piano that Castilla had sent for from Vienna to please one of his lover's many whims, a piano that nobody played and that rested like a meek and refined animal in the anteroom on the second floor.

Making love to Lucrecia on those premises was as insolent and audacious as profaning a cathedral. They became so addicted to each other, so blind, so reciprocally insatiable and frantic that, when they couldn't see each other at home, Lucrecia found ways to let Luis Benjamín know where she would be, and he went looking for her with the voracity of a madman, following her to processions, churches, shops, train stations and Sunday walks through the central alameda or the meadows of Chorrillos, always keeping a physical distance that only fed the temptation between them, and when he could no longer resist, they managed to coincide in some corner, where they kissed and touched with fleeting fervour.

The adrenaline spiral of that love triangle would dissolve after three months, when Lucrecia announced to the Poet that she was pregnant. When imagining that he would be a father, eighteen-year-old Luis Benjamín felt like his friend Ricardo Palma on the deck of the *Rímac* in the middle of a storm, or more precisely like the ship itself sinking into the horrendous throat of the Punta de San Juan.

Lucrecia broke with Marshal Castilla and he, furious, wounded to his core, not yet suspecting the existence of another man, let alone the pregnancy, shut her up first in the henhouse and then threw her out without giving her the chance to pack, tossing a couple of dresses after her into the street.

Anticipating this outcome, the Poet had rented a room high up in a convent near the house where he lived with his mother, from whom he carefully kept his machinations secret. Lucrecia moved in and over the following months Luis Benjamín dedicated his evenings to caring for her. He prepared tonics and infusions and caressed her bump, while recounting the latest from the Ministry or describing the drink-fuelled exploits of the Romantic Crows around the city centre bars, and lay awake until she was fast asleep, and only then would he tiptoe home and offer ever more inventive excuses to his mother, keeping Nicolasa's questions at bay, although to herself she never stopped wondering where her son went on these constant escapades.

The waters broke early one morning and the Poet urgently sent for the only person who could act as midwife while maintaining total discretion: Dominga Prieto. The black servant had stored away and been mixed up in so many secrets that one more would make no difference. Lucrecia lost a lot of blood but overcame the pain and pushed with all her might, refusing to give in. When the little head emerged through the swollen vagina, the umbilical cord was wrapped around the neck of the baby, which was a frightening shade of purple. Despite the complications and her shock at the tiny size of the premature baby, Dominga Prieto pulled it out with a single tug, announced in her gravelly voice that it was a girl, gave it a sharp smack on the bottom and wiped away the buttery substance that had been its cloak in the womb for the days and nights of gestation. The parents received the girl knowing that she would be called Elvira – Elvira Cisneros Colichón – and it would take them some time to learn to hold her without feeling that she was slipping through their nervous arms. Her minuscule presence illuminated the walls of that gloomy little room, unexpectedly making it look something like a home.

* * *

With the support of a handful of close friends, Lucrecia and the Poet lived like mice, growing used to being young parents who no one acknowledged as a family. Disguising, lying, devising subterfuges, acclimatising to tricks and life in the dark was an ordeal that lasted four seemingly endless years.

At this time Luis Benjamín was dividing his life

between the Ministry – where he had become head of the Department of Continental Affairs – and the secluded building on Velaochaga street where he moved with Lucrecia. He hadn't stopped writing poetry, nor staging works of theatre, nor feeling like a patriot, nor placing articles in the papers about the constant political wrangling. Nor had he stopped getting his lover pregnant: after Elvira, Lucrecia gave birth to Adelaida and moved straight on to María Luisa. For the Poet, those were years of breathless uncertainty, yet they brought him a strange kind of happiness.

All of that came to an end the morning that Lucrecia, tired of the faking, the simulation and the concealment, demanded that they be publicly married.

'I want everyone to know we live together and I want my daughters to be able to embrace their father in the sight and tolerance of all.'

Luis Benjamín didn't take the request well. His first fear was his mother's disappointment on being apprised of so many things at once. It wouldn't be easy for Nicolasa, he thought, to suddenly discover that her son lived in sin with the lover of the president, and much less that she was grandmother to three girls she'd never seen.

The Poet, anticipating the debacle, asked Lucrecia to reconsider. He understood her exasperated wish to legalise her family, but wasn't prepared to deal with the consequences that such a decision would unleash.

Lucrecia flew into a rage at his being such a milquetoast, and threatened to leave him. She was not prepared, she warned, to remain in a deviant relationship while watching her youth disappear.

From the sheer fright of hearing such talk, the Poet developed an insomnia that turned his eyes yellow and his ideas to dust. Every time he picked up a piece of paper and a pen, he produced nothing but smudges and hieroglyphics, as if he had suddenly forgotten how to write.

To top it all, Castilla was going through his most difficult period since he had been voted back into power in fixed elections. He had long given up his stance as the magnanimous governor who would abolish slavery, which had flourished in Peru for 300 years, setting him on a collision course with the hacienda owners, who believed in racial supremacy and could not conceive of a world without the subjection of black people. Before being sold to work on the plantations and spend their lives amid abuse, whippings, strappings, torture and other humiliations by their owners, black men, women and children spent their nights locked up in sheds that were real pigsties, at the mercy of disease, guarded by vicious dogs that barked constantly, and when they died their bodies weren't buried in coffins or even pits, but abandoned as carrion for the vultures to fight over.

By 1859, the Marshal had become an impassive and fickle despot won over by a court of sycophants who ran to kiss his hand and organise festivities for him that, as the Government Palace majordomos themselves recounted, were drunken revels where the Marshal, narcissistic like no other, assailed his guests with insufferable rants in which he compared himself to Alcibiades, Trajan and Alexander the Great.

Luis Benjamín knew that if Castilla were to learn of his betrayal, he wouldn't hesitate to order that he be skinned alive, and then would surely send his attack dog, the pitiless Mono Quintín, to mete out to Lucrecia and her daughters who knows what unmentionable retributions. In a hasty reaction that he would quickly regret, out of an overwhelming desire to break all contact with the government, the Poet renounced his position at the Foreign Ministry. Yet unemployment would only worsen his situation.

Lucrecia then cornered him with an ultimatum:

'If you have not announced the wedding within one month, I will leave Peru with the girls, penniless as I am.'

Luis Benjamín was driven crazy by the thought. He spent the following days wandering around the centre, getting drunk in taverns and shabby chinganas, from which he'd emerge without an alibi, thinking about how insignificant and unhappy he'd be without his daughters. He was troubled by his own indecision, his lack of courage, how easily he gave up at the first obstacle. He was troubled by how similar that made him to his father, Gregorio Cartagena, a man he had never fully known but who he identified as plagued by inconsistencies, hesitations and fear, the same fear that now crawled inside of him.

Nicolasa only had to run into him one night in the street, drunk, rattling between lampposts and other pedestrians, to see or to confirm that something was destroying her youngest son from the inside. She sent Dominga Prieto for him, sat him down at the kitchen table in the house on Peña Horadada, laid out a bowl of hot bean soup and waited until he had finished the last spoonful before confronting him:

'Will you tell me, or should I tell you?

And so the Poet, burying his face in his hands, stuttered out a few apprehensive words, before confessing everything between sobs, trembling like a freshly plucked bird.

Nicolasa listened intently, with no heed to the accumulated impact of so much shocking news. She felt the Poet's bewilderment so deeply that she wrapped her arms around him, begging him not to corrupt his spirit any further and, once he was calmer, enjoined him to leave everything behind, to be the one to leave 'that spurious household', to travel far away, and save his heart from the asphyxiating glut of misfortunes and from the shadows that were surely to come.

'Go to Paris! That's where you should be,' she said without hesitation. 'I'll look after your daughters,' she added, to encourage him.

Luis Benjamín rejected his mother's offer out of hand, but he reconsidered a few weeks later, when the inflexible Lucrecia blackmailed him by saying she would prevent him seeing the girls if he didn't arrange the ceremony 'tomorrow'.

The following lunchtime, taking advantage of Lucrecia's departure for the train station to collect her aunts who were arriving from Jauja, the Poet went into the room of Elvira, Adelaida and the infant María Luisa, dressed them in the first togs he could find in the sole wardrobe, stuffed their other clothes into a single suitcase and took them to Nicolasa's place as fast as he could.

As soon as she opened the door to find this clutch of little rag dolls, the grandmother's heart was won forever, and immediately forgetting the animosity stirred by the children's mother, she spoiled them with gifts and sweets prepared by Dominga Prieto, now a white-haired old woman who hobbled around, smiling like a fortune teller to see that the story of the Cisneros was nothing more than a prophecy condemned to be repeated again and again.

'How they love to screw up their lives,' she murmured to herself.

The Poet knelt down in front of Elvira, the eldest, the four-year-old who had been born two months premature and looked younger, and told her in a cracked voice that he had to leave on a long journey but that she mustn't worry, because grandma Nicolasa would look after her and her sisters. Elvira, with a knot in her throat, her pigtails all askew, asked for her mummy. Trying to calm her down, confronted with the choice of telling her the truth or continuing to lie, Luis Benjamín confused her by uttering an impulsive phrase that the girl would take years to come to terms with.

'From now on your grandma will be your mummy.'

Before leaving, he hugged all three with his remaining strength, stammered out some words of wisdom that they would immediately forget, planted a kiss on their foreheads and, looking back from the doorway, bit his lip and set his jaw so as not to dissolve into tears.

The next morning, shrouded by a mist that turned the port of Callao into a dense and mysterious forest, and clouded still further by the tribulations of travellers who, like him, seemed to be fleeing from a siege or persecution, the Poet embarked on a schooner for the city of Colón, Panama, and twenty-four hours later boarded the ship *Sharon*, bound for France. On the high seas, dejected but also with a feeling of release, he wrote the first lines of a poem that would be titled 'Aurora amor':

Where am I? I have wept...
On the bed
of the narrow solitary cabin,
I fall into the clutches of a mortal swoon.

CHAPTER 9

Paris, 1859

The Poet first set foot on French soil at four o'clock on a drizzly, lead-grey afternoon. His luggage amounted to a single suitcase. He spent a while observing the comings and goings of the port of Le Havre, getting used to the light, the horns of the boats, the voices, the language and the appearance of the people passing by. Without enough money for the train, he found a coachman who would take him to Paris for ten francs.

His first place of refuge was the room in a pension located at number 3, Rue de Lutèce, in the crowded Île de la Cité district, four blocks from Avenue Victoria. Nicolasa had given him a piece of paper with the address on it, but it wasn't until he was standing in front of the two-storey building that he asked himself how his mother had formed this contact. He never found out. 'They'll be expecting you' was the only instruction he was given.

The pension was ruled over by an older woman, somewhat soft in the head, Madame Georgette Leblanc, who made great efforts to understand the much-chewed-over French of her new South American lodger.

After registering, Luis Benjamín climbed the eleven treads of the staircase leading to his room and closed the door behind him. He found that it was a five-metre-square den with a single window – the wind rattled the timber frames – overlooking the Seine and the new Pont au Change, partially obscured by the dome of the Tribunal de Commerce. As he passed his gaze over the sagging matchbox of his bed, the jug and washbasin standing crooked on the woodwormed night table, and the rickety chair that threatened to collapse if he should have the gall to sit, Luis Benjamín recalled the precarious hovels where his daughters were born and felt thrust upon him all the pain that a man in his condition was capable of feeling.

In his first days in that ebullient, monumental, always hectic city, where people seemed indifferent to or even exhausted by the beauty around them, the Poet wrote dozens of letters to Lucrecia begging her forgiveness for fleeing Lima so abruptly. He never dared to send a single one of them. They were written, in reality, for himself, in a ritual of self-pity that lasted two months, and only ended upon receiving a missive from his brother Luciano recounting that Lucrecia, following an altercation in the street with Nicolasa, had finally accepted that the girls should be raised in their grandmother's house. It was Colichón herself who established that her visits to Elvira, Adelaida and María Luisa should be restricted to Sundays. Luis Benjamín was not surprised by this coldness: years earlier, she had allowed Castilla's wife to raise her son Agapito as her own, and hadn't even wanted to breastfeed him.

In his letters, Luciano related that Lucrecia had returned to live with the Marshal in their rustic mansion, to frequent the same salons together with her friends the mazorqueras, and to wear the crinolines that helped to disguise her pregnancies. He remarked that she had been seen at the Valvanera festival, at the Plaza de Acho, at the Quinta de Presa, and dancing cuecas and resbalosas at the soirées held by the aristocracy. And he also advised his brother of the rumour that Lucrecia had gone back to working for Hilario Buenaventura of an evening.

Luis Benjamín suffered greatly reading and rereading these pages, crumpling them against his chest and wondering how the mother of his children had gone back to being the same arrogant woman he'd first glimpsed in the theatre five years earlier, and realised that, by taking up her old life again, Lucrecia sought to erase or deny all the time she had spent by his side, and he suddenly felt that his love for her was nothing more than a passion gone sour, and that if it weren't for their three daughters they would have nothing in common. He was grieved to learn that his impact on Lucrecia's life had been so minimal, and felt ashamed, wishing he had not taken all those impetuous decisions that had ultimately delivered him into this forced exile.

Luis Benjamín made the best of his days in the city strolling along Avenue de l'Opéra or Rue de Rivoli, or down the Sébastapol and Saint-German boulevards. He liked to walk deep into the heart of Paris and drink in the chaos of the renovation works ordered by Emperor Louis Napoleon Bonaparte, Napoleon III, who had commissioned the Prefect of the Seine, Baron Haussmann, to lay out broad avenues, straight streets, and new boulevards, as well as restoring façades, remodelling parks, repairing monuments, creating sewers, and in short carrying out a complete transformation of the city. He wandered among the shells of the demolished houses in the ancient core of the city, he lingered under the iron hooks that swung around like arthritic puppets, he pondered the novel construction techniques, and he avidly explored the vast new embankment works along the river. Other days he stayed in his attic, isolated from the monotonous din of the machines and pulleys outside, immersed in books he happened upon, seeking to shake off the dull feelings instilled in him when Lima was at the centre of his musings.

One such morning he came across a book lying on the pension entrance hall table. It was a recently published novel called *Lui*, by one Louise Colet, daughter of Henriette Leblanc, the sister of Madame Leblanc, the owner of the guesthouse, who did nothing to conceal her antipathy towards her niece. It was thanks to his landlady that Luis Benjamín learned that Louise – whose maiden name was Révoil – was 'a pedantic and irascible blonde', 'a second-rate poetess with no other merit than having seduced Gustave Flaubert', that she was eleven years his senior and had been his lover for almost ten. After *Madame Bovary* had appeared two years earlier, and feeling that the character of Emma alluded to her in an unfavourable manner, Louise attempted a riposte in the form of *Lui*, which turned out to be a vicious little roman à clef that sank without trace.

From a Peruvian friend living in Paris, Luis Benjamín also learned that in 1838, eight years before meeting Flaubert, already married to the flautist Hippolyte Colet, Louise had become involved with the illustrious philosopher Victor Cousin, who would go on to become Education Minister and who fathered a child by her two years later. Hearing this story, Luis Benjamín could not fail to associate Louise Colet with Lucrecia Colichón: he superimposed on the former the latter's face, her voice, her false sweetness, the sometimes grotesque or prickly manner in which she acted in private. Even the surnames sounded similar – Colet, Colichón – and he felt that they must be twisted twin souls, volatile and telepathic souls that operated at a distance, kindred spirits giving each other mutual advice on how to harm the men who had loved or tried to love them. The comparison was hardly fair to Lucrecia, at least, since Louise was a manic depressive, not to say unbalanced. One day, a well-known French journalist, Alphonse Karr, had scathingly suggested that Louise Colet had committed adultery and insinuated that her unborn child had been fathered not by her husband the flautist, but by Minister Cousin. Using a satirical pun he claimed that the pregnancy was due to *une piqûre de Cousin* – 'a mosquito bite'. Reading the article, Louise felt sick, found out where Karr lived, banged on the door of his apartment and, when the journalist appeared, out of her wits by that point, threw herself at him and plunged a kitchen knife three times into his back. Incredibly, although the wounds were deep, they were not fatal. When he was released from hospital, Karr asked the police for the blood-stained knife and hung it on his living room wall with the inscription 'Gift of Madame Colet'.

This was the Paris into which my great-grandfather Luis Benjamín arrived with his premature lassitude at life. It was the late Second Empire Paris of Flaubert and Baudelaire, whose book *Les Fleurs du Mal* was denounced as 'lurid' by Ernest Pinard, the same government lawyer who months earlier had accused *Madame Bovary* of being an obscene novel (and who was later revealed to be a clandestine author of erotic stories as well as an enthu-siastic pornographer). It was the Paris that enjoyed the tales of Alexandre Dumas and the early speculations of Jules Verne. The Paris that not long before had mourned the deaths of Stendhal and Balzac, and that within a few years would celebrate the emergence of Mallarmé. It was the Paris rebuilt with aesthetic and political aspirations, capital of a France protected by armies, led by Napoleon

III, that were presently clashing with the Austrian forces in Solferino, in support of the Italian independence struggle embodied by Giuseppe Garibaldi. It was the Paris where popular idols flourished like Charles Blondin, who was not any old Blondin but the Great Blondin, a tightrope-walker who had recently become the first man to cross Niagara Falls. According to *Le Tour du Monde*, Blondin crossed a line 335 metres in length at a height of fifty metres above the water. Hundreds of Parisians – professionals, students and workers alike – travelled to the United States to experience with horror and chills the fantastic feat, the near-hallucination that the acrobat would later repeat against other backdrops, with increasingly reckless variations: on stilts, blindfolded or, the most bonkers of all, carrying his own manager on his back, even taking a chair with him to pause mid-rope and eat an omelette off a small table.

★ ★ ★

Luis Benjamín financed his first studies of French with the meagre funds that Nicolasa sent him. He attended free courses at the Sorbonne and – turning his back on the distractions of the Quartier Latin, the student quarter, where any young writer would naturally head – locked himself in his room to draft the chapters of his first novel, *Julia*.

As soon as it was complete, he sent it to Peru to try his luck, and within a few months received news of its publication. This boost to his spirits made him feel full and alive, as full and alive as he had felt the night he premiered his first play. When he learned that *Julia* had been well received in Lima, he understood that he was meant to write, and decided to remain in Paris indefinitely. He wanted to nourish himself, to connect with writers who could shape, smooth and enrich his style and personality. He enrolled in philosophy and literature courses, consulted professors outside of scheduled class hours, and purchased so many books and notebooks he found himself in debt. Whenever he returned to the pension on the Rue de Lutèce, he would have tea with Madame Leblanc, tell her about the novels he wanted to write in the future, and then shut himself away to do accounts and draw up plans, determined to remake himself far from Lima, and become someone else: a respected artist, an Old World intellectual.

Some nights, his dreams were brought to a grinding halt by enduring memories of the people he had left behind: his daughters, who were growing up without a father, just like he had; his ageing mother; his siblings, above all Luciano, with whom he would continue to plot patriotically about reuniting in Peru; his closest friends, Ricardo Palma and Casimiro Ulloa, known as El Rojo, husband to his sister Catalina, a true brother more than an in-law, another member of this proud family of bastards with a single surname. All of them floated weightlessly through Luis Benjamín's dreams, and he felt them speaking to him from some kind of watery galaxy of stars where the words were echoes or bubbles or clues whose meaning he uselessly tried to unravel. However he longed to put the past to rest, those names and visions dimmed him, slowed him down, becoming the bond that for a long time prevented him from drawing an imaginary but definitive line between who he had been and who he wanted to be. The only thing these memories achieved was to increase his anger at his own lies, his poor decisions, his lack of courage, an anger that translated into a sleeplessness so awful that the Poet sometimes came to believe he would never sleep again.

One November night, in the Café Guerbois on Boulevard des Batignolles – which years later would become the club for painters such as Manet, and writers like Zola and Maupassant – he met another young Peruvian, the journalist Narciso Álvarez, who had been settled in Paris for several years. He was the one who told Luis Benjamín the story of Louise Colet and Victor Cousin and, although they barely knew each other, took pity on his tight economic straits and invited him to share his apartment at number 11, Rue de la Sorbonne. The Poet had no idea that this move, provisional as he believed it to be, would come to define his future, not immediately but much later on: nine years later, to be precise.

The father of Narciso Álvarez was Don Gervasio Álvarez, a lifetime member of the Supreme Court of Lima. One day in January 1869 Don Gervasio would receive from the hands of the Poet Cisneros a package sent by his son Narciso from Paris. That day in the future, Luis Benjamín – on a visit to Lima – would walk down Mariquitas street in the city centre, between Quemado and Mogollón, and knock on the door of number 363. Don Gervasio was sitting at a table sorting a pack of cards, playing tresillo with his old friends from the Court: a half-dozen veteran flabby-cheeked magistrates puffing on clay pipes, expelling columns of smoke through half-open mouths delineated by trimmed moustaches, and sipping from their diminutive glasses of cognac.

From his chair, Don Gervasio instinctively trusted the Poet's voice. It didn't seem like the voice of the man who, as was rumoured all over Lima, had run off to France leaving behind his three illegitimate daughters with the best-known of Ramón Castilla's lovers. He stood up to welcome him, adjusting his waistcoat.

Luis Benjamín entered and came to a halt halfway, as if a memory had suddenly assailed him. It wasn't the tableau of the six magistrates vegetating around the table that shook him, but spying beyond them, in the courtyard adjacent to the kitchen garden, a young lady who, rather than simply playing the piano, was picking at the keys as if they were electrified. He observed her lucuma fruit-coloured hair woven into a plait and tied with a scarlet bow, her patent leather shoes, her pearl gloves, her taut skin, her pale lips. She was dressed in a white so pure that she looked like the spirit of a recently deceased adolescent. Who is she? Luis Benjamín wondered to himself. He would soon learn that she was Cristina Bustamante Álvarez, the sole granddaughter of Don Gervasio – who had adopted her – and thus the niece of his friend Narciso.

She felt the weight of new eyes upon her and turned to see who they belonged to.

Observing the exchange of glances, and intuiting the kind of promises they seemed to convey, the aged former judge was struck by a sense of foreboding and regretted asking the servant minutes earlier to let in 'the Poet Cisneros'. Wouldn't it have been better to receive the package at the door? In a matter of moments, Don Gervasio realised his error and, watching his grand-daughter from afar, sank into a gloom at what already felt inevitable.

'Dammit, the girl has gone to ruin,' he grumbled to himself, and to the astonishment of his companions, drained the rest of his cognac in one, before blowing his nose and spitting a thick gobbet of saliva onto the floor.

Over the following weeks, every time the virginal Cristina received the Poet to play the piano together or converse on the lounge sofas or the wicker chairs in the kitchen garden, the old man spied on them, seething with rage. As soon as Luis Benjamín said goodbye and stepped out onto the street, Gervasio hurried to poison his granddaughter's mind, telling her that her suitor was 'a phony', 'an uncaring father', 'a degenerate who lives like a poor bohemian in Paris, getting drunk on cheap liquor under fetid bridges, sleeping in rubbish-strewn alleyways, and disporting himself through the most sordid of dunghills to practise all kinds of sexual aberrations with depraved women, carriers of the black plague and God knows what disgusting venereal diseases'.

Seeing that his granddaughter paid no attention to these calumnies, Gervasio turned to silently cursing his son Narciso, as he failed to understand how his first-born could have sent such a miserable envoy from Paris, in what amounted to an inconceivable affront against the family. To add to his disgruntlement, his son-in-law, Cristina's father Arnaldo Bustamante, who appreciated the books and journalism of Luis Benjamín and hated Ramón Castilla, not only approved of the writer's courting but encouraged his daughter in the romance, ignoring the hysterical grumblings of his father-in-law and minimising another fact that the curmudgeonly Don Gervasio saw as an ineludible hindrance: Luis Benjamín was sixteen years older than Cristina, who had just turned fourteen and had not yet had her first period.

But all of that was to occur in the first months of 1869, nine years after my great-grandfather arrived in France.

In Paris, deducing that writing would make him poorer than he already was, the Poet set aside his literary studies and devoted himself to political economy. This was the recommendation of Eliseo Zevallos, his former boss at the Foreign Ministry, who having crossed paths with him by chance succeeded in getting him hired as consul at Le Havre, the same port where he had arrived so many months earlier.

Thus Luis Benjamín returned to diplomatic work, taking charge of a specific task: organising the distribution of Peruvian guano exported to France. He also spent time writing political articles he sent every two weeks to his friend Casimiro Ulloa, and working on his second novel, *Edgardo*, in which the Paris-based, Spanish-language publishing house Rosa & Bouret had expressed an interest.

At first he felt himself to be a faithless writer disguised as a civil servant, but soon he became a civil servant who wrote in his spare time, and not long after that a novice consul who missed writing and who was dazzled by the lavishness of the diplomatic world and by the characters he got to know in Le Havre, from the most distinguished to the most curious.

One such figure was Monsieur Fysquet.

Fysquet was a little man of some seventy years of age. He held down a modest post in the port management office but boasted about being a 'retired corsair with the honours of a Navy ensign,' asseverating to anyone who would listen that in 1816 he had 'pirated with Simón Bolívar on the voyage that took the Liberator from Santo Domingo to Venezuela on a ship called *El Bello Inca*'. With a speed of movement admirable in a rickety old body such as his, Fysquet offered no quarter to his interlocutors, befuddling them with soporific maritime anecdotes in which he played a leading role that bore no proportion whatsoever to the advanced myopia he had suffered since birth, his scrawny constitution, nor the evidently less-than-glorious history of his musculature.

After he was introduced to Luis Benjamín at the annual festivities held at the Hotel de Ville, Fysquet came calling every Sunday. He would turn up late at night like a rodent and in recounting his naval escapades for the umpteenth time would eventually and unfailingly invoke his 'animated discussions with Bolívar', although he never explained exactly what these had been about. One such night, having done the honours to five bottles of Burgundy, he finally confessed, ashamed, that his supposedly prolific dialogues with the Venezuelan military leader were limited to a few laconic words, a brief exchange on coastal navigation aboard a brig as they were flanking Isla Margarita.

'Petty officer Fysquet! Take your spyglass and tell me if that vessel ahead is flying a flag.'

'It is raising one this very moment, General.'

'Is it a Spanish flag?'

'No, General, it is an English flag.'

'And what is its bearing?'

'The same as ours, General.'

'In that case, there is no call for alarm.'

That was it.

The alcohol also led him to admit that during the fighting he'd seen as boatswain's mate he had not in fact climbed the mast, fired the rifles, or lit the fuse of the cannons as he had claimed on previous occasions, but was in charge of counting the losses, tossing the bodies overboard, cleaning the splashes of blood from the deck and dispelling the stink of death.

By contrast, Monsieur Fysquet was not exaggerating when he related that his involvement in that expedition had earned him gold medals from the governments of Colombia and Venezuela, the two most valuable in a collection of minor medals, all silver, granted for salvage operations in different French ports. At gala events, he would arrange the medals on the breast of his dress coat, always careful to leave space 'for the next one'.

This is how he was dressed the night he attended a dance at the Tuileries Palace with his lover, Evarista Charpentier, a frumpy, plump Breton villager who, at the suggestion of his own wife, he passed off in public as his adoptive daughter. The permissive Madame Fysquet claimed not to be troubled by her husband's autumnal flirtations with 'this hirsute peasant girl' as long as he behaved with prudence. When Fysquet confided how fortunate he felt to enjoy the attentions of both women without causing conflict, Luis Benjamín couldn't help thinking about Marshal Castilla, Lucrecia Colichón and Francisca Diez Canseco, that other love triangle that he had temporarily thrown awry, in the previous life that his past now seemed to him.

That night in 1862, won over by the stubbornness of his French friend, Luis Benjamín also attended the dance at the Tuileries.

It was an experience he would never forget.

There he participated in the hand-kissing of Emperor Napoleon III, whom the servants called 'The Sphinx' behind his back, in reference to the many hours he could spend in motionless meditative trances in the most unexpected corners of the palace. And while he was struck by the monarch's satiny attire – the blue and red uniform of the Grenadiers – he was more impressed with the palatial paraphernalia that successively revealed itself as he entered the monumental construction: the elegance of the open-top carriages; the steel helmets of the elite unit of the Cent-gardes Squadron, lined up motionless like mannequins or wax soldiers; the majesty of the spherical pavilions; the vastness of the galleries; the splendour of the pointed vaults; the superb domes with heraldic motifs; the Roman porticoes with stone parapets; the red gold of the window frames; the Murano glass of the chandeliers; the granite of the anteroom floors; the brilliance of the Venetian mirrors; the thickness of the Chinese rugs; the velvet of the Damascus curtains; the naval shields embroidered on panels that covered entire walls; the Persian screens that separated chambers and cabinets; the rural love scenes depicted in Flemish wall hangings; the tapestries from Brussels with their bucolic themes; the carved ivory of the vases from Peking; the ebony altarpieces that appeared to have been looted from some monastery; the elegance of the staircases with their landings and double flights; the porcelain swans at the back of a dozen Gothic clocks with pendulums that marked different times; the African canaries that seemed to be sleeping in their bronze aviaries, and always, everywhere, up above, those unattainable ceilings adorned with remarkable frescoes depicting allegories of the Last Judgment.

There was something magnetic and disturbing about the gleaming corridors which led Luis Benjamín out to broad terraces where centuries earlier Catherine de' Medici, the capricious designer of the palace, had walked, her head clouded by the predictions of an astrologer who had said she would die in those rooms, with the result that she decided to endow them with even greater distinction, ordering the construction of the ostentatious marble entrance arch and extending the extravagant Florentine gardens, whose paths, pergolas, benches, fish ponds, and squares bearing the names of the continents replaced the sand quarries that had occupied the area, and which would be the only part to survive the fire of 1870, when after the collapse of the Second Empire the Tuileries Palace was doused with oil and tar to ensure the greatest symbol of the Ancien Régime went up in a proper blaze.

Luis Benjamín contemplated all this courtly nobility from a quiet spot in the garden and watched, surrounded by orchids, white lilies and other more unfamiliar flowers, as a soft snow began to fall, almost to the beat of the waltzes the orchestra was playing, causing a stir among the guests, who included the poets Théophile Gautier and Charles Baudelaire, Baron Taylor, and the painters Henri Fantin and Édouard Manet, who a few days later would paint a scene depicting that very celebration entitled *Music in the Tuileries Gardens*.

* * *

He would never again attend such a dance in all the years that followed: he preferred not to be distracted by entertainments now that diplomacy occupied his every hour, including those that until recently he had dedicated to writing. More a consul than a poet now, Luis Benjamín devoted himself to learning commercial law and discovered in trade relations the best manner of supporting Peru's interests. By his twenty-fifth birthday, he had unwittingly become an expert in transactions, prices, freight, profits and fiscal income.

It was about this time that the letters sent by his brother Luciano informed him of the fall of President Ramón Castilla and later of the swift succession of replacements, a sequence of events that operated on his mind in such a way that he suddenly wanted to travel to Lima, to put his personal life there in order and only then return to Europe, as he confessed in writing to his friend Casimiro Ulloa:

> Dear Rojo, I want to travel to Lima, marry, establish a home and return for a time to France. I have serious work planned on civilisation, the history of Spain and of Peru. I pray that God takes pity on my ambition.

He also shared his concern about the interest of the European governments in the new republics of Latin America, and expressed his intuition that the same could happen in Peru as was currently taking place in Mexico, which had been invaded by Napoleon III after President Benito Juárez froze repayments of the foreign debt it had contracted with France. To the surprise of Casimiro Ulloa, who had treated this foreboding as overblown and misguided, Luis Benjamín's hunch proved correct when in April 1865 Spain took possession of the Chincha islands and began a campaign of harassment against Peru, demanding it pay the supposed 'costs' of the war of independence.

The Poet received a visit from his friend Ricardo Palma in Le Havre, with whom he walked around the busy streets of the port, enjoying the views of Normandy and speaking about the many things that had happened since they last saw each other in Lima. In my great-grand-father's diary there is a note that, given the date, may reasonably be connected to this visit from Palma: 'I can spout off with him, and for hours at a time I am back in the motherland.'

Inspired by his presence, Luis Benjamín set aside his consular work and shut himself up to write prose, poetry, essays and articles that he sent to Lima and which appeared in *La Revista de Lima* and in *La República*, the new periodical published by El Rojo Ulloa. This creative fervour was short-lived and left him so spent that he soon returned to his diplomatic labours, and in any case the political situation in Peru was intensifying, demanding his full attention, especially once President Mariano Ignacio Prado, in alliance with Chile, declared war on Spain.

The government assigned my great-grandfather the task of contacting the various Peruvian politicians and military men who would be arriving in Europe over the following days – 'I have made contact with a Peruvian admiral by the name of Miguel Grau, who is in England preparing the departure of two ships, *Huáscar* and

Independencia, essential to countering the Spanish attack,' he wrote to Casimiro Ulloa. However, from one day to the next, without providing any explanation – perhaps due to an administrative oversight – the new Foreign Ministry cancelled his consul's licence and Luis Benjamín found himself obliged to move back to Paris from Le Havre. He took advantage of the circumstances to organise a flying visit to Lima, where he hoped to see his mother Nicolasa, who was fighting tuberculosis and spent her days in bed, subjected to tiresome inhalations of tar vapours.

A few months before leaving Paris he had heard of the death of a childhood friend, José Gálvez, in the combat of 2 May. Sad but imbued with his perennial patriotism, he wrote to El Rojo Ulloa:

I received the great news of the disaster suffered by the Spanish at Callao and of our glorious triumph. The Peruvian colony talks of little else. All the newspapers, and notably those from Le Havre, have set out the details of the events, ascribing them all the significance they deserve. The triumph of 2 May has been Peru's alone; from this perspective it is an even greater honour than that of Ayacucho. In these parts, as indeed among many Peruvians, the surprise is great, for until now they have believed us weaker than we are. We have risen 90 percent in the estimation of all Europe. Those countries who call themselves powers now know that all the countries of Spanish America are united and that we can and will defend ourselves. This date shall, in my view, mark a new era in foreign relations and internal renewal. My satisfaction knows no bounds, my dear Rojo. I had lost many of my illusions about my country, and I myself feel a resurrection in my spirit. I lament the death of José Gálvez as his country will sorely miss him, but as his friend I do not weep for him. Gálvez could only die this way, and for myself I would relish such a death.

* * *

During those months and years several events had fractured Luis Benjamín's life, heightening his fatalism, hardening him in sadness and resentment. First the death of his sister Francisca in 1865, then that of his brother Feliciano in 1866 and now, just a year later, in January 1867, that of his own mother. The telegram from his brother Luciano informing him that Nicolasa had just died found him on the deck of the ship that was taking him to Lima. Only when he finished reading did Luis Benjamín become aware of the relentless wind, the persistent splashing of salt water on his skin and, above all, the lurching of the ship. And as he watched the passengers run here and there in terror, in defiance of the crew's orders to stay put – some even leaning dangerously over the railings to see the violence with which the choppy sea hit the metal hull of the boat – he noticed his complete indifference to the possibility of a shipwreck and, upon returning to his cabin, as he rounded the last funnel, he felt like an orphan for the first time. It was on his mother's pleading that he had left for Paris and it was because of her that he was returning to Peru, and as a result the unprecedented pain of her death was deepened by his inability to repay her either materially or emotionally for her wise exhortations at the time of Lucrecia Colichón's snake-like threats and blackmail, tricky days when Nicolasa encouraged him to go abroad and overcome the fear that was making him ill. And while it was true that in France his life had stabilised and his character had toughened to the point that all trace of his former accidie had disappeared, that stormy morning of January 1867, with the news of his mother's death, realising that he wouldn't be able to say goodbye to her, the Poet again fell victim to his former uncertainty, and when hours later it was his turn to disembark, he crossed the gangway out of pure inertia, and as he was about to step onto the dock at Callao and rejoin the city he had fled so many years ago, he saw himself again as the timid and abandoned child he had perhaps always been.

In the following moments he became resigned to the idea of dealing with the funeral, arranging a marble tomb with an inscription that read – he decided it right then and there – 'her children will love her always', and bury her in the place she had indicated in her will and that she had long set aside in the Presbítero Maestro cemetery: niche 253, in the San Job sector, alongside the tomb of that man that Luis Benjamín and his siblings had already forgotten they hated, and whose name caused them to catch their breath even after all this time: Gregorio Cartagena.

The morning of the burial, when General Pedro Cisneros realised that the mortal remains of his sister Nicolasa were about to be placed beside those of the priest, he ordered the gravediggers to halt – 'don't move that coffin another centimetre, dammit!' – and immediately demanded to speak to the cemetery manager to exhume Cartagena's bones and move them, not to another plot or sector, but to another graveyard altogether. The short, nearly bald man who was in charge of the Public Welfare office received him and, despite the viciousness with which Pedro set upon him, refused to yield to his demands. In a fury, the general lifted him up by the lapels with one hand, as if he were a scarecrow, shoved him against the wall, and would have given him a couple of slaps with the back of his free hand – his four-fingered hand – had the short-arsed fellow, with his legs dangling in the air, his comb-over in disarray, not stuttered out in a reedy voice: 'Do you really fail to see that your sister and the priest wished to rot here together?' Pedro had been deaf for so long that he made no attempt to read the official's lips, but held him there quivering for a few more seconds before dropping him to the floor.

The only thing that kept the Poet going was his excitement at the chance to see his three daughters again: Elvira, Adelaida and María Luisa. However, the day he saw them, returning from the burial, he soon noticed – not only in their changed faces but in the way they looked at him – the passage of the years. Seven years without seeing them, hearing them or touching them. Seven years that now felt like twenty. Their hugs were stiff, their kisses perfunctory, their gestures lifeless, their gazes hardened. Luis Benjamín sensed their animosity, smelled their rejection, realised that any love they had felt for him had long dissipated, and knew that it would be near impossible to break through the solid walls that had been erected between him and his daughters.

Before returning to Paris, with his position as consul at Le Havre restored, he entrusted the care of the girls to his sister Catalina. The day of his departure, Elvira, the eldest – who was twelve but looked like she could be seven – insisted on accompanying him, more out of eagerness to see the world than of having the chance to be close to her father at last. Luis Benjamín accepted, thinking that this way the girl's animus would soften, and perhaps he could even recover her affection. Once in Le Havre, however, realising that his work prevented him from looking after her, and that the girl spent her days wandering around the port, he found no other solution than to send her to board in a German convent – a place that felt more like an orphanage – inevitably shattering Elvira's heart. From then on, she would forever see her father as an indolent and distant man.

CHAPTER 10

Lima, 1869

Luis Benjamín returned to Lima for a meeting with the new president, José Balta, and at the request of his friend Narciso availed of the journey to deliver some packages to the latter's father, Don Gervasio Álvarez.

It was there, on Mariquitas street, that he first saw Cristina, the angelical fourteen-year-old pianist whose hand in marriage he requested just two weeks later. While her parents, Amelia and Arnaldo, quickly granted their full consent, grandpa Gervasio exploded in a rage on learning that his granddaughter, a minor, was to wed Luis Benjamín Cisneros.

'However much of a diplomat he may be, that man has three illegitimate daughters with an adulterer, not to speak of his reputation in Europe as a perverted good-for-nothing,' he protested. (If he had only known that the groom was the bastard son of a priest and that his surname was entirely made-up, the indignation really would have done him in.)

The religious wedding was held in the grandfather's own home, at the same time and place as he usually met with his old friends from the Supreme Court. Hours earlier, when he learned that his game of tresillo would be cancelled for the ceremony, the old man shut himself up in his bedroom, growling threats.

'I'm going to hang myself from the rafters!' he bellowed.

No one was especially concerned. It was one of his usual old man's tantrums that served no purpose but to chafe at his liver, choke his lungs and deepen his wrinkles. In the end, talked down by his granddaughter, who even persuaded him to act as witness, Gervasio scribbled his signature on the certificate, gritting his teeth, making no attempt to conceal his disapproval from the guests, in particular the priest, at whom he wagged a resentful finger, disgusted that he'd offered the groom 'some knock-off blessings that won't go far when it comes to erasing his sins'.

In order to marry Cristina without the Bustamante or Álvarez families learning of his true origins, Luis Benjamín turned to the only priest in the world who would cover for him: the Bishop of Huánuco, Don Leandro Teodoro del Valle, brother of Catalina del Valle, wife of his brother Manuel Benjamín. The bishop, who was well aware of the story of Nicolasa and Gregorio Cartagena, and had wed and protected each of the bastard children without a trace of remorse, travelled to Lima solely to officiate this new marriage and signed the certificate in full knowledge that it contained adulterated information. The Poet, like his siblings before him, asked to appear in the papers as the 'legitimate son of Roberto Benjamín and Nicolasa Cisneros'. Whenever he was asked about his father, he mechanically repeated the lines that Nicolasa had prepared so long ago: 'he is somewhere on one of his endless trips'.

The newlyweds spent their first night together at

the home of Cristina's relatives. The next day – a cold morning with lowering clouds – they sailed for Europe. As the boat moved off, squealing against the wharf, lurching in the grey-green sea and startling the guano birds, the new couple stood on the deck and waved to their family and friends gathered on the quayside, accompanied by the band hired by Don Arnaldo Bustamente to endow the departure of his only daughter with a sense of occasion. Taking advantage of Cristina's distraction as she bade farewell to everyone she held dear, Luis Benjamín put his arm around her, rested his chin on her right shoulder, caressed the curve of her upper back with both hands, kissed the nape of her neck, and covertly slipped a handkerchief into her dress pocket. Cristina would only unroll it once the land had receded from view, and discover stitched on it some verses, illegible at first, but which she would read over and over until she learned them by heart, and would in fact never forget. Many years later she would recite them to her children as she got them ready for school each morning, or put them to bed, telling them proudly and vainly that their father had written them for her on the first day of their honeymoon. They, easily distracted and generally forgetful, would transcribe those eight lines and insert them in a little wooden frame that was passed on, gradually yellowing, from hand to hand, wall to wall, home to home, century to century, until one fine day it got lost and wound up in that unfathomable repository for belongings that the dead wrench from the living as punishment for failing to take proper care of them.

> Bouquet of white blossoms,
> symbol of your purity,
> crown of your head,
> garland of your beauty:

why as I outstretch my hand
does it seem to besmirch you?
Why just to look at you
do I tremble with joy?

★ ★ ★

Arriving in London, my great-grandfather and Cristina
spent three nights at a hotel on Paternoster Row. On
their second day, as they breakfasted at a café in St Paul's
Churchyard, they saw a throng of people and horse-
drawn coaches heading for the south side of the city. They
soon joined the crowd of curious onlookers and watched
as Queen Victoria – a woman now in her fifties, with
chubby cheeks and a cow-like build, her central parting
severely marked beneath the tiara and veil – officially
opened the redesigned Blackfriars Bridge, which had
become a popular site for lovelorn Londoners to hurl
themselves into the leaden waters of the Thames.

From London they moved on to Paris, where one
night they attended the opera to hear arias by Rossini
and Donnizetti sung by Adelina Patti, an Italian soprano
who stunned the audience with her waif-like figure and
copious jewellery, but also because in one passage of the
spectacle, making an extraordinary effort to reach a note
almost beyond the range of human hearing, she fainted
and began to bleed from her ears, much to the perplexity
of the musicians, who carried on playing their instru-
ments as the singer was carried from the stage.

In Paris too they once saw Napoleon III, accompanied by his wife the Empress Eugenia and the heir
prince, at the head of a military parade. As they looked
on, Luis Benjamín, seeking to impress his young bride,
recounted that seven years earlier, in the Tuileries Palace,
he had met and kissed the hands of these figures who

now seemed so unreachable. Cristina looked at him wide-eyed, and kissed his forehead with a mix of incredulity and compassion.

Leaving Paris, they moved to Le Havre, into a riverside chalet in the commune of Sainte-Adresse, where they would spend the next few years. Days after their arrival, they learned that the old lady who lived in the crenelated castle next door was the former Queen Consort of Spain, Maria Christina of the Two Sicilies, who had been exiled in France for over two decades, deprived of the lifetime pension granted by the Spanish Parliament, and who had recently been accused by the authorities in her country of thieving jewels worth millions.

When she learned of the presence of a Peruvian couple in the neighbourhood, the former Queen invited the couple to dine with her, establishing a friendship that would grow closer over the following months, seasons and years. 'I place myself entirely at your disposal, your grace,' was Luis Benjamín's reply when one evening the former monarch requested his services 'as a man of letters' to organise her personal archive, which comprised a first draft of her will and voluminous correspondence that had never been seen by anyone else, and to which he was afforded unrestricted access. My great-grandfather had to sign a confidentiality agreement before spending a series of afternoons among the turquoise trees of the castle gardens reading these letters in which Maria Christina delved into the minutiae – covered-up by the crown – of her first marriage to her uncle, King Ferdinand VII, who had taken advantage of her on their wedding night and would die of a heart attack just four years later. She also wrote about her morganatic marriage to a sergeant from her royal guard, performed in secret by a sympathetic priest three months after she became a widow; about the periods she spent in far-flung estates to conceal the eight pregnancies resulting from this forbidden relationship; and about the falsification of passports for her children, who she had to send away from Spain as soon as they were born to avoid arousing the suspicions of her political enemies, constantly seeking excuses to dislodge her from the throne.

Luis Benjamín found these stories of illegitimate loves so familiar, and felt his mother and himself so present in their lines that, over the days to come, as he classified the documents with a diligence and speed that surprised even him, he had the unpleasant sensation that he was re-examining and putting in order certain unknown chapters of his own biography.

★ ★ ★

The Poet was most grateful for the payment he received from Maria Christina for this task, even though the most urgent financial straits were behind him and he earned money by involving himself in certain thorny legal matters relating to Peruvian politics, the most famous being the case of one August Dreyfus. He had proposed to President José Balta that a single official agent, based in Europe, purchase all of Peru's guano. At that time, guano was offered to consignees, merchants who sold the product independently for very high profits, but the system was so carelessly managed that it put the country's coffers in serious jeopardy. Luis Benjamín oversaw the signing of a contract with August Dreyfus, a prosperous French banker of Jewish origin, married to a Peruvian lady he had met by chance in Paris in an Italian bookstore on Rue de Rivoli. After persuading Dreyfus to take over the administration of the guano imports under a more advantageous system, Luis Benjamín contacted President Balta, who approved the idea despite the political upheaval it promised to unleash. Months later, following a great deal of controversy whipped up by the former consignees, who fought to the bitter end, Congress approved the new procedure for the sale of this precious natural resource. In a letter to Casimiro Ulloa, Luis Benjamín celebrated the conclusion of the deal:

> By now, the telegraph will have announced the results of the subscription for the Peruvian railways loan. Six times oversubscribed! A loan of twelve million pounds sterling! Dreyfus has opened up this new and vast future for the benefit of Peru. We can now be certain that not only the routes currently under construction will be completed, but many more. We can pat ourselves on the back for encouraging Dreyfus to negotiate this proposal with the government, for having placed the parties in contact, and for having afforded him our tutelage. I have no doubt that the reception across Peru will be most gratifying.

The peace they found in Le Havre would prove short-lived. With all of Paris abuzz at the fall of the Second Empire after Napoleon III's defeat to the Prussians at the Battle of Sedan, and with the occupation of the city a distinct possibility, Luis Benjamín sent Cristina to England. Five months pregnant with their first child, she was hosted by a friend of the Poet and the secretary of the Peruvian delegation in London, Ernesto Jaramillo, at number 39, Gloucester Place. My great-grandfather joined her three months later, following the French capitulation at Metz and just before the Siege of Paris, from which a number of people escaped by the most unlikely of means, even using homemade hot-air balloons that disappeared like great birds into the heavens, from where they tossed handfuls of pamphlets that – as Luis Benjamín wrote to his friend Ulloa – contained ineffectual revolutionary propaganda against the invading regime, and ended up scattered on the ground like the useless scraps of paper they were, blown away with the autumn leaves:

> In this last fortnight the greatest hopes of victory for France and the Republic against the Germans have been dashed. You won't believe it, Casimiro, but Metz capitulated without Marshal Bazaine even attempting a desperate action! With one hundred and fifty thousand men, three thousand guns and forty million francs! This disaster is greater than Sedan and everything already suggests that France will be forced to sign a false peace, which will be nothing but a truce. Even so, Paris is still standing and can do something great and glorious.

One frozen midnight of a London November, weakened by twelve bedbound days, the fifteen-year-old Cristina gave birth to her first daughter, Helena. The baby looked like a doll in the young arms of her mother, who sobbed with both happiness and disappointment, since she had hoped for a boy. Luis Benjamín tried to calm her, saying 'it's better she's a girl, at least she won't start a war or a revolution'.

They moved to a flat on the second floor of 45, Paddington Street and hired a Peruvian wet-nurse, Clodomira Bustíos, who Helena called 'Mamaína' once she began to talk.

London had become an industrial city, driven by engines, flanked by docks and naval factories, crisscrossed by rails. Locomotives connected stations that proliferated even beyond the outskirts, where hawkers and fishmongers gathered in long lines every morning, while masses of strikers protested for better wages, leaving the nights to prostitutes, ruffians, vagrants and bellicose drunks, whose fights with broken brandy bottles dragged on well into the new day.

Cristina and Luis Benjamín eagerly threw themselves into this new landscape. They would first skirt the boundaries of the East End, avoiding the district of Lambeth, infamous for the squalor of its bleak alleyways, where packs of starving children with torn shoes picked their noses while their parents in threadbare clothes thronged the public latrines and opium dens; pestilential streets that just twenty years later would be the birthplace of Charlie Chaplin and the backdrop to the crimes of Jack the Ripper.

Then they would tour the wealthy sectors of the west, to the sound of waltzes played by organ grinders in the squares, where the high cornices of the mansions and the portentous public buildings were silhouetted against the evening light. At five o'clock sharp they saw crowds of employees dressed in shirts and ties pour from their workplaces, thirsty to finish off the day at one of the numberless pubs in the area, which bore names like Dog and Duck, Bear and Bottle, Iron Duke or Black Bull. It was the dark, romantic London where it had become fashionable to take long walks at night to 'discover the anxieties of a great city that stirs and starts before falling asleep', in the words of Charles Dickens, who had died suddenly of a stroke just five months earlier. This mood impregnated the country, but especially its capital, with a foggy despondency that lingered in the air and from which no one seemed to have been cured.

Cristina and my great-grandfather established a regular morning routine: they headed to Piccadilly Circus, stopped for breakfast at the Café Royal on Regent Street, and then visited the British Museum, where they never ceased to marvel at the mummies and sarcophagi in the Egyptian collection. If it was raining, they took refuge in the opera, where the ballet companies offered daily matinées, and when it cleared they wandered towards Trafalgar Square. Once, at midday, they saw Queen Victoria drive past for a second time. She was very ailing by then, transformed in the distance into a tiny pearl, yet still resplendent among a crowd that spread around her like a stain.

Each time they returned to the flat, Cristina prepared the tea, Mamaína served biscuits or scones and Luis Benjamín rocked baby Helena in his arms with a paternal affection he had never shown any of his three previous daughters. It was as if physical and emotional changes had taken place inside him that he could only now begin to grasp. He imagined his body as a vast and bewildering city where whole districts – blocks of houses, pavements, parks, inhabitants and all – would suddenly rise up and seek out their fellows, forming convenient groupings out of an instinct for survival or preservation, anxious to save themselves from the chaos, and to imbue these landscapes with a peaceful and settled appearance. The Poet acknowledged this new and healthy inner choreography and lamented that his older daughters were unable to benefit from the harmony that now flourished in him and seemed to orchestrate his life. They had grown up amid secrecy, illegitimacy and silence, suffering from the pusillanimous actions of a young and hesitant father who had seen his horizons shrink too soon. By contrast, Helena and the six children who would follow grew up in a sound, comfortable, organised household, with the love and dedication of their diplomat father, who was proud of his legitimate marriage to his wife, and as a result their early years would be infused with a pleasant sensation of having been born in the right time and place.

Luis Benjamín decided to send two of his older daughters, Adelaida and María Luisa, fifteen and thirteen respectively, to the Sante Infance boarding school in Versailles, hoping an Old World education would shore up the cracks in their relationship. And although the older girls travelled to Europe and enjoyed this long period spent in France and did indeed receive an outstanding education, making lifelong friends and traveling all over the continent, it was too little to compensate. The gaping holes in their lives opened up by their father's long absence were coloured by a disappointment too deep to recover from. Something had ruptured between my great-grandfather and his older daughters, and however much they all tried, the wound could never be healed.

* * *

Luis Benjamín found himself forced back to Peru when the government asked him to manage the Lima-Chancay railway, which ran along the cliffs of Ancón. As on previous occasions, he accepted the role without really knowing what he was getting into.

In Lima he reassembled his forces.

In Lima his daughters Adriana and Olga were born.

In Lima he invested his money in bonds, achieving a level of economic wellbeing that was reflected in various luxuries: he purchased a lofty house on La Cueva street, facing the Church of La Encarnación; he rented a first-rate box in the theatre; and he gained several kilos organising dinners frequently attended by General Mariano Ignacio Prado, a man with an authoritarian air and cobwebbed beard who had served and would again serve as president, and whom no one had ever seen without his worn boots made – he claimed – from freshwater caiman skin.

It was during this period that the Poet recovered something of his literary drive: he wrote poems and plays, and began to attend sessions of a literary club with his friends Ricardo Palma and Numa Pompilio, a society that would later become El Ateneo, the leading cultural centre in Lima of the day. However, within just a few months of recovering a certain tenacity in his preferred field, he found himself once more held to ransom by his political pursuits, accepting the post of manager of the Compañía Salitrera and postponing numerous personal projects, most of which he would never return to.

In a high-risk transaction, he invested all of his savings in the company he now found himself in charge of, obsessed with increasing his already abundant capital. A few years later, during the War of the Pacific, when Chile occupied Tarapacá and expelled workers from the salt mines, appropriating them to 'pay for the costs of the conflict', Luis Benjamín lost his entire patrimony. The little savings he kept at home were used up in a matter of days.

To keep his children from realising that they now lived on the edge of poverty, my great-grandfather engaged in all kinds of sleight-of-hand, even going so far as to institute make-believe Christian traditions in the home: he appealed to non-existent saints and invented calendar dates on which lunches had to be frugal, while abstaining from dinner three days a week, reusing the same garments, and dispensing with any sign of ostentation.

One night, Cristina finally gave birth to the son she had yearned for. They called him Gonzalo and when he was baptised at five weeks, Luis Benjamín's friends laid on a party at which – aware of his precarious financial condition – the wine flowed in abundance. The high point of the night was when the host himself, the poet Carlos Augusto Salaverry, recalling the golden age of the first literary soirées held by the bohemian poets, climbed onto the piano in a state of moderate inebriation and improvised a sonnet to the newborn:

What I envisage in the face that peers above
the infant's crib, your first and tender nest,
has something of the goldfinch and the dove.
A dream for Caesar is a dream to lose,
for you, my boy, will be Don Juan instead,
born of a kiss between Poet and Muse.

Gonzalo's birth offered only a brief respite from the chaos unleashed by the war with Chile. In May 1879, Peru found itself in a deep economic depression, requiring concerted efforts to prevent it from collapsing altogether. Along with other colleagues, and on the initiative of his brother-in-law Casimiro Ulloa, Luis Benjamín volunteered for the reserve army and was designated head of an ambulance section. For her part, Cristina – as Nicolasa had done a generation earlier to subsidise the independence struggle – donated necklaces, rings and expensive brooches that contributed to the purchase of ships, and organised a group of women who raised funds to protect orphans and widows of the conflict.

One October night, as they were eating Cristina's birthday supper in the house on La Cueva street – the usually joyous occasion diminished by the harsh reality of war – they heard the sound of an approaching carriage. The coachman brought news that plunged guests and servants alike into gloom: during the Chilean capture of the ironclad *Huáscar*, Admiral Miguel Grau had been killed. He was a dear friend of Luis Benjamín and godfather of Cristina, who in turn was godmother to his eighth daughter, Victoria. My great-grandfather asked for a minute of silence in honour of the man who would go on to be recognised as the greatest hero in the history of Peru.

The war had begun on the border between Peru and Chile, but it hadn't taken long to spread northwards and reach as far as Lima, where in January 1881 cannon battles were fought in the districts of Chorrillos, San Juan and Miraflores. It was the worst summer the city's denizens could remember in a long time, both for the number of troops marching past as they watched from their doors, windows and balconies, and due to the heavy losses. The Chilean soldiers, over 10,000 in number, easily defeated the lines of Peruvian defence, taking prisoners every day; by night they'd get drunk in their trenches and shoot their hostages or slit their throats while they planned their next assault. Together with other civilians, Luis Benjamín did what he could, whether it was responding to emergencies, transferring the dying to the damaged hospitals, accounting for the deceased, searching for the disappeared, or coming to the assistance of women raped by the opposing army in the course of its savage raids and looting of museums, churches, libraries, schools, palaces, cemeteries and private homes.

Meanwhile, the families of Peruvian soldiers and reservists had taken refuge in churches and schools provisioned to withstand the relentless disturbances, fires, assaults and lynchings. There was a widespread sense of mourning. The Poet's family had to spend twelve nights in the Colegio Belén, which was largely spared the vandalism of the invaders. Early one morning, guided by the mother superior, acting as midwife, with the assistance of Mamaína and two other women who held up oil torches, Cristina gave birth to Alfonso, her fifth child. Outside, shots rang out and they could hear the clamour of the dying. As soon as the baby was put to her chest, Cristina embraced him, rejoicing, and all those present began to weep and clap at this breath of humanity amid all the horror.

Informed that Luis Benjamín was protecting and feeding the refugees, the Chileans began to threaten him. He didn't take the hint, but when the hostilities intensified into written warnings that mentioned his children, he became convinced that they had no choice but to leave the country. So he moved his library and some valuables to a neighbour's house, auctioned off furniture and belongings among his acquaintances, and offered all the money raised to a Chilean military officer to secure passports for him, Cristina, Mamaína and the five children. The bribery worked and two nights later, bringing nothing but the nightclothes on their backs, they were transferred to the port of Callao and, following the instructions of an emissary, boarded a cargo ship and crowded into a cabin which they were forbidden to leave. Within two hours, they were on their way back to France. Only once the ship's engines started up did Cristina sit down on the bed to feed Alfonso. Luis Benjamín repeated over and over that everything would be all right, though he himself was sure of nothing. Little Helena, Adriana, Olga and Gonzalo, clustered around the skirts of Mamaína, the vigorous maid they had grown so fond of, stared at each other in silence, perplexed by all the coming and going, allowing themselves to be swept along by it, entertained or perhaps intrigued by the oscillation of the boundless sea that turned from blue to black through the porthole as the hours passed, and whose vastness and motion suggested a great sheet beneath which intermingled and mated all the animals of creation.

★ ★ ★

Once in France, they settled once again in the port that had become like a second home: Le Havre. There they felt safe from the strife of war, though news of death would soon reach them there too. In the first days of 1882, a brief telegram sent from Paris by Luciano informed Luis Benjamín that their brother Manuel, the second of the bastards, had died. Luciano did not specify if it was from illness or in battle. All he said was 'Manuel is no more. Mourn him with me.'

But my great-grandfather would soon receive a yet worse blow. Attacked from one day to the next by a severe case of croup, his son Gonzalo died from an inflamed trachea before reaching his fourth birthday. He died in hospital, in the arms of a frantic Luis Benjamín, who refused to allow this tragedy to take place before his very eyes. He watched over the little body for two nights, and then decided to leave Le Havre without even discussing it with Cristina. The port city where they had been so happy had become grim and unliveable to him. His brother Luciano accompanied him to bury his son's coffin at the top of the Sainte Marie cemetery, and persuaded him to come and spend some time together in his Paris home.

When he heard of Gonzalo's tragic death, the poet Salaverry, perhaps to compensate for his improvised performance at the child's baptism that had turned into such a poor sonnet of augury, wrote a condolence letter ending with a poem that, instead of easing Luis Benjamín's pain, only served to inflame it.

> Turn to the prophets: in their holy tome
> filled with the treasures of divine laments
> and in the lyric world that song intones,
> the finest singers are known for tears spent.
> Take up your lyre, and let blind envy learn

your stanzas till it has them memorised:
it's what the shadow of your son most yearns
for your dear homeland and its majesty.

CHAPTER 11

Paris, 1882

Luciano did his best to distract Luis Benjamín from the loss of his son, and took him on walks around the Quartier Latin, to attend the Universal Expositions, the comedies at the Théâtre Historique, the musicals at the Théâtre du Vaudeville, to visit clandestine gambling halls, and even to observe the prostitutes who swarmed the Tuileries, Notre-Dame and the Italian quarter, but none of it softened in his younger brother's face the sorrow that began to seem indelible.

Luis Benjamín was not only downhearted but had also lost his appetite, barely touching the dishes Luciano prepared for him at breakfast, lunch and dinner, and nor did bottles of bourbon or gin, once synonymous with celebration, and which he was always the first to open and serve, do anything to revive him or get him out of his funk.

The Poet fell into depression when he thought about returning to Le Havre, so he stayed in Paris, moving with Cristina, their children and the tireless Clodomira Bustíos to number 59, Avenue Marceu, and later a fifth-floor flat at 16, Rue Christophe Colomb, where they lived in some austerity, since the Dreyfus Company continued to dodge the debts they owed.

Meanwhile, back in Lima, his remaining uncles were dying one after another: first Gerónimo and then Pedro, the general with the abundant sideburns, the man lacking both a finger and his hearing who tried but failed to take revenge on Gregorio Cartagena, the only uncle who saw the bastard children grow up and by far the one who loved them the most.

Luis Benjamín didn't smile again until November 1882 on the day his sixth and penultimate child was born: Fernán, my grandfather.

Without money to pay school fees, he took the risk of home-schooling the older children himself, preparing a strict routine two or three days a week from nine in the morning until lunchtime. He took them to see museums, monuments, factories, libraries, historical buildings and gardens whose significance and development he described in advance. He patiently gave them general lessons in art, history, geography and literature, as well as on how paper, porcelain, chocolate and bread were made, while asking them to repeat together each explanation and then write it down in their notebooks. He taught them to keep themselves well-groomed, brush their clothes, snip dangling threads from jackets and dresses, sew buttons, tie their shoelaces, and walk with the proper bearing, without hugging the walls or dragging their feet, however tired they were. When they arrived home he wouldn't tolerate anyone sitting down to eat at the table without brushing their hair, and checked their hands and fingernails for the least sign of muck. Each child had to speak in turn, but if they did so with their mouth full they would receive a rap on the head with his knuckles; likewise if they expressed themselves unclearly once corrected. As a good nineteenth-century man, Luis Benjamín distrusted casual language, which he saw as vulgar, and obliged the children to use pompous or outlandish nouns and adjectives, such as *latent, impious, irate, stupefaction, vainglorious*. On Saturdays they bought pastries at the Stohrer bakery and on Sundays they attended mass, where he translated the epistles of the priest for them, quietly indicating the correct way of kneeling and following the order of service. At night, if some ephemeral fear kept them awake, he would stand at the foot of the bed like a sentinel, and his sole presence was like a kind of silent lullaby that succeeded in sending the children to sleep.

When he wasn't teaching the children, the Poet wrote methodically, returning to the poems he'd abandoned years earlier. But it was never the same again. The nights he couldn't write, he went out for solitary walks, with the energy and openness to chance he'd lacked the first time he lived in Paris, more than fifteen years prior. And so, wandering streets he'd never been down before, he discovered the cellars of Montmartre, converted into nocturnal clubs with sloping ceilings. In one of those stifling rooms, with its dim oil lamps, dense tobacco smoke, voices and sweat, crowded with men of a salty and degenerate air who roamed around looking like they were intellectuals or wanted to be, he met Ernest Renan, who introduced himself by saying 'I am the greatest writer and artist of my time'. Then – charmed by the philosophical elucubrations Renan employed to draw attention to himself – who should sit down at the same table but Dr Louis Pasteur and Alexander Dumas *fils*, the author of *Camille* and already a prominent writer. For several months, the four of them would gather at night in these blue-hued bars stuffed with picturesque characters, to debate literature and have long meandering discussions in which Luis Benjamín played the part of attentive listener, both fascinated and frustrated because, deep down, he wanted to be as much of a writer as they were, to know what they knew, look the way they looked, remember the way they remembered; he wanted to have a mind capable of fantasising with greater fertility, a memory that could encompass and reproduce everything he had seen and read; he wanted to be and act like a bohemian in Paris, not like a lacklustre immigrant who missed his old petit-bourgeois life; and while the others spoke with real authority, he scolded himself for having become so involved in politics, for letting himself be carried away by insubstantial, muddy currents, for channelling his energies towards exhausting patriotic or bureaucratic tasks, allowing himself to forget that he was above all else a writer, although now, in those cellars that teemed with poets, he was no longer so sure, fearing that, with more than forty years behind him, it was too late to become one and he shouldn't kid himself, and the more he drank the more his guts clenched with rage, the more implacable he was with himself, the more ashamed that he hadn't dared to be a real writer, that he had settled for being a patriotic diplomat who wrote trifling books that would likely not survive him, a pseudo-writer, a barren writer who lacked obsession and tenacity, and he suddenly remembered that he was bankrupt, that he had lost all his money to an absurd war, and he told himself that his poverty would have been more worthy, more splendid, if he had at least surrendered completely to the vice of writing, and he felt an inexplicable, anguished desire to be a penniless poet in Paris, a poor yet fervent poet, anything but this timorous novelist who had always been afraid to act like the free man he was meant to be.

One day, Renan, Pasteur and Luis Benjamín headed to the French Institute where they met an eighty-three-year-old man, enthroned on an imperial chair, who seemed to gaze out with a certain ennui as he chatted with a score of young writers who regarded him as if he were not just an eminence but a granite pyramid. The old man was Victor Hugo. His forehead was furrowed with irregular lines, his nose massive, his jaw overwhelming, his broad shoulders like uneven terraces, his ring like a prosthesis on the index finger of his left hand, his six-button waistcoat tight, his nails clean but uncut, half his face sunken into knots of silvery beard and, under his lids, pronounced bags that seemed to contain the dilated memory of eyes that had travelled and suffered like no one else's. Rapt and pale, the three listened to the genius reflect on his republican ideals and talk about his father, a French general with a devotion to reading and to Spain; of his four dead children, especially of Leopoldine, drowned in the Seine, whose disappearance he learned of from a newspaper; of his admiration for Chateaubriand; of his experiments with spiritualism; of his visceral repudiation of the 'ominous usurper' Napoleon III; and of his exile in a medieval building on the Grand Place in Brussels. His voice was thick and he dragged out the words as if he were chewing crushed glass. Such was the impression that they immediately declared themselves his unconditional disciples. Luis Benjamín didn't have a cent to his name, but he only needed to hear this wise old man for a minute to feel he was standing before an oracle, enveloped by a faith as hard and tangible as stone. When just a month later Victor Hugo passed away, the three friends felt that his death united them, marked them, compelled them to sign a pact they could not name. The day of the funeral, they slipped into a tall building to watch from a balcony as the cortège headed down Place de l'Étoile, escorted by a legion of mounted guards, and they looked at each other, unaware they were living through a future chapter of world history. As they followed the uncertain path of the coffin, which lurched above the crowd's heads like a bottle sent out by a castaway, they saw how at the door of each house it passed, and in the windows, and on the roofs, people were weeping and reciting verses from *Les Contemplations*, *The Hunchback of Notre-Dame* and *Les Misérables* as if they were hymns to the dead or prayers learned at some key moment of their childhood. The next morning, all three attended the wake beneath the Arc de Triomphe and accompanied the procession bound for the Pantheon, where the cadaver of Victor Hugo, wrapped in a shroud, would be buried in a crypt that they, in a final surge of dedication or friendship, would watch over until the following morning, like guardians or sentinels, wielding torches soaked in pitch.

★ ★ ★

My great-grandfather Luis Benjamín returned to Peru with his family at the end of August 1885, the same year that General Andrés A. Cáceres ousted President Iglesias, and also the year his sister Catalina died. Diminished by this new loss, as well as by the disaster of the war with Chile, and without an income to provide the least economic relief, let alone the opulent lifestyle of yore, he wrote new poems that he read in the centre of Lima on the stages of El Ateneo and the Casino Español, at stowed-out recitals from which he emerged consoled, at least artistically.

For the first time he seemed to forget about politics, even disregarding an offer from President Cáceres to become his Treasury Secretary. Instead, in order to manage his many debts and support his family, he agreed to oversee the construction of the Teatro Nacional, at the request of the mayor of Lima.

Although his daughters Helena, Adriana and Olga were boarding at the Belén school, Luis Benjamín made an effort to give them lessons again, just as he had in Paris, and on their days off he took them on walks to the Parque de la Exposición, the Alameda de los Descalzos and the Plaza de Armas, pointing out the majesty of each building, the genesis of each construction, the significance of each site, the secrets of each monument. Force-fed with so much information, the girls wound up exhausted and longing for these walks to end with their usual stop on Las Mantas street, where they were allowed lime sorbets at the Leonard bazaar, run by an old Pole with a permanently sun-struck air by the name of Felix Jawooski, who for some obscure reason everyone knew as Leonard, and who spoke French as if he had a forked tongue, and who also offered certain viscous medicinal potions under the counter that my great-grandfather would soon find himself in urgent need of.

One Sunday, as he was visiting his daughters in the quadrangle of their school, one of them, Adriana, now sixteen years old, observed a nervous tic in her father: a slight, barely perceptible but constant movement that caused him to rotate his head from side to side, as if denying everything. Luis Benjamín told her not to worry, that it was just a sign of tension, nothing that couldn't be fixed with the homemade remedies of Leonard the Pole.

A month later, however, Luis Benjamín's tremors became more persistent and severe, when Adriana – the 'generous and selfless', the Poet's favourite – fell ill from a typhoid fever so lethal that it snuffed out her life in seven days without anyone being able to do anything, or even believe it was happening. Just as with little Gonzalo before her, the death of Adriana led him to despise himself and feel adrift in the world.

Initially he attempted to get over the awful loss of his daughter and wrote what he could, almost by way of therapy, and insisted on continuing the instructive yet increasingly dull walks through the city centre with his remaining children, until one day he felt unable to keep up these useless, flailing gestures and, weakened and eaten up by his many sorrows, he lost control of his body and began to shake like an epileptic.

A team of doctors led by his friend Casimiro Ulloa treated him with electric baths and local cauterisation, but after weeks of failing to make a diagnosis, they recommended that he seek the opinion of doctors in Europe.

My great-grandfather no longer had enough money to cover these new expenses, having leased a ranch in Barranco for his whole family, and so his depression backed him into a corner, aggravating the nameless illness that was beginning to deprive him of sleep, cause him constant migraines, and atrophy his muscles.

His friends begged President Cáceres to secure some kind of position for him in Europe, anything at all, so that he could afford his treatment. In January 1889 Cáceres named him vice-consul in Bordeaux and wrote these lines to his wife Cristina, whom he knew from his youth: 'Nothing brings me such satisfaction as complying with your and your family's instructions; and I only regret that obstacles contrary to my wishes so often delay the manifestations of the friendly deference that I hold for you all.'

Before setting up their new home in Bordeaux they stopped in Paris, where Luis Benjamín found new energy to wander the streets that he had once enjoyed at his leisure. Reaching a crossroads, he turned as if following a premonition and glimpsed in the distance the rundown bars of Montmartre. Later, passing through the Tuileries, he remembered his conversations with the curious

Monsieur Fysquet, and before the day was out visited a number of old friends who were as ill as he, or worse. Galvanised by these memories and reencounters, he braved the third and highest platform of the iron tower that had just opened bearing the name of its architect, Gustave Eiffel.

On the day before the doctors examined him, he arranged to meet his daughter Adelaida in a café near Pont Neuf. He hadn't seen her for over fifteen years, when he sent her to board at a school in Versailles. Perhaps for this reason he expected to find a resentful little girl, rather than the poised woman he took several minutes even to recognise. Whether it was tempered by Luis Benjamín's evident state of ill health, or because she suddenly realised that the long-harboured discord and hatred had since dissolved into complete disinterest, Adelaida displayed a compassionate air throughout the conversation that she never would have thought herself capable of: an air hardly typical of children who know they have been neglected, who grew up feeling like a hindrance. As she spoke to her father, she beheld him without suspicion, leading him to believe that they were reconciled, and by conceding this relief to him, seeing his face relax – empty now as it was of its old vitality and fury – she saw there would be no further opportunities of the kind, and thought that perhaps it would not be so difficult to forgive this tired, condemned old man who only inspired pity.

The next day, Luis Benjamín placed himself in the hands of two neurologists, the doctors Charcot and Babinski, who subjected him to tests and probings over a period of ten weeks. One afternoon the following spring, they confirmed that he was suffering from an illness that would progressively erode his nervous system, destroying his ability to make voluntary actions and leading to paralysis and, eventually, death. 'It is a disease that has no name,' they told him, although the symptoms resembled those described in the book *An Essay on the Shaking Palsy* published in England by a doctor by the name of James Parkinson.

Stricken by the greatest sorrow of the many he had suffered, he embarked on what would be his final journey back to Peru. The death of his mother, his children and brothers, the eviction, the bankruptcy: it had all diminished everything that he had come to trust. One morning he felt his body was bursting into smithereens and that the splinters of his bones were shooting in different directions, and the resulting sand or dust was the only thing that belonged to him any longer. He felt as if someone had smashed his sternum, as if some cavity of his heart was the burrow for a small, decomposing animal. In thrall to these fantasies, one night he got too close to the rail of the ship en route to Lima, and gripping tight to it, he watched the surging of the waves and thought how easy it would be to throw himself overboard. Yet just as with so many choices that life had laid before him, he lacked the courage; or perhaps he only preferred the dramatic idea to the reality.

And then one morning, as they crossed the choppy waves of the Caribbean, all this urgency and spite was transformed into fuel as, holding his hand steady for the last time, with his final portents and intuitions, he wrote a poem, 'The Sea and the Man', which he recited to himself with his gaze fixed on the roiling waters.

★ ★ ★

Once in Lima, he shut himself up in the ranch at Barranco for three weeks. His illness stopped up his tongue, made his head wobble uncontrollably, spread vibrations through his hands, punished the joints in his legs and shot his talent to pieces. In the face of these difficulties he turned to his second-to-last child, the youngest son, my grandfather Fernán, to dictate his poems, his letters to Ricardo Palma, and a series of documents addressed to various ministries.

From the first line he wrote at his father's request, Fernán understood the magnitude and transcendence of every word. He knew they weren't his own, but taking them down in his handwriting somehow made them so. 'They are', he thought, 'the words of both of us.' Luis Benjamín, tremulous, spoke through the intermediary of his son, and his son knew that while his father lived – or rather so that he could live – he had to transform himself and offer him his writing, giving him oxygen and relief with these phrases and lines that belonged to them both, though more to his father.

In Barranco he received daily visits from the few loyal friends he had left. In Barranco too his final daughter Zulema was born, conceived before his illness became too severe. In Barranco he saw harsh poverty come down on his family like a vengeful fury and, with no money to maintain a dignified livelihood, sold off his scant remaining shares in the near-bankrupt Compañía Salitrera at bargain-basement prices, flogged his wife's jewellery and trinkets, and wangled places for his sons Alfonso and Fernán at schools run by his friends who, out of sheer reverence for him, refused to charge any fees.

And when, with great pain, he advised old Mamaína that he would have to dispense with her services after twenty years, she told him, weeping: 'There's no need to pay me, Don Luis. Your children are my children, how could I leave them. Where would I go anyway?'

'Are you sure about this, Clodomira?'

'Of course I am, Don Luis.'

'I am so grateful.'

'Don't be. We poor people need to help each other out.'

A letter came, announcing the death in Arequipa of Casimiro Ulloa, El Rojo, the doctor who had been more of a brother and confidant than friend and in-law. The Poet shut himself up once more in his hideaway of tears to write, with Fernán's help, a series of grief-stricken texts that one morning, in an outburst of either fury or apathy, without his son's knowledge, he tossed into the rubbish and set on fire with a match that danced in his fingers, as he struggled against his tremors.

His great friend Ricardo Palma had to travel to Spain around the same time and asked him to replace him as temporary director of the National Library of Lima. Luis Benjamín understood that this was a charitable offer, as he had no physical capacity to take up this nor any other position, but he accepted the interim assignment and moved to a two-storey house with balconies located at 164, Sacristía de San Marcelo street, very close to the library. His wife and children followed him to what would be his final place of residence.

When Palma returned and took over the position again, the Poet, now retired from all external activity, shut up in his room, bearing the rigours of Parkinson's without any palliatives, spent the next months dictating more poems to Fernán and receiving visits. Even so, he didn't give up all contact with the outside world and continued to ask about the delicate political situation and for all the local gossip.

Andrés A. Cáceres had returned to power following the death of President Remigio Morales Bermúdez; but on a tense day in March, before he had completed a year in office, he was overthrown by Nicolás de Piérola, known as El Califa, who arrived in Lima on horseback, pistol at the ready, wearing a white cap and pantaloons, at the head of 3,000 montoneros. Entering the city through the Cocharcas district, they took a well-protected route along Teatro street, fought their way to the Government Palace and defeated Cáceres after a bloody forty-eight hour battle that left over a thousand bodies scattered in the streets, swelling and stinking in the sun by the following day.

Amid the affray, some brigands on Cáceres' side lit fires that rapidly spread to the surroundings of the Palace. One of the buildings affected was my great-grandfather's house with its box balconies. Barely able to move, he cried out wildly for help when he saw the flames licking closer and closer. His sons Alfonso and Fernán managed to rescue him from his study and carried him – soaked, blackened by smoke, with first-degree burns on his hands, his scant hair singed – over the adjacent roofs until they reached the house of a neighbour, who offered shelter to the whole family for the weeks it took to make repairs to their home, where two rooms on the first floor had been charred.

Around this time, the Poet found his material privations and enervating illness compensated to some extent with unexpected recognition for his work. The Piérola government named him director of the National Archive, where he went every day together with his principal amanuensis, his son Fernán, now fifteen, who pushed him along the city's streets in his squeaking wheelchair.

He was also invited to take part in a patriotic gathering at the Machine Hall of the Exhibition Palace to celebrate the anniversary of Peruvian independence. For the occasion he composed his poem 'The Supreme Moment', but the day of the ceremony he was in too much pain to get out of bed and asked Fernán to take his place.

It was to be a memorable night. On the stage, his son – my future grandfather – was sweating with nerves. Someone brought him a chair so he would feel less awkward. It took him a few minutes to gain his composure. Yet when he began to recite he did so with eloquence and grace, with his father's aplomb. If in recent days he had lent his hands to write these verses, now he was lending his voice to share them in public. When the final line left his dry mouth, he heard the eager applause, and no longer knew if they were clapping for him or his sick father, and for a moment believed he *was* his father, or that his father had taken possession of him, and discovered an inescapable mission in life: to embody his father, to personify him, to follow him like an idol and extend that fading life through his own. For a few minutes Fernán was Luis Benjamín. The body was the son's, the poetry the father's, and this fusion was sealed with the ovation by the hundreds of strangers looking up at him entranced while he stared back down at them in amazement, blinded by the lights.

From the stage, Fernán managed to identify Ricardo Palma and the poet José Santos Chocano, a young man with fastidiously back-combed hair and a waxed black moustache that resembled bison horns. They both approached to embrace him just as they would have embraced his father, and thanked one as they would have thanked the other, and told him how happy they were that Luis Benjamín had found in his youngest son the heir to his talents. And in the midst of all the affection, cheers and accolades, Fernán smiled proudly, grasping that this was precisely what awaited him: a vocation only recently gestated, discovered, or recognised, because he already had it inside him. The difference was that now it had revealed itself and boldly emerged from this riot of sensations.

There stood my grandfather Fernán, smiling before the auditorium, oblivious to the tragic burden of this inheritance. Because together with the words and the poetry, he would also come to inherit his father's need to discover his origins. And he would someday become curious about Nicolasa, about the priest Gregorio Cartagena, characters whose names hadn't yet reached his ears, but who already tormented him without his even knowing.

* * *

It was his friends José Santos Chocano, Ricardo Palma, Juan Francisco Pazos and Javier Prado who proposed to the director of El Ateneo that Luis Benjamín Cisneros be crowned the National Poet; a homage like the one made in Granada to the Spanish poet José Zorrilla. The director of El Ateneo took to the idea immediately, and promised to sponsor the ceremony. Hearing of this, the Poet dictated a letter of gratitude to his son Fernán, taking three whole days to do so amidst the reverses of his debilitating illness.

I find myself deeply moved by the exceptional distinction you seek to bestow on me, one you could have granted to any of our eminent writers with reputations in America and Europe; and I accept it only in the thought that perhaps it may reward the ardent love I have always professed for poetry itself, noble and lofty as it is, and my steadfast worship of this art throughout my life. My hope is also that this unexpected honour, intended to venerate poetry in my name, will reflect on our beloved motherland, and be passed on to my children; and therefore it is not my place to reject it. The symptoms of my

171

neurotic illness notwithstanding, I promise to make every effort to attend any ceremony that you should arrange.

And so, one Monday evening in August, at seven o'clock sharp, Luis Benjamín, gripping tight to the arms of his sons Alfonso and Fernán, entered El Ateneo's halls at the top of the National Library. He tapped at the floor ahead of him with a gold-handled cane. From the lapels of his suit hung the worn insignia of Academician and Commander of Isabel La Católica. His rheumatic gait expressed the lack of haste of a snail, his pale body was rocked by spasms, of clicking bones that only he could hear, and his eyes shifted nervously, flooded with tears. The place was packed with three hundred people, perhaps more. His friends filled the second row, behind his wife Cristina. Every scientific and literary institution in the country had a representative there. Only President Piérola was absent because, he explained later, a niece had died after swallowing a needle.

Luciano spoke first in the name of his brother, who even if he hadn't been so ill would barely have been able to utter a groan, so moved and exhausted was he. A bishop stepped up to gird the laurel wreath on that head whose translucent skin already revealed its skull, followed by cheers and acclamations that persisted for several minutes, even when a group of students broke with protocol to hand him a card with gold inscriptions. Then came recitals of poems by José Santos Chocano, Numa Pompilio and a long list of younger poets. The last to speak was his son Fernán, who read 'The Sea and the Man', the poem that Luis Benjamín had written about the waters of the Caribbean when he was certain of his illness and his heart was crippled by the death of little Adriana. Fernán again entered a kind of trance, and brought the whole event to a close with a grand finale. Altogether it was three extenuating hours for Luis Benjamín, who felt a little less haggard with all these honours foisted upon him.

The following day, all the newspapers reported on the events at El Ateneo, and a journalist recounted the participation of fifteen-year-old Fernán:

> The poet found a faithful interpreter in his worthy offspring, and everyone foresaw the atavistic succession of his genius. What propriety of attitude, what intelligent inflection of voice, what exact understanding of expression! It was the son embracing the father, proving his worth.

* * *

Luis Benjamín worked for a little longer in the archive, arriving always with Fernán, taking the last animal-hauled trams that crossed the city, pulled by skinny horses with plaited manes. At quiet moments, which were many, he wrote new poems and made an effort to polish older texts, discussing them with the few colleagues he was still in touch with. In 1900, now barely able to move, he made his final two appearances in public when he asked his sons to help him attend the presentation of the first phonograph to reach Lima – a noisy contraption built of cylinders – and one of the earliest film screenings at the Olimpo theatre.

What followed was an acute and extremely painful worsening of the disease. One morning his wife, seeing him crawl out of bed, angrily ordered him not to move. The Poet took her literally and, with surprising discipline, remained prostrate for days, not moving an inch. He gave up the archive, spent mornings, afternoons and evenings sitting in a velvet chair, waiting for someone to feed him mashed vegetables or read him the newspapers, magazines and books sent by his relatives. Mamaína was the first to step in, but he, with the conceit of the truly ancient, asked his daughter Olga – whom he affectionately referred to as 'ma soeur de charité' – to act as his nurse, and she began to bathe and dress him, overcoming the shame of seeing her father naked or pretending not to look while soaping his body.

Fernán continued writing out the poems that his father dictated to him with the worn threads of his voice; sometimes joining the lines together through sheer instinct. By the end of 1903, his final book, *Free Wings*, was ready.

In summer 1904 his symptoms worsened. The Poet trembled constantly, complained of hernias and new afflictions and, once the paralysis had extended to the rest of his limbs, it became hard to understand not only his speech but his gestures. His head shook as if it would fall off, and no one could sleep in the two-storey house any longer, what with his tachycardia, the creaking of his femurs and the groaning of his spirit.

The doctors redoubled their efforts, Cristina swathed him in poultices, Mamaína prepared curative potions for him, but it was all to no avail. A Jesuit priest, Father Íñigo Covadonga, offered him confession over a number of afternoons, and one morning another priest, Ludovico Rivero, read him passages from the Gospel before daubing his forehead with the chrism of extreme unction. At ten o'clock in the morning of 29 January, the Poet stoically demanded to be moved to the sofa in his bedroom. 'It's in very poor taste to die in bed,' he murmured. In his delirium, by means of signs, he asked his son Fernán to cut a vein in his right wrist as soon as the doctors declared his death, and to place under the pillow in his coffin the copy of the complete works of Lord Byron that lived on his bedside table. To calm him, Fernán agreed, knowing full well that when the moment came he would not dare to follow through. The five children and Clodomira Bustíos sat praying in silence, some for the Poet to stay alive, others for him to expire and to suffer no longer the merciless trials of his humiliating paralysis. At two in the afternoon a torpor settled over the bedroom. Cristina placed her husband's arms in a cross and sank a crucifix between his rough fingers. Ten minutes later, with his eyes fixed in an astonishing certainty of solitude, Luis Benjamín exhaled his last breath. He was sixty-six years old, but with death upon him he looked like a hundred.

★ ★ ★

Obituaries were published in every newspaper.

El Comercio: 'You will live forever, maestro, king of the strophe, emperor of verse.'

La Opinión Nacional: 'We all weep for this illustrious man. Literature, science, society and the motherland all lament his passing.'

El Tiempo: 'Like a sun descending into the sea of history, casting until the very end the resplendent rays of his outstanding talent, the national poet has been extinguished.'

And Ricardo Palma bade him farewell with a public letter: 'Though today you abandon me, illustrious poet and unforgettable friend, your absence will not be for long. Goodbye dear brother, and until soon.'

The government of Manuel Candamo covered the costs of the funeral, which was attended by political and ecclesiastical authorities, ministers and former ministers, diplomats from home and abroad, intellectuals, judges and lawyers, bankers and businessmen, journalists and poets. There were also a dozen funeral orations and eulogies prepared by his children and close friends, each of whom took one of the white ribbons hanging from the coffin. Former presidents Nicolás de Piérola and Andrés A. Cáceres were seen stepping forward from the crowd and asking to carry the coffin together. The two old and bitter adversaries, who had clashed all their lives over political matters, made a truce and set aside their enmity before the tomb of Luis Benjamín.

After the burial, the Congress voted to provide a decent pension for the widow and her children. Six years later, thanks to Fernán's efforts, *Free Wings* was published in a posthumous edition, and in 1935, at an anniversary celebration for the founding of Lima, a bronze plaque was placed on the house on Peña Horadada street where Luis Benjamín was born. Finally, in 1937, on the centenary of his birth, the government published his *Complete Works*.

My grandfather Fernán was twenty-two years old when his father died and was the closest witness to the circumstances of this event, which would become both his inheritance and his obsession. To come to terms with Luis Benjamín's death, the other children sought to remember happier days the Poet had spent with Cristina in so many different places. Not Fernán. Unsatisfied by these memories, he understood that his father lived on in him. He firmly believed it. He felt that something deeply intimate and secret had been forged between them during those silent walks along the beaches of Barranco and Chorrillos, during the sunset strolls along the Puente de Palo and the Plaza de Acho, during the readings of Amado Nervo, Byron, Espronceda and Victor Hugo, during the days that his father dictated to him, and especially on that night when he publicly recited his father's poems, standing on a chair, and received the applause that both was and was not for him. Since then, he was convinced that he should be like his father, a version or extension of him, but he knew that he would first need to do something fundamental, something that, despite their closeness, despite the affection and the friendship he had shared with Luis Benjamín, he had never quite managed: to actually know him.

He needed to know who Luis Benjamín Cisneros had been beneath his medals, his laurel crown, his undeniable fame and, above all, beneath that single surname his mother once gave him so that no one would ever dare to call him a bastard.

CHAPTER 12

Lima, 2014

One morning, when I was eight or nine years old, I opened the encyclopaedia where I'd been told I'd find the name of my grandfather. 'Luis Benjamín Cisneros, poet, liberal politician, diplomat, economist.' A charcoal-drawn portrait emphasised his ancient, querulous expression. Looking at it, I didn't feel anything. Beside the image, a few lines gave an account of his books, his work in Europe, his coronation as national poet. His biography was exhausted in a paragraph.

I also learned around that time that the Cisneros esplanade in the Miraflores district – that long winding road that looks out over the Pacific from the edge of Lima – owes its name to Luis Benjamín, though I don't recall this prompting me to learn anything more about him. At that age, the esplanade was the place where I'd go to ride my bicycle, passing the La Marina lighthouse and the yellow-painted bridge then favoured by suicides. I wasn't interested in my great-grandfather: the brief encyclopaedia entry sufficed in the rare moments when I was struck with a faint, distant need to find out more.

Later, at those family reunions, when my uncles would tell stories about his literary adventures, I found it hard to disguise my yawns. The merits he achieved during his lifetime sounded as tedious as the notable figures he had the chance to meet. I could only associate their names with the places, buildings and establishments that were part of the twentieth-century city I'd been born in. Ricardo Palma was a clinic. Casimiro Ulloa a hospital. Piérola and Salaverry the names of two avenues. It was as if time, habit and custom had poured thick immovable layers of concrete over the memory of my great-grand-father and the people he had most loved. If Luis Benjamín was anything to me it was this: solid cement or rock. A grey and impenetrable mass. A noble yet abandoned monolith that formed a part of the historic backdrop of the Cisneros family.

I was no more concerned to learn, a little older now, that in the centre of Lima, deep in the Barrios Altos, there was a boys' school that bore his name. I later found out that this building was in fact the mansion on Peña Horadada street where he was born and spent his early years. In the 1960s it was levelled by an earthquake and rebuilt as a school.

Very close by, as it happened, stood the office of the newspaper where I worked for ten years, *El Mundo*. One day, my boss, the editor of the news desk, assigned me to cover a political event not far from the city centre. I decided to go on foot. It was an unusually warm June morning. As I walked, distracted by the bustle of the crowded streets and the sunlight glancing off the open windows of the tallest buildings, I passed the school. It wasn't intentional. I only realised after running into a hundred kids practising a military march, as if preparing for a parade. They wore white shirts, grey trousers and skinny black ties. Observing the large building constructed part from brick, part in the traditional quincha or wattle and daub style, from which they came and went like ants, I noticed the number of the school campus, No. 937, inscribed together with the distinctive shield, containing three white letters in a red circle against an electric blue background: L.B.C. All it took was a glimpse of my great-grandfather's initials – seen so many times in the books our uncles made us read – for them to spell out his name in my head. Below it, a small plaque read:

The Municipality commemorates the Romantic writer Luis Benjamín Cisneros, the first poet to be crowned with laurels by an adoring city.

The boys then formed four columns in the middle of the street, to the curiosity of passers-by, who paused to watch. With martial poise, standing to attention, they put one hand to their chests and raised their chins. Their expressions were almost adult. I thought they were about to sing the national anthem, but instead it was the school song they sang a cappella:

Here was born Cisneros, the Poet here was born,
let us pay tribute with love and admiration.
His steps ring out here, we hear his voice,
his warbling like a sublime nightingale.

At the first line, I was left dumbstruck. I had the impression people were looking or pointing at me, as if the heat had instantly begun to melt away my mask as a journalist and reveal my true face. Seeing these comradely teenagers singing the praises of Luis Benjamín with such solemnity and pomp, I remember feeling, more than intrigue, something like envy. It was clear that my great-grandfather's name was well known to these kids. Later I learned that they professed a veritable cult of Cisneros: they knew his legacy, they saw him every day in the photograph that hung on one wall of the library, they considered him an influence, a subject of study, they drew him in art contests with his moustaches, pen and parchments. Meanwhile, I was completely in the dark. I could barely recall what I'd once read about him in the encyclopaedia. I didn't even know exactly why he was so famous.

Watching this crowd of schoolkids break ranks after crying out in unison 'I am a Cisneros', I felt a discomfort somewhere in my body I couldn't quite identify, and hurried on my way to keep it from spreading.

* * *

In the sky the stars,
in the field the thorns,
and in my breast
the Republic of Argentina.

This quatrain by José Piñeiro – a Spaniard who in 1896 stowed away on a ship bound for Argentina, looking for his father – was one I heard recited countless times by my father and my uncles who had been born in Buenos Aires. They repeated it before and after toasts made at family lunches throughout my childhood. At first I enjoyed its sonorous rhythms and my siblings and I composed less patriotic variations that made everyone laugh. Later, it was the image of the sky and the fields full of stars and thorns that I most liked about these touching verses. How different they were, the stars and the thorns. One remote, celestial, luminous, unreachable; the other spiky as needles and painful when they pierce your skin. One a signpost for the lost sailor; the other protection for flowers attacked by herbivorous beasts. Piñeiro's quatrain returned like an arrow the afternoon I happened to pass school No. 937, Luis Benjamín Cisneros, and minutes later, as I attended the political event my editor at *El Mundo* had sent me to cover, I caught myself writing it down in my notebook two or three times over.

In the sky the stars, in the field the thorns…

I wouldn't be able to explain why, but I suspect this was the moment I first opened myself to probing questions of my own provenance. Does every star belong to a constellation? Is every thorn an extension of a larger stem? I didn't yet know how to answer myself, but I was aware as never before of the unfathomable distance that separated me from the first men of my family, those almost biblical characters who had established mysterious norms to which – I suddenly understood – I was not united, but bound.

The second time I was invaded by such a feeling was in my early years as a university lecturer. At the end of a class, a student came up and bombarded me with questions, wishing to learn if I was 'connected' to Luis Benjamín Cisneros. She told me she was preparing her thesis in comparative literature on 'the most representative authors of Peruvian Romanticism' and quite reasonably imagined that I could offer some insight into the Poet. I told her that I was indeed his great-grandson, but felt instantly embarrassed at how little I knew about the works she described with striking erudition.

That was a long time ago.

Everything I now know about Luis Benjamín I owe, above all, to a book that Uncle Gustavo wrote about the public life of my great-grandfather, which nevertheless leaves out – due to an enduring inhibition that none of my family has attempted or wished to overcome – the most decisive episodes of his private life, which are precisely the ones that most fascinate and disconcert me. If I've been able to reconstruct this private life, or rather peer into it, it was thanks to copies of the correspondence Luis Benjamín exchanged with a number of different recipients, well preserved in some milk crates by Uncle Gustavo; to further documents scattered between Lima and Huánuco; and to the intense exchange of letters between his children Alfonso and Fernán, who as adults wrote revealing pages about their father, pages they swore would never be made public, in which they picked through everything they knew, thought they knew or imagined alone over the years. Rich in subtext and marked by tacit and easily deciphered shame, these letters sketch out my great-grandfather's private life. There, the great deeds and splendour of the public figure disappear and are replaced by the emotional suffering of the man. These letters are the trace of something that endures even to this day. Something immanent, irrefutable, nameless. Something that impinges upon me, that stalks my life, that makes me who I am.

★ ★ ★

The day we went to eat in a restaurant on Tarapacá street, after the visit to the cemetery, I waited for Uncle Gustavo to finish telling the family story before I launched into all the questions that had accumulated in my head.

'Aren't you surprised by all the secrets?'

'I was surprised at first, but then I realised I had nothing to gain by obsessing about it. All families have secrets,' he replied, almost laughing, without raising his gaze from the lemon fish fillet he had just been served.

'All families have secrets, but not all know they have them. The problem isn't having secrets, but finding out what they are. What do you do with this information once you gain access to it? They're not just anecdotes, is what I mean.'

'Perhaps it's best not to know.'

'We have a problem: we know the secrets and the lies.'

'What's wrong with that?'

'I don't mean it's bad, but you can't deny that it comes with a certain commitment.'

'Commitment? To what?'

'I don't know. To tell it, to say it, to inform the others, bring them up to date.'

'That would be a temptation, not a commitment.'

'OK then, a temptation.'

'Clearly you want to publish your family's private business. Go on, say it, you don't have to make excuses. Not with me, at least.' Uncle Gustavo said this with his mouth full, and laughed again.

'Is that what you think?'

'Yes. You're a gossip, just like me.'

'I can assure you of one thing: writing this story isn't going to rid me of this feeling I have.'

'And what feeling is that?'

'Disappointment, basically.'

'Let's see, what is it that affects you so much?'

'Everything! That my great-grandfather grew up believing that his father was a traveling businessman who didn't even exist. That he spent so many years unaware he was someone else's son. And then he suddenly learned that the man was a priest. Do you think that's nothing?'

'Those were different times.'

'I disagree. This is a scandal at any time – nineteenth, twentieth or twenty-first century.'

'You can't look at the past with today's eyes. It's not fair to judge that period with our criteria.'

'Of course you can. Imagine if you couldn't. There'd be no history, no archaeology. No religion, too. We all revisit and judge the past.'

'That doesn't make it any fairer.'

'Can you be fair about things that affect you?'

'Sure.'

'No, Uncle. Not fair. Not objective. Not impartial. Not neutral.'

'I mean the morals of the time. It was a different moral code. If women got pregnant out of wedlock, they had to keep it quiet. It didn't matter if they were poor or high class, they were looked down on. Think about Nicolasa: an influential, forward-thinking woman, with connections. She couldn't say anything.'

'It's the same moral code as today. Perhaps there was more fear or more hypocrisy, I can understand that, but at bottom people thought the same way.'

'No. Everything was harder. Much harder. You've no idea.'

'OK, Nicolasa's situation wasn't easy, but Luis Benjamín's was worse: being a bastard, in the dark about it all, condemned to spend his life dealing with his orphanhood…'

'Hang on, hang on. Where do you get the idea that he felt "condemned" from?'

'Haven't you read his poetry? It's all there. He won't say it literally, but it's clear enough. He needed to resolve his traumas.'

'You use that word a lot: resolve.'

'What word do you suggest?'

'I don't know, but you're exaggerating. It's not such a big deal. We all have wounds and that doesn't mean our lives are nothing but frustration and trauma.'

'Be honest, don't you think that Luis Benjamín came into the world with a heavier burden than other people, a different kind of wound, a kind of birthmark?'

'But not just him. His siblings too! They were all children of the priest. In any case, Juan, the eldest, the one who vanished in the jungle, was the worst affected. Why focus on Luis Benjamín?'

'Perhaps the older ones suffered the same, there's no way to know. For me it's obvious that Luis Benjamín was the most damaged…'

'Damaged?'

'Yes. I think that he was first to understand their origins, and processed it more than the others, and that's why he suffered the most harm.'

'You can't be sure of that.'

'I can deduce it.'

'Then it's a biased interpretation.'

'And what interpretation isn't, Uncle?'

'Well, I'm telling you these things not for you to interpret them, but for you to know them. That's it.'

'And if you're so interested in sharing them, why didn't you include them in the biography you wrote about Luis Benjamín?'

'Because I only wanted to talk about his public life. I had no interest in getting into the rest.'

'Were you frightened that some relative would object?'

'I simply didn't want aspects of my grandfather's private life to become the focus of morbid interest and to cloud his public and literary merits.'

'…'

'In any case, I'm not the right person to do it…'

'Why not?'

'For years I've organised our family reunions, I'm known as the uncle who brings the Cisneros family together. Why publish a book full of disloyalties? They'd all turn against me.'

'So you don't mind me doing it?

'I've told you already: if you don't, then these things will be forgotten.'

'You're not going to stop talking to me?'

'I'm too old for resentment. Write the damn book. Though I don't know what the rest will have to say about it.'

'They won't have to worry. I'm going to write a novel, not a biography.'

'They'll complain all the same.'

'I can already imagine the arguments: "How dare you dig up the family's skeletons!"'

'Well, I'd understand them. No one's prepared for someone else to rake through their secrets.'

'That's the issue. Are they theirs alone? Aren't they *my* secrets too? Don't we inherit these things?'

Uncle Gustavo gestured to the waiter, asking for another whisky. I was spinning out what remained in my glass: although there was a voice recorder on the table, I wanted to retain aspects of the conversation that the machine wouldn't capture, and that I intended to note down in my journal as soon as my uncle got up to go to the loo. I had to stay lucid.

'Let's talk about the bastards.'

'Another unnecessary term!' Uncle Gustavo made a face.

'Why's that?'

'No one uses that word any more.'

'The word is the least of it. It's what it signifies.'

'It's just that "bastards" sounds so tragic.'

'Sorry, but your father denying your existence is pretty tragic, right?'

'Luis Benjamín and his siblings were "natural children", unrecognised children, something that was very common in the nineteenth century, and more recently too. To this day there are countless children without a father. Do people yell "bastard" at them in the street?'

'It's one thing not to have a father, another to have one invented for you. Roberto Benjamín was an invention.'

'Nicolasa did what she had to do.'

'She didn't tell the truth.'

'Here's the way I see it: if you're missing a leg, they need to get you a prosthesis, right?'

'Is that your best analogy? A prosthesis…'

'If it helps to make up for what's missing, it works.'

The more Uncle Gustavo tried to avoid or proscribe the word 'bastard', the more he made me want to say it. Telling him that his grandfather had been a bastard was outrageous, blasphemous, but there was something liberating in the outrage, something restorative in the blasphemy. In any case, why such fear of calling things by their name? Being a bastard, after all, is an involuntary condition of birth, and therefore free of moral judgement. No one chooses to be a bastard. No one opts whether or not to have a father. On the other hand, there's something undeniably coarse about bastardy. The implications aren't the same for an ordinary person as for a bastard. Even less so for a bastard poet. Even less so for a Peruvian bastard poet crowned by a society that considers difference repellent.

'Do you find the term dishonourable?'

'Initially yes, very much so. I was influenced by my uncles, my older cousins, my siblings. No one talked about this. *No one*. The mere fact of asking about my grandfather they'd have seen as immoral.'

'It doesn't shock or embarrass me in the slightest. Don't ask me why, but this halo of illegitimacy around Luis Benjamín makes me even fonder of him. I'd even go so far as to say I like the fact he was a bastard.'

'If they could hear you, several of your relatives would accuse you of heresy!'

'And I'd accuse them of cowardice for concealing all of this.'

'You have to understand that until a few years ago

these things were a real social handicap. It was better to keep quiet about them. Once when I was a child, I tried to draw the family tree and when I asked my dad and Uncle Alfonso about their grandparents, they sent me packing.'

'And the day I called Aunt Elena to talk about Gregorio Cartagena – do you remember? – she put the phone down on me!'

'Well, what can I tell you? That she'd have been delighted to discuss the old priest?'

'Why not?'

'Because all of that was a stigma, a source of shame. It still is.'

'But Nicolasa and the priest was two centuries ago! At this point, all this reticence just seems like affectation.'

'There are people who don't like airing their dirty laundry in public.'

'They prefer the muck to build up.'

'Why are you so surprised? This is Lima prudishness. That's how folk are here, prudish. Most of our family are prudes. They're horrified, indignant at the lurid details of others' lives, but say nothing about their own.'

'Or they only whisper about it.'

'Or they simply don't care.'

'I think they do care.'

'Come on, let's not fool ourselves. This thing about the "origin" of our family, about discovering our ancestors, is something you and me and a handful of others care about. Most of them don't give a shit. Or are you going to tell me people are deeply concerned about where they came from. Bollocks! Most people care only about the future, not the past.'

'Cheers to the past, then.'

'Cheers!'

We clinked glasses.

'Instead of world history, schools should teach the personal history of each pupil.'

'This history isn't taught, but discovered.'

'But we should be able to gain access to it earlier, don't you think?'

'A course in genealogy, you mean?'

'One that recounts the pre-history of your family, but with plenty of details. Who were the founders, the heroes, the traitors, the marginalised, the pariahs. Biographies and secrets of each ancestor. Generic data, but also hard and uncomfortable facts. Personal triumphs, defeats, illnesses, disloyalties, plots. Battles won and lost. Moments of glory and tragedy. Can you imagine? With photographs, documents, slides. Everything. Emblematic dates. Myths. Rumours. What is known, denied, surmised. The public, the private, the secret.'

'I guess it's probably more practical to teach world history after all.'

'Practical, yes, but sometimes unnecessary.'

'Well, it's part of a general cultural education.'

'I think I prefer individual culture.'

'They're not mutually exclusive.'

'I just find it a little ridiculous to learn about, I don't know, the pyramids of Egypt, the genesis of Mesopotamia, or the names of Chinese dynasties instead of learning about where you come from, who you're descended from.'

As the discussion went on, I realised that there were still questions swirling around in me, things that neither Uncle Gustavo nor anyone else would be able to answer either then or later. What did my great-grandfather do with the fondness he originally felt for this Roberto Benjamín, the 'ornamental' father invented for him and his siblings by their mother? Where did those feelings go when he found out the truth? And what did he do with the sudden aversion towards Gregorio Cartagena, whom he had always seen as a family friend, whom for years he called 'Uncle Gregorio', never suspecting he was his father? Did he really hate him? Where did this bitterness end up? How much of it was worked out through poetry and how much kept ringing inside him, scraping at those nerves that were already in shreds by the time he reached sixty? How much of that frustration travelled across generations and settled in his children and grandchildren, many of whom perhaps never identified the source of their own jealousies, resentments and illnesses? Why was nothing ever said in my house about the bastards? And why have I taken so long to find out about it, when Luis Benjamín – just like his parents in their respective wills – left written clues to his secrets, as if he acknowledged them as potential traumas, perhaps trusting that someone would find them and unblock them, deactivate them, neutralise them to halt the blast wave?

My bastard great-grandfather. His blast wave.

It is no coincidence, it now occurs to me, that his poems contain no allusions to his father at all. There is not a single line or verse or metaphor that refers to the invisible man manufactured by his mother, nor to the priest who engendered him. The figure of the father doesn't exist in his poems, not even in negative form. He's simply not there. And if a father doesn't exist in his son's literary universe, if he doesn't even have a place there, it's because a powerful animus has tried to strike him out.

'Doesn't it surprise you that Luis Benjamín already had a daughter by the age of eighteen?'

'It surprises me even more that by twenty-two he had three…'

'How did he manage?'

'That was also perfectly normal in the mid-nine-teenth century.'

'It's not so much the children, but who he had them with. The president's mistress. That is bold, to put it lightly.'

'He could have chosen another woman, that's for sure.'

'He could? You think so?'

'It would have been wiser, certainly.'

'What I mean is, do you really believe that people *choose* these things? Don't you think they're already determined, written down? Wasn't meeting Lucrecia Colichón a question of fate?'

'No. No. That's all nonsense. Fate is what you make of it. A man chooses a woman and a woman a man, and that's it. There is risk and sometimes there is luck, but nothing else. Fate is the word used later on to tell the story, to make it sound grander.'

'Seen from up close, sure, it looks like a choice, but if you go back over our whole genealogy and see it from a broader viewpoint, all these "choices" together make up a pattern. Or suggest one. You'll deny it, but I see in almost all our Cisneros ancestors, both men and women, a clear tendency to get themselves into trouble, a toxic calling.'

'Which is even more noticeable in Luis Benjamín, who got involved with Castilla's mistress shortly after the president himself invited him to work in the Foreign Ministry.'

'Why do you think he did that? Why do you think he betrayed him?'

'Because Castilla was an enemy of the family, an adversary of his uncle Pedro.'

'I think his transgression had another objective, a less conscious one.'

'And what's that then?'

'To return to the clandestinity of his own origins.'

I only thought of it later, but this is another word that emerges from my family story and that weighs as heavily as the heat of that night I spent conversing with Uncle Gustavo: clandestine. Many chapters of our past and present have been consumed in its name. Clandestinity, for many Cisneros, has been a refuge, a dwelling place. Sometimes even a purpose. Or a fate. Is that the destiny of my family? The destiny of my clan? My *clan-destiny*?

'I don't know. Perhaps he wanted, as you say, unconsciously, to repeat the story of his parents. It's complicated. What I do find unquestionable is that Luis Benjamín saw Lucrecia as a projection of Nicolasa. At bottom, he had a bad case of the Oedipus complex. In his books, his poems, it's extraordinary how religiously he acclaims and eulogises Nicolasa. He puts her on a pedestal. He didn't talk about her as a mother, but as a saint. More than her son, he was her devotee.'

'Can you imagine how overwhelming it must have been for Nicolasa to realise from one day to the next that he, her youngest son, had three daughters with the president's mistress?'

'The most incredible thing of all was that after finding out, becoming disenchanted, cursing and reprimanding him, she convinced Luis Benjamín to go to Paris. And not just for him to get away from Lucrecia, but to become a writer! She sent him to France to write! She forced him to discover the world! How many mothers did that in Lima in 1860? How many mothers do that today? What a marvellous woman, dammit! Cheers to her!'

Whether out of effusiveness or the whisky, Uncle Gustavo's eyes began to shine. Then, looking through the window over the busy Arequipa avenue, as if these streets offered inspiration, he uttered a few of his grandfather's verses he knew by heart. Slowly, as if expressing his memories.

'What happened to Lucrecia Colichón's daughters when Luis Benjamín went to France: Elvira, Adelaida and María Luisa?'

'They were left in the custody of Nicolasa.'

'But how did they feel?'

'Abandoned, betrayed. It's only logical.'

'And later?'

'None of them forgave Luis Benjamín for having married Cristina Bustamante, even less for having seven children with her. For the older daughters, each child he had with Cristina was a dagger thrust, one reason more to distance themselves from their father. There is a very harsh letter from Elvira in which she tells him "I know that we are your spoiled fruit."'

'Yet the three were the product of a more, how should I say, truthful relationship, weren't they? How would you define Luis Benjamín's relationship with Lucrecia?'

'Sick.'

'Sure, but at the beginning it was impassioned, full of desire.'

'Yes, but it was totally unsustainable. That's why it ended like it did: defeated by the circumstances.'

'His love for Cristina, meanwhile, was more conscientious.'

'There was a certain coldness about his marriage to Cristina. He wanted to have a formal wife. Don't forget the letter he wrote to Casimiro Ulloa: "I want to travel to Lima, marry, start a family, and return to spend a period in France."'

'Marrying Cristina wasn't a dream, but a plan.'

'Right. He wanted to do things "properly" to satisfy Nicolasa. There is a poem in which it seems that his mother tells him about a suitable woman.'

'Do you remember it?'

Uncle Gustavo looked through the window again to recollect his scattered memories.

A woman who under the white veil
of chaste innocence
and the blushing cheek
can bring to the altar
her serene temple raised
to the orange blossom
of the crown of rays
that fall from the sun
through the ogive tinged
in resplendent colours.
Does the woman you love respond
to this ideal? The tears you shed
very clearly say 'no', and you understand
with cruel remorse
the danger you run
and the fatal abyss into which you descend,
moment by moment.

'So the "abyss" is… Lucrecia?'

'Evidently.'

'And yet, I still think she was the woman who brought him to life.'

'Without a doubt. Lucrecia left a mark on Luis Benjamín. Afterwards he loved Cristina, my grandmother, but what they had together was… different.'

'More formal.'

'Formal, but above all cold, perhaps even false.'

'But Cristina benefited from Nicolasa's approval, right?'

'Nicolasa wanted all her children to be married. That was what she approved of, the formality.'

'My grandfather experienced something similar.'

'Yes, with his wife Hermelinda, and with my mother.'

'And then you all carried on with the habit.'

'What habit?'

'I don't know if habit is the right word, but it seems like a tendency or tradition.'

'What does?'

'The way the men of our family love one woman desperately, another one responsibly, but end up having children with both.'

'Do you mean your father? Because he fell in love with your mother when he was already married?'

'Him… but you too.'

'That's different. I was widowed.'

'Sure. Aunt Marta.'

'Yes. Marta Ferreira.'

'What did she die from?'

'Stomach cancer, a very rare tumour called… Krukenberg.'

Uncle Gustavo fell silent, his gaze lost in the distance.

'What is it?'

'I've never been able to get that name out of my head all these years: Krukenberg.'

'…'

'…'

'After her, came Aunt Liliana?'

'Yes. A long time after Martita died I met Liliana and, true to my nature, I married again.'

'You say that you married again, not that you fell in love again.'

Uncle Gustavo gave a half-smile.

'Losing Marta was very hard, too hard. Imagine finding yourself alone, at the age of thirty, with three children. Liliana appeared and she was great company. I loved her, I love her, we have four children together, but now she lives far away and it's no longer the same. I could never fall in love with her or anyone else as I did with Martita. I've never stopped being a widower.'

'But on paper, you're still Aunt Liliana's husband.'

'That's right.'

'But weren't you also with a Nancy?'

'Nancy was much younger than me. There was love, but we met too late.'

'And Patricia?'

'A rebound.'

'And Begonia?'

'A fling.'

'And Soledad?'

'A mistake.'

'And María Elena?'

'Dammit! You're raking through the whole file now!'

Certain men on my father's side of the family are like this. Or were like this. Insatiably acquisitive. Predators. Womanisers. They had women they loved blindly and impetuously. Women who left them wounded, in a bad way. Then they met others that perhaps they didn't love altogether but married them, made alliances that in theory were sensible, correct and definitive; and later − or rather in parallel − sought out new illicit and risky lovers with whom they could enjoy a second youth. The custom of the double life has been repeated in each generation. If this is not a habit, a pattern, a trend, I don't know what it is. An enduring coincidence? A hereditary gene? A vice, an illness, an infection? An echo? How to escape it? Can atavistic viruses be eliminated? Can contagion be avoided? Can this intangible, genetically transmissible part of us ever be decontaminated, or does it become intrinsic from the start and all we can do is bear it? How can we be sure what is ours, our own, and what is passed on if everything comes to us melted down and mixed up at birth? Were the men of my family aware of obeying an established mould? Did they ever set out to correct that tradition, or were they simply carried along by it? Am I yet another such man? Will I repeat the story I am writing? Or am I writing it down in order not to repeat it?

Before the final whiskies, when the restaurant was almost empty and the waiters, already changed into civvies and their hair freshly combed, were watching us out of the corners of their eyes, wondering how much longer we were going to stay, Uncle Gustavo opened his briefcase and pulled out a sheaf of documents.

'Look, this is the marriage certificate of Luis Benjamín and Cristina.'

'The one we found in the archbishop's office…'

'The very same. I made two copies of it. I don't know if you'd realised, but here he declares Roberto Benjamín to be his *legitimate* father, despite the fact that in 1869 the rumour that he was the son of a priest had been heard all across Lima. Look.'

I scanned the page, squinting to make sense of the old-fashioned calligraphy.

'Was this marriage valid, or pretend?'

'It was totally valid.'

'And why didn't he just put the name of his mother, Nicolasa?'

'And run the risk of appearing not to have a father at all? That would have been worse.'

'But strictly speaking… he didn't.'

'He must have done it to protect himself and to protect the honour of his mother at the same time.'

'But Nicolasa had declared herself single in her will.'

'That was private information, not public.'

'In any case, she was dead. Why should he bother?'

'Don't you think even dead ladies deserve to be properly married?'

'But at least to a real dead husband, not a false one.'

'Not false; artificial.'

'Do you have any idea if Luis Benjamín ever spoke to anyone about this?'

'Only with his brother Luciano, and only through letters. They were close friends, as close as my father and my Uncle Alfonso, or your father and Juvenal.'

'It sounds like each generation needs a pair of brothers ready to protect each other's backs, and keep the family secrets…'

'Sure, but as you can tell it didn't do them much good. In the long run everything comes out. And when it began to be rumoured that the Cisneros were all descended from some priest, things got heated.'

'Were there attacks?'

'Direct ones.'

Uncle Gustavo went on to describe a clash between Luciano Benjamín and a civil attorney who brought his origins to light and made his bastard status public as part of a smear campaign. This was in 1870, during the Supreme Court trial over the Dreyfus contract, which Luciano was defending on behalf of the Dreyfus Company. The contract had replaced the extortionate system of guano consignments with one of direct sales, ending a twenty-year commercial dictatorship, and according to a number of studies saving Peru from bankruptcy. But the beneficiaries of the old system wouldn't take it lying down, and filed a lawsuit to have their unwonted privileges restored. Hundreds of citizens interested in hearing the arguments of both parties attended the trial.

After Luciano demonstrated, in his opening remarks, that the complaint filed by the consignees was unfounded, the lawyer for the prosecution, by the name of Pativilca, lacking arguments for a counterattack, paralysed by helplessness and under pressure from his clients, stood up and threw his hemlock:

'And tell me, doctor, do you know all this by your own letter or by another's? A *Carta-ajena*, perhaps?'

insinuating the name of the priest with a clever pun.

The courtroom was frozen into silence. Not a viscous, but a mineral silence. The air became almost palpably stiff. All those present grasped Pativilca's disloyal trick. Everyone was too embarrassed to make eye contact. The low blow disfigured Luciano's face for an instant. But then he turned his indignation into self-esteem, when the noise of throats being cleared began to spread, addressing the judge while he continued to point at Pativilca:

'All I know, Your Honour, is that this individual is a knave, a blockhead and a wretch!'

Thunderous clapping swept down from the Pierolist galleries like a herd of horses. Luciano combed his hand through his hair and, without wasting time asking his aggressor to retract, focusing on the matter of the trial so as not to bog himself down any further, he delivered a convincing piece of oratory that would be enough to win the trial.

'Look, here I have what none other than Raúl Porras Barrenechea said about Luciano's intervention.'

Uncle Gustavo took a dusty, hardcover history book out of his briefcase. He opened it to a page he'd marked.

...the defence offered by Luciano Benjamín Cisneros of the legitimacy of the Dreyfus contract may be one of the most notable ever to be uttered in our court, given the social significance of the matter at hand, the struggle between formidable economic interests and the political and social rivalries involved, and above all due to its popular repercussions. The Dreyfus issue was no mere private negotiation but a weaponless revolution that profoundly shook the country, later leading to abuses and excesses, yet first paved the way for hope and historic and social transformation.

That was Luciano. Far from quaking in fear, he replied sarcastically to diatribes and gave twice as good as he got, knowing his words contained shrapnel that could forever undermine the self-esteem of anyone who sought to revile him or ridicule him for his illegitimacy. He earned a lot of money as a lawyer but, like his brother, my great-grandfather, he fell into poverty as a result of the Pacific War, losing almost all his capital and property at the hands of the Chileans who occupied Lima by force. Of the two, Luis Benjamín was the most affected financially. His account statement – the only piece of paper that remained after his death – includes some share certificates from the Compañía Salitrera, which by then were not even worth half a real.

'He didn't have any property left either?'

'None. They sold everything, even the house on Peña Horadada street.'

'What happened to that house?'

'Have you heard of Antonio Raimondi?'

'The Italian scientist? The Estela Raimondi one?'

'The very same. He bought it. He completed his first studies on the natural resources of Peru, which later won him global fame, in the same room where Luis Benjamín was born.'

'When they sold that house, did Luis Benjamín already have Parkinson's?'

'That's another thing that strikes me: the illness that prevented him looking after himself, from writing...'

'But that ironically brought him closer to Fernán. When Luis Benjamín could no longer sit down and hold a pen, my father became his right hand, his secretary, his scribe, his guide dog, his interpreter.'

'His father's paralysis is what made him a writer in turn.'

'He was the most sensitive of all Luis Benjamín's

children. Perhaps the only one who could clearly express what his old man wanted to say… If I'm not mistaken, somewhere here I have a letter from my father that talks about him.'

After digging around in his briefcase for a moment, Uncle Gustavo pulled out a yellowed page so translucent that the two typewritten paragraphs could be read from the rear. It was a letter from another century, so thin and fragile that even holding it gently between the fingertips risked damaging it. Uncle Gustavo put on his glasses and began to read:

> The old man in his wheelchair. What a spectacle, the tortured heart constantly composing rhymes in silence. What a spectacle, that peaceful and generous gaze amid the gloominess of his prison and the afflictions of his body.

Unlike Luis Benjamín, who did not draw at all on his priest father, Fernán drew all too deeply on his writer father. Too much brilliance, too much fame, too much learning. Also, too much silence.

A long time before he died as a result of the degenerative consequences of Parkinson's, Luis Benjamín had already decided to lock away certain things from his past. He never told his children who he was, where he came from, nor who Gregorio Cartagena had been.

For this reason, because he lived so close to his father but had no access to the hiding places of his childhood or the labyrinth of his fears, even without having been born into illegitimacy, Fernán, my grandfather, plotted a course towards this condition and reproduced it on his own, without extenuating circumstances.

'There's one more thing, Uncle.'

'What's that?'

The sole remaining waiter brought us the bill and removed our empty glasses. It was almost six. The noise from outside had faded though soon, as dark fell over the city, the chaos of the streets would start up again. The chairs had been placed upside down on the tables, giving the impression they too were exhausted and recovering, or regaining their strength to bear the weight of the next lot of diners.

'Our surname, Cisneros…'

'What about it?'

'It's not the right one.'

'…'

'Don't tell me you've never thought about it.'

'Yes, tons of times, but what good does thinking do by now…'

'We should be called Cartagena, like the priest.'

'Or Benjamín, like Roberto.'

'No, no. Roberto was an invention. Cartagena was real. We should bear his name.'

'You're forgetting something: if anyone didn't want that name passed on, it was the priest. He didn't want to be found out. What do you think the children felt once they discovered that Roberto Benjamín didn't exist and Gregorio was their father? Did they feel proud? No. They hated him! That's why they decided to take their mother's name.'

'But they were the priest's children. There was nothing they could do about that. Even if they used another name they were his blood. That's irreversible.'

'And?'

'It's not normal to live with the wrong surname.'

'Tell me one thing: do you feel like a Cartagena or like a Cisneros?'

'A Cisneros.'

'What's the big deal, then? Do you really want to

change your name?'

'I just want to talk about it. If someone discovers that their real surname is something different, it's only natural for there to be questions, confusion, doubts, don't you think?'

'If the children of the priest didn't care about it, why should you?'

'Do you really believe they didn't care? Do you really believe that?'

'Do you have any idea how many people live with a name that isn't their own?'

'Millions, no doubt, but that's no consolation.'

'It shouldn't be a dilemma, either.'

'You don't get to choose your dilemmas.'

'But you do choose to turn them into a big drama.'

'Do you reckon I'm being dramatic?'

'You're playing the victim.'

'Please explain.'

'In this country, where people are dying of hunger, of cold, of fear, of poverty, worrying about the origin of your surname is a little…'

'Frivolous? Graceless?'

'Yes, graceless. The right word, at last.'

'Let me remind you, Uncle, that this is *your* subject. You started this whole investigation.'

'Because I wanted to know, not to question.'

'But knowing is questioning.'

'You're just as stubborn as your father. You refuse to acknowledge that you're whipping up a storm in a teacup.'

'Our personal origins may not be a problem of the first degree, but that doesn't mean to say they're not a problem. Don't pass it off as something banal. If everyone had the time and means, I'm sure they would take an interest in their identity, their background, their ancestors, their roots.'

'I doubt it.'

'I don't.'

'I do. People who don't have any money, which in this country are the majority, only worry about how to get some. They're preoccupied with surviving, with feeding their kids. Do you really imagine that they're losing sleep over their origin? Forget it!'

'You're generalising.'

'You're interested in these things because you're well-educated, you live comfortably, you don't lack for anything. You can allow yourself the luxury.'

'How do you know I don't lack for anything?'

'I can tell.'

'Perhaps I lack things you can't see, or don't want to see.'

'Like what?'

'Right now, a little more openness and less irony on your part. You're being pretty cynical, I reckon.'

'Cynical?'

'Uncle, please remember it was you and the rest of them who were always talking about "the Cisneros". For years, at countless family reunions. You sang, recited poetry, danced. You talked about Fernán and Luis Benjamín. Being a Cisneros was a real party.'

'It is.'

'It was.'

'Good times. They didn't last.'

'In the home of our grandparents in La Paz, there was a plaque on the wall that read "This is the house of the Cisneros"…'

'Yeah, a ceramic plaque written in gothic letters. We had it made…'

'I grew up in that house, I grew up seeing that plaque with that illegitimate surname.'

'What do you mean, illegitimate?'

'Well: mistaken, erroneous, incorrect.'

'We are Cisneros because of Nicolasa.'

'*We* have no reason to be. My great-grandfather should have been called Luis Cartagena Cisneros; my grandfather, Fernán Cartagena Bustamante; you and your siblings should be Cartagena Vizquerra. I should be Cartagena Zaldívar. Cisneros is a forced, imposed, artificial surname. A surname that should have been lost and left behind. You are the expert in these things. You should know better than anyone.'

'All I know is that two centuries have passed and there are many generations of Cisneros who are very proud to bear their name.'

'I wonder how many of them know that Cartagena is our real surname.'

'You keep insisting on that. Is it really so important?'

'You were the ones who taught us it was important! You repeated it to the point of exhaustion, every Sunday, that the paternal surname is the one that is inherited, passed down, the one that endures, the mark of prestige. You told us that this was our heritage, our patrimony, our DNA. A load of patriarchal machismo, now that I come to think of it. Don't look at me like that, Uncle, these are the things you all told us. It's only logical that they lodged in our heads. They certainly did in mine.'

'You're practically claiming we brainwashed you.'

'More than brainwashing, it was an evangelisation. A very effective one at that.'

'Is this another complaint?'

'All I want is for us to speak clearly and for you to admit that you hammered it into us, this admiration for the wrong surname.'

'The only thing we did was provide you with the same foundations that we had been given.'

'You said it: establish the foundations.'

'Is that a sin, too? Now it seems like we failed in everything. Is it such a bad thing to pass on the history of your family?'

'If it's based on a lie, and you know it's a lie, then you have to take responsibility sooner or later.'

'Is that what you want me to say? That the Cisneros are a lie? Hypocrites? Phonies? Would you feel better?'

'Say whatever you want, as long as it's true.'

'I don't know what to say to you any more. I'm a Cisneros. I feel like a Cisneros. I've always felt like a Cisneros, even when I learned about the priest. That's why I defended Nicolasa's surname. That's why I organise the reunions. That's why I struggle to keep us together. That's it. There's nothing traumatic in this. There's no reason to keep raking it over. I have no reason to feel bad. You neither – you need to stop making so much of it. You are what you feel you are.'

'What you feel you are? Or what it falls to you to be?'

'What you feel. Period. Stop with this now.'

PART THREE

CHAPTER 13

Montevideo, 19 April 1935

Brother Alfonso:

Take a seat and answer me this: do you think that I could write a biography about Dad? I think you're going to say yes. I turn the idea over in my head, and I like it more and more because it would lead me to very interesting social and political observations. I have excellent documentation of this nature. Yet there is an elementary *but* that is one of life's ironies: the fact that, out of discretion, I have never asked anything about Dad, and know nothing of his childhood or his youth. When I was old enough for him to tell me more about himself, he had lost, together with his tongue, the faculty of offering paternal confidences. A biography written by a son cannot just feel its way blindly. I pass back and forth through our old man's life without stumbling, indeed with celestial clarity, from the house on Sacristía de San Marcelo, yet in all this I cling to memories that may be more like whimsical interpretations than memories per se, I no longer know.

So discreet have I been that I don't know if I've recounted to you a scene that is still burdened by tears in my recollection. In 1899, when I was already working on Dad's archive, I received a huge surprise one evening. The old man was sitting in his armchair facing the door, and myself at the little table in the farthest corner, the silence of the room occasionally broken by his convulsions, when a woman suddenly appeared who ran towards Dad, kneeled at his feet, and pressed him to her, sobbing loudly. I, who had no idea what was going on, tiptoed to close the door. The woman stood up again, approached and embraced me too, silently weeping. Dad was also in tears and trembling more than ever. I couldn't hold back my tears either, and I drew up a chair for her. I was about to return to my table when Dad, with a gruff voice that betrayed the huge effort he was making, said 'Son, this is your sister!' I turned to her and embraced her.

It was Adelaida.

Not long afterwards, our old man, as if he wished to complete the revelation, dictated his will to me, amid emotions you can well imagine. In it, he names three older daughters whom I had never heard of, Elvira, Adelaida and María Luisa, 'born of a single mother', and formally recognises them. When Adelaida returned to Paris, I saw her off. I later met Elvira at *La Prensa*. A short woman called for me and we spoke in the lobby. Later, for a period, I kept an eye on her son when he joined the same newspaper. And then I saw her on her deathbed and accompanied her coffin to her final resting place. After that I began a correspondence with Adelaida, who wrote to thank me for these kindnesses to her sister. Finally, I have recently exchanged letters with her, who is now very old and living in complete solitude, having lost her companion of many years, a woman who was her teacher as a young girl in Paris and with whom she lived for over forty-five years.

Well, brother, I don't know any more about this or anything else.

And the only reason I want to know is to get my bearings, not to tell the story. Why don't I know anything about our grandfather? Why do I know nothing about our grandmother, Nicolasa? Not even how many children they had, or what they did? I'd want, I'd need to know everything. I'd need exact information about the great-uncles, an overview of their relationships. I'd need a proper biography of Uncle Luciano. I'd need what we'd call a precise itinerary for Dad. Years he travelled. Places he travelled to. His life in Europe. Friends he had there, Peruvian and otherwise. The major events he witnessed. The Franco-Prussian war. The death of Victor Hugo. I'd need a faithful account of what happened to our family during the war with Chile. Why did they return to Europe in 1882?

In short, you can tell that I know nothing. I beg your advice, brother. I'd sure if you had the time you could provide many of these details. Perhaps the ones that demand most discretion. My sisters could give me the rest. Write to them. Tell them what this is about. Tell them I don't want to end my life without having laid a stone for our father's monument, and I am determined to seize this single moment of diplomatic opportunity, as it is rapidly running out, lest pain and effort render me helpless once more.

All my love to your family and hugs to you.

F.

My grandfather Fernán was fifty-three years old when he put his initial to this letter. He had lived for over half a century without knowing the truth about his family, relying on intuition. He had made inferences and conjectures based on his father's will, but he lacked decisive certainty, anchors to stabilise the rocking ship of his life. His encounters with his step-sisters Elvira and Adelaida were pleasant but too sporadic for them to establish a real relationship.

His brother Alfonso was fifty-five at the time. They had never spoken about the gaps in their past, until the time came to face them together and try to overcome those obstinate voids. 'I'd want, I'd need to know everything,' Fernán wrote, offering a glimpse of the desperation that troubles children, or some children, when we reach a certain point in our lives and find we know nothing definite about our parents, and that finding out is somehow essential in order to glimpse the meaning of our own existence.

Fernán appended to his letter a long list detailing his many questions and speculations, in the hope Alfonso could illuminate him:

> What did our grandparents do in Huánuco? Who was General Pedro Cisneros? Which school did our father first attend? What position did the family hold in the government of Ramón Castilla? And what about love? Who was the mother of our father's first children? Did he not marry her because he saw her as inferior, or because Nicolasa was opposed to it? Is it true that President Castilla was involved in that relationship in some way? Is the scene with his mother that appears in the verses of 'Aurora Amor' true to life? Who were his closest friends in France? Who were his hosts and landlords? When

he returned to Peru, did his daughters come too? Where did he meet our mother? Who blessed their marriage? Were they in fact married?

The questions continue with this blend of curiosity and anxiety. And as I reread them, I'd like to answer them one by one because, unlike Fernán, I do want to know so I can tell the story. And I wish I'd been there to dispel their ignorance, open their eyes and tell them what I know now. That their grandfather was a priest by the name of Gregorio Cartagena. That their grandmother, Nicolasa Cisneros, accepted the lies and pretence imposed by that priest. I'd like to tell them that the love they shared was true, but hidden. That their father Luis Benjamín and his six siblings were bastards who grew up believing they were children of a non-existent traveling salesman. That Benjamín was not a second name but a made-up surname. That the woman with whom their father conceived his first three daughters was Lucrecia Colichón, the mistress of President Ramón Castilla. And that Adelaida, their sister-in-law, who had lived 'with her female companion for forty-five years', was evidently a lesbian.

I wish I could say all of this to that dead man who is my grandfather, that pile of dust and bones I only know through photographs, whom I've glimpsed through his letters and books, but above all through the silences that for me are like virgin forests, arduous nocturnal paths I've been wandering for years now.

In his reply to Fernán, Alfonso unveiled all the truths he did know. I haven't found that letter anywhere, but it must have been heartrending.

Days later, my grandfather responded with the following lines.

Montevideo, 10 May, 1935

Brother Alfonso:

I greet you with a fraternal embrace and all my gratitude for the news you have sent me. I have remained in silence for twenty-four hours now. I knew since my youth that I was surrounded by a thick fog no one cared to part. I once took up pen and paper to draw the family tree, but I was only offered the most recent names and benevolent smiles. That, and the silence of those who could have chosen to say more, only intensified my tact towards the mystery. Of course, this tact was intuition. In my college days, someone, I don't remember who, mentioned that 'Benjamín', which I thought was a second name, was a surname, and I remember asking Uncle Carlos about this. He gave me to understand that it was, but that the change had happened long ago. Since then many people have asked me the same thing and I, ignoring Uncle Carlos' pious explanation, have invariably said that it was not true. But the doubt was still coiled up inside, and told me to keep quiet.

While we're sharing confidences, let me tell you that I once approached Dr Sánchez Concha with a health-related question. Books and other doctors had ascribed my nasal problem a specific probable origin I was sure I could never have acquired. I thought there must be darker antecedents. Dad's illness, which was never diagnosed, not even when he died, together with the death of his older brothers with symptoms of 'ataxia', felt like revelations. I wanted to learn as much as I could, in order to seek treatment. I told Sánchez Concha that an illness like mine, which had first appeared in adolescence, could only have come from farther back, and that I needed a whole cabal of doctors to cure me. He expunged the notion from my mind with great conviction and paternal warmth, said that our father had undergone extensive studies in Europe, and the treatment prescribed by the doctors was not at all what I had thought. He attributed the illness to an overly sensitive nature and the sudden failure of his businesses and hopes. I was left almost wholly convinced, or at least enough to stay calm each time my illness and other old symptoms of physical weakness renewed my suspicion.

Your painful revelation, which above all else has brought me the balm of truth, illuminates our father's spiritual and physical life and gives me closer insight into the worries, pains and loves that weighed on his psychology and physiology since childhood. The uncertainty at the root of that home doesn't frighten or even trouble me, given the children's exemplary path. For me, his origin is always illuminated by the selfless mother that Doña Nicolasa was, intelligent, severe, tender, deserving of better luck, and the pain I feel is from imagining her heroic strength and the nervous weariness of each hidden gestation. Here, I believe, lies the cause of the deterioration in the children's nervous constitution, and the prevalence of the psychic over the physical. This also explains why filial tenderness, harboured by the pristine hearts characteristic of their time, increased with gratitude and compassion. All of this helps me to love our father as a father and as the man in whom the family secret, locked away under seven keys, ended up cutting the knot of the nerves, shaken by the inevitable setbacks of life.

You see, brother, that I am grateful for this information, which arrives better late than never.

To finish with the matter once and for all, I shall say that the existence of Don Roberto Benjamín is as great an unknown as ever, and may be a complete fantasy. I find it telling that the religious witness should call Nicolasa by her maiden name in a public document that also mentions her children. The baptismal records, on the other hand, may well be concessions to social mores, and the marriage certificate, which I understand General Pedro Cisneros once demanded to see, has never been found. Mind you, when it came to settling the inheritance, there is no question that the true identity had to be revealed in order to identify the correct beneficiaries.

Enough! Pain, if it brings truth, is always a good thing.

The name of Lucrecia Colichón has stirred my memory. I suspected there was something in it. A long time ago someone asked me if I wanted to visit their home and meet a crippled old woman who knew me well and would be glad to talk to me. That must have been Lucrecia, and who knows whether she still lives.

Well, there we have it. I embrace you once more, brother, in silence, full of love and veneration for our family.

F.

Of all that Fernán wrote over his long life, nothing compares to these two letters for me. He strips himself bare, sheds the lyrical garb of his poems, the camouflage of his ambassadorial speeches, the idealism of his essays, the moral bent of his newspaper articles. His father too had used all those rhetorical masks, but in Fernán they were plainer to see. His romantic verses were armour, a shield to avoid speaking directly of the pain that flooded from his eye sockets when he was moved. In the face of a truth he already suspected, the panic of being misunderstood – a refraction of his father's panic at being persecuted as a bastard – was expressed in the distracting rhymes that muffled the cries inside him.

The two letters to his brother Alfonso, by contrast, contain a genuine innocence and matchless fury. There he confronts his past, his circumstances and the vulgarity of his fate. In these letters he is subjugated to the 'silence' of his spirit, fed up with the 'thick fog no one cared to part' and free at the same time of 'a doubt still coiled up inside, that told me to keep quiet'. Alfonso's revelations made him realise that there were 'darker antecedents' behind Luis Benjamín's undiagnosed nervous illness. His father's condition, he understood, was the symptom of a serious emotional imbalance produced by all the years he'd spent believing himself the son of a non-existent man, a man who was a 'complete fantasy', and then discovering this falsehood. This neurological disorder, Fernán saw and I now see so many decades later, was caused by having had to adulterate reality in order to protect himself from it. This was the origin of that perturbation known as 'ataxia'.

Fernán also persuaded himself that his own respiratory illness came 'from farther back'. Could this be the case of the acute asthmatic crises that I myself suffered as a child in the house in La Paz, crises that no one associated with any family precedent and that forced me to sleep sitting up night after night? Could those endless pulmonary suffocations and torturous chest whistles also have come 'from farther back'? How many things come to us 'from farther back'? I like to think that 'farther back' is a tiny compass point that expands over the years until it becomes ungraspable. A word that names not the past, but the geographical forms we give to the past. Arid, frozen forms. The past as a kind of attic. A crypt. A sinkhole. Or as a moment that began as all that and then eventually mutated into a boundless landscape, at once near and distant. The past as a bleak plain with ups and downs, a sometimes muddy or slippery plain, dotted with trees that commemorate triumphant and painful – or perhaps merely painful – memories, trees that from a distance seem tiny, but up close intimidate like the fossils of a prehistoric animal.

* * *

All the Cisneros – or at least all the ones who concern me here – have a trace of that nervous agitation, that laboured breathing. 'The nerves shaken by the inevitable setbacks of life.' For my grandfather Fernán these revelations were imperatives, because he knew their curative effect. Yet when he learned the warp and weft of his family history and the origin of his surname, and assimilated its meaning, his 'tact towards the mystery' reappeared. When it came to his children – including my father, the Gaucho – my grandfather maintained his ambassador's sense of diplomacy, his double standard, and said nothing.

He threw in the towel in every sense, because he never again wrote poetry, either. Learning the truth of his life, he renounced the truth of literature. It wasn't gradual but immediate, like someone abandoning a room they loved because something exploded inside it, leaving behind a body that soon began to rot.

The last 'literary' thing my grandfather Fernán wrote was, precisely, these two letters to Alfonso, and I want to believe that, in not destroying them, but preserving them, he made a decision to perpetuate the truth, hoping that this material would one day fall into the right hands.

When Uncle Gustavo got hold of these letters and with them the inescapable certainties they contained, he was sixty years old. A scandal. Sixty years of ignorance and darkness. He tried to share them as soon as possible with his remaining siblings, but didn't receive the response he expected. No one pushed him to investigate further. Uncle Reynaldo offered lukewarm encouragement; Aunt Carlota ventured a few words; but the others, including my father, ignored him. They had no desire to understand or clear away the dense clouds that shrouded their world. They did not believe that 'pain, if it brings truth, is always a good thing'.

CHAPTER 14

Lima, 1890

The sorrows and paradoxes of my grandfather's life began with early conflicts of identity. He was born in Paris, to a household plunged into gloom, eighteen days after the death of Gonzalo, the three-year-old brother he never met.

Can the birth of a child temper the disappearance of another? Can the presence of a new boy neutralise the vivid memory of the absent one? Can an angel overthrow a ghost? Can life impose itself so quickly on death? I don't see how: death brutally crushes life. The signs of death cancel out the signs of life so effectively that, after a few years, we remember far better the day our loved ones went to their graves than the day they were born, we remember with greater precision how long they've been dead, and it is increasingly difficult for us to calculate how old they'd have been if they were still among us. The date of the funeral, tragic, definitive, stamps itself over the date of birth, to the point that the birthdays of the dead, or of the living before they die, end up losing their meaning and significance.

Such were the circumstances of Fernán's birth: a haggard home, bereft of smiles, or where any smiles masked pain. His childhood was marked by his father's decline. As Fernán grew taller, Luis Benjamín buckled under the rigours of his illness. Something of that decrepitude must have shaped the boy's demeanour, infusing his early views of the world with pessimism and caution.

Fernán held his father in such reverence that he dedicated secret poems to him, like an infatuated child trying to impress the object of his affections without knowing how, and who in frustration would rather maintain a certain contemplative distance than fail altogether. My grandfather was so close to his father that he took pains to channel what energies he had when Luis Benjamín first took ill. But his father was an illustrious man with a reputation, and this renown, while inducing surges of pride in the son, also overwhelmed and diminished him. His love for this man made him believe that he would never amount to more than his disciple. He was aware that the closer he stayed to him, the less anyone else would notice him; and he knew that, by sharing his father's interests and perspectives, individual existence would be a monumental challenge. But he didn't care.

Only once Luis Benjamín was dead did Fernán feel he could flourish. He was twenty-two years old. He couldn't have done it any earlier. To distinguish himself sooner would have been a parricidal act he was incapable of perpetrating. He couldn't even dream of surpassing Luis Benjamín, and in any case he lacked the talent either to stand out or to shine with a similar intensity. He lacked his father's hunger, depths, and oceanic breadth of gaze. He hadn't experienced his father's dramas. He did have his own dramas, but at twenty-two he was still far from identifying and calling them by their name.

Without autonomy, subordinated to his condition as 'son of the first crowned poet of Peru', he felt like a satellite, an appendix, an accessory.

One day in 1897, when Fernán received his graduation diploma from Labarthe school, he saw that the certificate read 'Luis Benjamín Cisneros'. Someone had got his name mixed up, as if the only Cisneros worthy of appearing on a diploma was his father. His mother promised to have the error rectified but it never happened, and it hung there for years, a constant reminder of his non-existence.

His own birth certificate, issued in Paris, also contained an error: it didn't read 'Fernán' but 'Ferdinand'. The official had translated the name without asking anyone's permission, and when Luis Benjamín went to collect the document he didn't have the nerve to point out the mistake to the evasive and bad-tempered character across the counter, and left it for his son to correct at some point in the future.

In any case, no one called my grandfather by his real name. At the Labarthe school he was called 'Cabezón', or 'Bighead', and when he entered San Marcos University the other students referred to him as 'Cisneritos'. It was no surprise that he signed his first newspaper articles – while his father was still alive – with pseudonyms. In *El Tiempo* he wrote five-line poems for a column called *The Weekend*, and used the byline 'Don Tito'. Later he signed his parliamentary sketches and theatrical reviews as 'Zeta', 'Juan Peruano' and 'Cavaradossi', covering plays, operas, zarzuelas and sharing backstage gossip about 'actors trading blows in the dressing rooms over their favourite actresses'. His reports on bullfights, meanwhile, appeared under the nickname 'Retazos', or 'Snippets'.

While the use of pseudonyms was part and parcel of journalistic practice at the time, in his case it was no mere fad but a sign of his timid, laconic, withdrawn character. A way of not asserting his place in the world. Not speaking up for himself. Perhaps he was uncomfortable with his name, or thought that, while his father lived, he must settle for being the invisible son of a literary celebrity (one of his first opinion articles begins with the line 'I am a nobody'). And since he loved his father, and only wanted the old man to recover from his tremors, perhaps he came to believe that his way of bringing this about was avoiding the limelight and any possible brazenness. My grandfather assumed that his father would fall into depression or his illness would worsen if the latter sensed that interest in him was fading, however unintentionally, and he was ready to sacrifice himself, to deprive himself of any glory so that his father might recuperate and live a few more years, even if this meant remaining submerged, anchored, out of the spotlight that illuminated one man only: Luis Benjamín Cisneros.

When his father died, my grandfather was horrified to glimpse the torrent of a new freedom flowing beneath the bitterness of loss. He had spent years suspecting that he would be overcome when his father was gone, and now he found this to be false. Once he felt the purifying effects unleashed within, he didn't want to give them up. It was all a haze at first, but gradually, Fernán perceived concrete changes, irreversible alignments in his mind, and he sensed at last how nuts and bolts that had been kept asunder for too long, jumbled and disconnected, were assembling inside him, waiting for the right time to fasten together and start up a mechanism that would otherwise have been left unused. Only once his father died did Fernán stop postponing. Then he emerged. Took off. Saved himself. He felt light. He dared to face the future. And he began to sign articles under his own name. And for the first time he believed it was possible to be someone. To be different. To exist.

★ ★ ★

The letters my grandfather sent to his brother Alfonso are postmarked Montevideo, 1935: fourteen years before President Augusto Bernardino Leguía deported him from Peru, an event that decided his fate and marked that of his children and grandchildren in ways Fernán could barely imagine the afternoon he departed from the port of Callao.

It all began with the newspaper *La Prensa*.

Ever since it was established in 1903, *La Prensa* had maintained a critical opposition to the civil government of Manuel Candamo, questioning the statements of both the president and his ministers, especially the ambitious Treasury Minister, one Augusto B. Leguía. Years later, when the latter came to power, relations were further strained.

★ ★ ★

The morning of 1906 that he first arrived at *La Prensa*, Fernán stood for a while admiring the colonial façade of number 745, Baquíjano street on the Jirón de la Unión, before entering the lobby and asking the concierge which floor the newspaper offices were on.

'Second floor, up the stairs on the left,' he replied without looking up.

The marble steps seemed interminable.

He saw two young couriers hurrying out a doorway, and deduced this was the office he was looking for. He peered inside. Desks were crammed into a space rather smaller than he had imagined. Heavy brass-limbed lamps hung threateningly from the ceiling. On the largest wall, between a blackboard and a clock marked with Roman numerals, the portrait of the founder, Pablo de Olazábal, appeared to protect or rather keep an eye on the twenty or so men smoking and talking among themselves as they wrote out by hand the pieces for the following day. From the first floor came the clattering rumble of the new printing press that had been installed just days earlier. As he crossed the threshold, inhaled the thick air, saw the disordered heaps of paper, watched the editors passing each other documents with a sense of confidentiality, and heard them discussing matters that sounded like they might change the history of Peru forever, Fernán felt he was in the temple professing the one religion he could swear allegiance to. He had just turned twenty-three, and although he had written trivial pieces for *El Tiempo* and *El Redondel*, it was only in the offices of *La Prensa*, beside these besuited and moustached men who were now scrutinising him indifferently but who would become his close friends, that he hardened himself to the satisfactions, perils and disappointments of journalism.

He threw himself into it right away, gathering as much information as possible for each commission, writing even minor articles with the scrupulousness of a watchmaker, avoiding redundancy and set phrases, in the hope of winning the respect not only of his colleagues – all seasoned reporters – but of the editor, Don Alberto Ulises Calle, a fifty-something fellow with a prominent jaw and massive paunch who intimidated everyone not with his appearance but rather his mercurial personality: if a reporter brought him copy he judged not up to scratch, he could lose his rag in a moment and the hapless hack would find the chair that minutes earlier he had been invited to sit down on whistling past his head.

In those first overwhelming weeks, Fernán could never have imagined that, just two years later, he would find himself suddenly obliged to take the helm as the director of the newspaper.

This was in 1908. The new president Augusto Bernardino Leguía had imprisoned the directors of *La Prensa* and several of its lead journalists – starting with Alberto Ulises Calle – for supporting an uprising against the government in the central sierra. Faced with this emergency, my grandfather was chosen to head up the decimated editorial team.

In those days prison was a regular punishment for non-conforming journalists, and in general for anyone the regime saw as its detractors. Fernán himself wound up behind bars in June 1909 on the whim of Leguía, or more precisely as the result of a blunder by one Boris Kirchhoff, a German technician who had come to *La Prensa* a few years earlier to install a more modern printing machine and supervise the running of the rotary press on the first floor. Mr Kirchhoff was an amateur marksman, and while he lived in Peru participated in various contests, winning the most important shooting championship of the day, the Juan Gildemeister Prize. He owned a number of sporting rifles, which he stored in an office at *La Prensa* as the training ground was just a couple of blocks distant. This would be of little relevance were it not because in that very month, June 1909, twelve hours after the uprising led by brothers Amadeo and Isaías Piérola – a violent episode that plunged the country into uncertainty and saw an attack on the Government Palace and the temporary kidnapping of President Leguía, who was driven around the streets and unsuccessfully pressured to resign – the government ordered a police search of the newspaper's offices. The president was certain that *La Prensa*, now run by Fernán Cisneros, had coordinated this manoeuvre that had endangered his life and the continuity of his administration.

The armed police burst into the building, kicking down doors, overturning desks, breaking glass, swiping at anyone who got in their way, and accusing them of conspiring against the regime. Fernán was in his office, his jacket draped over the back of his chair, his fingers dipping like dragonflies over a black Remington, writing the story of the Piérola brothers' uprising. The officers barged in angrily, shouting that they would search every corner. Startled, Fernán acquiesced, warning them they wouldn't find a thing. It wasn't long before they uncovered the two Mauser pistols and three rifles that Boris Kirchhoff had hidden in a filing cabinet. The police scoffed at his argument that these were 'sporting weapons', and based on this sole piece of evidence the government shut down *La Prensa* and jailed Fernán for a fortnight.

His second imprisonment a few months later was more prolonged: 120 days in the sinister penitentiary known as the Panopticon, for attempting to publish a clandestine edition of *La Prensa*. There, my grandfather spent whole nights reading Zola novels aloud – ignoring the sound of the bell for lights out – at the insistence of his cellmates, three illiterate indigenous lads doing life sentences for murder, for whom Fernán's voice and words acted as salvation from the worst nightmare of confinement: falling asleep and dreaming of the free life they'd had before they committed their crimes.

Ten years later, in 1921, when Leguía returned to power as dictator, my grandfather's avatars also returned. In those days the government was preparing to commemorate the first centenary of independence and set about constructing monuments, hotels and a broad avenue to be named after the president. In the editorial pages of

La Prensa, Fernán revealed that the government intended to spend the then extraordinary sum of fifty million US dollars. The headline asked the question: Why must the celebration be so profligate? The next morning, an ordinary day in March, having barely taken a hundred steps from his house, as he took in the sight of the sun sparkling on Plaza Bolognesi, he was surrounded by government thugs who abducted him before he knew what was happening. From the police station he was transferred to the naval prefecture and then, by boat, to Isla San Lorenzo, where a jail for 'political prisoners' had been built. His detention sparked popular protest and statements issued by politicians and student groups. The pressure grew so strong that eventually Leguía let him go.

However, Fernán didn't rest: within days of being freed, he called a demonstration in front of the law faculty of San Marcos University, where he spoke out in the name of those still imprisoned. The crowd filled the plaza chanting for justice and applauding this obstinate orator who seemed obsessed with getting on the president's nerves. As he was carried off on their shoulders, flashing gestures of V for victory, a military unit entered the square and scattered the crowd by firing their weapons in the air. Realising that they were after him, my grandfather first sought protection in the doorway of the Club Nacional, then made a daring zigzagging dash to the offices of *La Prensa*, where he locked himself inside to write a scathing editorial on the thuggish behaviour of the soldiers disrupting a successful meeting at San Marcos. At midnight, the police intendent, Braulio Godoy, arrived at the office with a decree ordering 'the expropriation of *La Prensa*, including all its facilities, for public utility.' Fernán tore open the envelope, read the contents and ripped the letter to pieces before Godoy's face.

'This decree has no basis in law, do you hear me!'

His burst of dignity cost him dear. They knocked him out with a single blow and the next day he found himself lying face up on a concrete bed, staring at the featureless prison ceiling, surrounded haphazardly by a chamber pot, a bowl, a jug, a spoon, a scrubbing brush and a comb.

A further public outcry achieved his release within hours. And so my grandfather headed straight back to the offices of *La Prensa*, where he found to his astonishment that the government had already confiscated the printing presses and altered the latest edition, whipping up an editorial praising Leguía, without providing any explanation for what had happened to the journalists the previous night. Seeing that the newspaper he and his colleagues had done so much to defend had been turned into an apocryphal rag, Fernán turned up at the offices of *El Comercio*, where they agreed to publish a letter denouncing the usurpation of *La Prensa* at the hands of Leguía's henchmen.

In those days many opposition figures were caught in raids and exiled to distant countries. Knowing a similar fate could befall him, my grandfather opted not to act too hastily. His good judgment lasted barely a few weeks. One night he called editors and linotypists to his house and persuaded them to print and distribute a clandestine edition of *La Prensa* in tabloid format 'to denounce the outrages of the regime'. The men initially showed little willing, reminding him that they had taken a similar tack with disastrous consequences just a few years earlier. 'This time we'll be more careful,' Fernán chivvied them. The clandestine newspaper would be called *La Prensa Chica*.

This underground 'mini-edition' of the newspaper successfully circulated despite the Minister of the Interior himself being on my grandfather's trail.

The minister in question was Germán Leguía Martínez, a cousin of the president nicknamed the Tiger Leguía. He had been a theatre actor and was a natural on the stage, but had failed to establish a career there due to a vision defect: he was cross-eyed. His strabismus, however, was no impediment to the schemes of the president who, knowing his surly temperament and unscrupulousness, assigned him the exclusive mission of quelling dissent.

Playing the executioner, Tiger set about persecuting journalists, shutting down secret meetings, carrying out deportations, intervening in the media and imprisoning opposition politicians on Isla San Lorenzo, with a particular predilection for members of the Civilist party. 'The best Civilist is a jailed Civilist,' was the slogan he uttered with thespian grandiloquence. He had the twisted idea of reviving the fearful Isla de Taquile prison, located in the middle of Lake Titicaca, over 3,000 metres above sea level, where the least gust of wind sucked the breath from the hardiest man, and where the guards forced prisoners to confess their errors and betray their companions by crushing their toes with pliers.

Yet none of these tactics served the Tiger to prevent *La Prensa Chica* appearing on 4 July 1921, the very day of the anniversary of his cousin's revolution, a symbolic journalistic victory for the opposition. When the paper reached his hands, his eyes began to cross compulsively. He examined it line by line, which took him the whole day, and once he had read the editorial signed by Fernán he felt his anger grow and intensify into the desire for revenge.

Here we are and shall remain, pursued or not, imprisoned or not, disappeared or not. We bear, as we shall continue to bear, the conviction that sincerity and abnegation are the weapons that shall put an end to despotism forever, delivering it to the shame of history. *La Prensa* has been, and to its great honour continues to be, the nightmare of those who believe that in taking over the government they have taken over Peru, its freedom, and the interests and lives of Peruvians.

FC

'Don't torture him, just bring him to me,' the Tiger ordered his jackals, who carried out an efficient pursuit that ended with Fernán in prison once more, accused of conspiring against the government.

This time he was taken from the naval prefecture to Isla San Lorenzo, and from there to Panama on board the *Mantaro*, a two-engined steamboat with ancient boilers that opened asymmetrical furrows in the sea as it advanced.

My grandfather's exile began on 21 July 1921, almost exactly a century after independence. He was thirty-eight years old.

I think now of the many exiles in this story and try to see them as episodes brought together by chance: the exile of the name of my great-great-grandfather Gregorio Cartagena, erased from the map by his descendants (and who had once been exiled to the high puna by Pedro Cisneros); the emotional exile of my great-grandfather Luis Benjamín, who left Peru at the urging of his mother to reinvent himself in Paris; the political exile of my grandfather Fernán, who spent thirty years between Panama, Ecuador, Argentina, Uruguay, Mexico and Brazil, countries where he discovered himself as a diplomat, established himself as a journalist and became diluted as a poet; the ethical exile of my father, the Gaucho, the soldier and former minister, who at twenty-one had to leave Argentina, the country of his birth, for Peru, without wanting or needing to. And finally, my own voluntary exile, here in Madrid, where I shut myself every day in a room with a large window, through which I watch the shapes of men and women pass, people with whom I share no connection nor specific feeling save the heartfelt sensation of being in the right place. The only possible place where I can sit and write these words.

CHAPTER 15

Lima, 1905

In Lima, long before his deportation, with his father already dead, Fernán had married his fiancée Hermelinda Caicedo, who had presumably fallen pregnant that night of 1905 on which they both went to bed determined to lose their virginity together.

At the age of twenty-two, Fernán was on the point of joining *La Prensa*. He was still that downcast lad who doubted himself morning, noon and night. Hermelinda was just sixteen and had no more plans for her future than to win herself a husband who would keep her in the same comfort she had grown accustomed to thanks to the wealth of her father, Don Ilegario Caicedo, a doctor specialising in smallpox and whooping cough. Such diseases were so widespread in Lima in those days that he couldn't cope with all the cases, some of whom would even turn up at the door of his house in critical condition.

Fernán had no desire to marry so soon, but he was under direct pressure from Don Ilegario, who insisted on marriage as the only dignified manner of quelling the public humiliation at his daughter's unwanted pregnancy. In the days prior to the wedding, she was already carrying a belly too big for any dress to conceal what many of her own relatives, diehard Catholics, considered a mortal sin.

Once married, they went to live in the Caicedo residence, where Hermelinda gave birth to a daughter they named Bernarda.

Fatherhood didn't make Fernán any fonder of his wife, but he did make a commitment to her and to their incipient family. At least, that was the case for the eight years Bernarda lived. She died in 1913 from a whooping cough so aggressive that her grandfather was helpless to cure it.

Mere hours after her death, as the girl wasn't baptised, Hermelinda went to the centre of Lima to seek Adolphe Dubreuil, director of the Courret photography studio, for him to immortalise Bernarda in an 'eyes-open' daguerreotype. This was the custom at the time for children who hadn't received the sacrament, in the belief that only thus could they 'enter heaven and see the glory of the Lord'. Dubreuil had a very effective technique that many found shocking: he sat the little bodies on a chair, attaching their arms to the chairback to keep them in place, and used glue on the eyelids to create the rather grisly desired effect of eyes that looked strangely alive.

With the loss of her daughter, Hermelinda seemed to age twenty years. One morning, she got up and put on a black veil and wandered around her father's two-storey house in a state of complete distraction. In each room she decreed that Bernarda's name must never again be mentioned in her presence. Next, she begged Fernán to take her somewhere else, fearing that her daughter's restless spirit would trouble her forever.

The later children would deny for many years the existence of that first-born daughter, perhaps because acknowledging her would be a way of admitting their parents' union was a forced one; while also reviving the most unfortunate chapter for the Caicedo family, above all for Don Ilegario, long plagued with guilt at his failure to save his first grandchild. That is why they got rid of the daguerreotype showing Bernarda after her death, and even sought unsuccessfully to suppress from an anthology of Fernán's poetry the words that were the principal testimony of the life cut short, eloquently titled *My Dead Daughter.*

Confronted with the image of my daughter, dead,
her parted lips still red,
her hands entwined in tender supplication,
I snuffed my soul and closed her lids,
then shut my own again.

To take their minds off the tragedy and attempt a new start, the couple rented a pink-walled single-storey house opposite Plaza Bolognesi. There were born Sarino, Rosaura, Fortunato and Magdalena. For many years Fernán performed miracles with the fifty-seven pounds he brought home from *La Prensa* each month to meet their household's basic needs and provide his children with a minimal level of wellbeing. By March 1916, when the last was born, the third boy, named Belisario but called Benito, the family was accustomed to overcoming economic hardship. In Hermelinda's eyes, Fernán wasted his meagre salary on his friends at the newspaper, at the cost of the family budget. 'You always have enough money for the street!' she would imprecate him, and he didn't dare deny it, leaving her to mutter accusations that were not without truth; because after work Fernán did indeed frequent the crowded downtown chicherías, where among the greasy tables, voices raspy with brandy, tinkling glasses, clamour of waiters and fingerclicking of clientele he found a strange peace that sustained him far from the ups and downs of domestic life.

The arrival of Benito brought about a truce in the household. The daily recriminations ceased and some of the former stability was restored, like a scene change at the theatre. The tightened straits continued, but for a few months the couple lived or believed they were living in an atmosphere of harmony. They had no way of knowing it would not last long. By December, the nascent rips in the backdrop had grown into a gaping hole.

The night of Saturday, 2 December, Fernán said he had a commission from *La Prensa*, though it was really an excuse to attend a performance at the Teatro Municipal. A Spanish dancer had recently arrived in Lima, brought by local businessmen who sought to dissipate the depression of the Great War by staging shows. Her fame preceded her: she was a Sevillian who had previously performed in Buenos Aires, Santa Fe, Montevideo, Santiago, Vienna, Paris and Madrid, and the theatre critics agreed that she won the audience's affections every time. She was a woman of immaculate skin and large eyes like black candies, who performed Oriental dances with bare feet and painted insteps, who didn't wear corsets, much to the delight of the male audiences, and who was said to be 'the reincarnation of Salomé', 'the heir of Isadora Duncan', and 'the successor of Mata Hari'. Her name was Carmén Valencia but in the world of glitz and glamour she was known as Tórtola.

Her début in Lima was an outstanding triumph. Just like everyone else who crammed the theatre that rainy night, Fernán was left dazzled by her superlative beauty and lascivious, writhing style.

Immediately after the almost two-hour performance, my grandfather hurried to the dressing rooms, claiming he wanted to secure an interview with the Spanish diva. A cluster of businessmen, reporters, photographers and other onlookers all fought to catch a glimpse from close up. Amid the pandemonium, a woman stuck her head out of the dressing rooms and announced that the artist would grant a single interview. The men protested, waving their canes and umbrellas in the air. Short and slight, Fernán got ahead of the pack, slipping through the jungle of legs to the front, where he stood up straight inside his coat and offered his mischievous smile, one hand fluttering his felt hat, the other gesturing with the rhythm of his words, and introduced himself in a low voice to the woman as 'poet and lead chronicler of *La Prensa* newspaper', flashing his credentials. Tórtola's assistant yielded to his gallant grins and, seeing that he was calm and appeared harmless, she chose him over the other thronging men. 'Come this way,' she said. Fernán ignored the whistles of discontent and warily entered a room, advanced over rugs with motifs that looked Japanese to him but were in fact Egyptian, and felt his way along the white walls until he came to the end of a narrow corridor.

There he saw her. Tórtola Valencia was seated before a mirror, removing one by one the beauty spots painted on her face, radiant beneath the flickering red bulbs of the dressing table, still barefoot, her eyes like wet stones, the silk dress marking the arch of her hips. Seeing him standing there motionless, she invited Fernán to sit, offered him a drink and asked her assistant not to interrupt them for the next two hours. They gazed at each other. They liked each other. They connected.

She started talking, leaping from one subject to the next with the same rhythm she danced to, and Fernán dedicated himself to listening and contemplating her; from time to time, he would drop in an erudite note, improvise a line of verse, try to make her laugh and ask her questions as if he were really going to write a review for the next day. She stressed several times that she felt 'as-ton-ish-ed' to have achieved so much success, being who she was: 'The poor illegitimate daughter of a seminarian.' The daughter of a priest, no more, no less. If my grandfather had known the truth of his own family at this point, the dancer's confession would surely have drilled into his brain.

After a few minutes, Fernán's curiosity was drawn to the striking necklace hanging around Tórtola's neck and he asked what it was made from. 'The teeth and cartilage of a Moroccan sultan who fell in love with me, but as he couldn't have me he ended up falling on his own sword,' she replied, sipping her champagne with an air of vanity that disarmed him and left him dumbstruck.

Fernán wanted to stretch out the night and keep soaking up the fanciful flights of this over-the-top Spaniard, whose neck he now desired to kiss and nibble, and he felt tempted to offer his services as a guide to the city the following day, as if, for one thing, he didn't have to take his children to school in the morning. From one moment to the next he turned serious, grave, overly journalistic, and took up the conversation again asking about the 'Andean motifs' of a dance in her show.

'That is a homage to an aboriginal chief who threw himself into a crater after I refused to kiss him,' she rambled, laughing again and taking another draught of the champagne, which Fernán pictured slipping down her throat.

Tórtola lit a cigarette and blew the smoke straight into the face of my grandfather, who, enveloped in this brief cloud, no longer knew if what this enchanting woman had told him was true and cared little to find out. He let her babble on, and feigned making notes that were no more than pirouettes of his hand over a sheet of paper that many hours later would still be blank.

Believing herself to be the star of some tabloid headline, Tórtola proclaimed herself 'the world's bride', 'Goya's niece', a 'sexual predator', and boasted of the kings, princes and arch-dukes chasing her skirts across Europe, and of harvesting lovers among the latest intellectuals, including Pío Baroja, Rubén Darío, Valle Inclán, and other less famous writers who had wrecked their marriages and ruined their lives 'just to appraise my skin for a few minutes'.

Fernán took her hand, reminded her that he too was a poet, uttered a few of his father's verses, mentioned books he hadn't yet written nor ever would, and penetrated her with his pupils until he filled her eyes entire.

The rest was silence.

Silence and dreams. Dreams and champagne.

My grandfather ended up improvising sophisticated ballet steps in the dressing room and imitating Tórtola's own writhing, dishevelled or rather inebriated, perhaps even in a state of undress, submissively allowing her to paint beauty spots on his body with her make-up pencils before throwing him onto the Egyptian rugs that looked Japanese and mounting him with abandon.

The only trace that remained of that encounter is a poem of Fernán's, 'The Chopin March, Danced by Tórtola Valencia', which begins with this line:

'The heart gallops in the darkness like a pipe organ…'

I understand the disillusionment or even the scepticism of my grandfather years later when he read repeated references in the press to the supposed homosexuality of the delightful Tórtola Valencia, who was said to maintain relations with a young woman by the name of Ángeles, thirteen years her junior, who acted as her personal secretary and whom she would later adopt as her legal daughter.

This extramarital adventure raised a hatch, pulled aside a veil, broke a taboo. Without intending to, Fernán had made room for the possibility of the inappropriate, for the lie as resource, for egotism as method. He allowed himself to be corrupted as if he already knew himself to be the fruit of a forbidden sowing. Throwing off repression, exploring another intimacy and allowing himself to be swept along by an exultant and alien body faced him with a hitherto unknown part of himself.

That night of December 1916 the waters overflowed their habitual course. A riot erupted in Fernán's mind, and he felt that one of the many men who inhabited him – disregarding the well-intentioned but milquetoast person he had been – was rebelling and fleeing in no clear direction, burning his bridges, provoking a collapse that would take years to play itself out.

A few days later, early on Monday, 4 December, standing before one of the tall windows of *La Prensa*'s offices, his gaze fixed on one of the chequered black and white paving slabs on Jirón de la Unión, Fernán was distracted by a young woman passing by on swift and stealthy feet. 'She looks like a sad cat,' he thought. Then he noted the girl's features, hard or sweet depending on the angle presented to the light, the hooded eyelids and small eyes that seemed fixed on some withered thought. Her hair was black and wavy. She was the same young woman who always wore shift dresses he had seen the week before, and whom he would see the following days at the same time, always stationed on the same threshold, attentive but retreating like a cautious sniper.

The young lady, who click-clacked her heels back and forth from Casa Welsch, where she was lead sales girl in the imported goods department, paid no attention to the envious eyes gazing at her from all sides. She was only twenty, but something in her gestures made her seem older: whether it was losing her parents at the age of four, or perhaps her experience working, now in the centre of Lima but previously, when still a child, in the northern region of Chancay, on the cotton and sugarcane fields of her parents' Hacienda Vizquerra, from which she remembered the wagons emerging piled high with oranges, wagons now rented out to street pedlars to stave off the worst of their poverty.

Or perhaps her gloomy countenance had more to do with her sworn commitment to Tomás Cazorla, a dandy with no known trade who got drunk daily, both in the carpeted halls of the Club Nacional and in the dingy chinganas on Argentina avenue. He was once a sought-after bachelor, but the gossip about his soft spot for liquor had been scaring off women for years. Everywhere it was claimed that, in addition to being an alcoholic, he had become rude, depraved and a gambler.

The courtship had been arranged by her older sisters, Apolonia and Rufina, who didn't wait for her consent on the morning they decided to visit Cazorla at home in the Magdalena neighbourhood to propose a prenuptial agreement that seemed to suit both parties: he would guarantee money and social contact, while the youngest of the Vizquerras – the sisters promised – would take care that he did not fall prey to his vices and would assume, 'both in public and in private', all her marital responsibilities. From that day on, Tomás began to send flowers to his future wife, but she, impervious to gestures she found manipulative, returned them twenty-four hours after they arrived. If she kept them overnight, it was just to see if their scent could dissolve the gloom suffusing that house.

Something of all the solitudes etched into the young woman's face was captivating to Fernán, who, as the weeks went by, rushed with ever greater anxiety to the newspaper office windows, waiting for her to emerge from the shop on Jirón de la Unión with her worried little face. Every Friday, in the glare of early evening, as soon as she left his field of vision, he realised that he would have to wait until nine in the morning of the following Monday to see her reenter the screen of the window, whose glass, it seemed to him, only then recovered its light, sharpness, and transparency.

Fernán grew to hate Saturdays and Sundays stuck at home, deadening and endless days, nothing but a tedious succession of hours spent attending to his children and tolerating Hermelinda, this stressed, reproachful woman he no longer got on with and had forgotten how to love, or had never loved sufficiently in the first place.

One day the lethargic routine was abruptly altered. It was Sunday, 24 December, Christmas Eve. The Plaza de Acho provided the backdrop.

Fernán arrived to cover the last bullfight of the day, planning to head to the newsroom to write the weekly bullfighting chronicle that he signed with the pseudonym 'Retazos'. It wasn't just any bullfight. The poster announced the presentation of the Sevillian right-handers 'Joselito' and 'Belmonte', as well as the long-awaited debut of the Mexican Rodolfo Gaona, the 'Maestro de León de los Aldamas', 'El Califa', 'El Indio Grande', the first international bullfighter to visit Rímac at its height, charging 15,000 soles per appearance, an unprecedented sum. The 10,000-seat bullring was at capacity. When Gaona appeared with the cuadrilla, the deafening pasodoble 'olé, Gaona', composed especially for the occasion, reverberated around the bullring, shaking even the slopes of the San Cristóbal hill, crowded with people unable to see what was happening but content to interpret the noises coming from inside. After the greeting before the stands and the cheers, just as the

Mexican was diligently awaiting the first bull, Fernán spotted the young Casa Welsch salesgirl sitting in the stalls on the sun side, a few metres from the ring, and felt an irrepressible desire to do some trick or perform some stunt in order to catch her attention. He turned around as if looking for an accomplice and found three colleagues, the fat Julio Portal, known as Tío Cencerro; Saturnino Durand, chronicler of Prisma; and Fausto Gastañeta, the bullfighting specialist for the weekly *Actualidades*. Gastañeta was a small, coquettish, short-necked fellow fond of interrupting, good at hunting down information and spreading vicious rumours. He had been a fixture at the early meetings of *La Prensa* and was a habitué of the Spanish bookshop, so Fernán knew him well and saw him as honest and obliging. He approached the three men, apologised to Portal and Durand and took Gastañeta to one side, telling him about the Casa Welsch girl and asking him to get her name without delay.

Twenty minutes later, as 'El Califa' Gaona left the crowd dumbstruck with a defiant desplante posture, followed by a fearful pass that saw him swap the muleta to his other hand behind his back, just ten centimetres from the bulls' horns, the bloodhound Gastañeta returned with double the information requested.

'Fernán!' he called. 'Listen up: the girl's name is Esperanza Vizquerra and she's just turned twenty. The guy at her side – do you see him? – is Tomás Cazorla, her boyfriend. Little Tomás here is a barroom bullfighter. The other two, the old ladies who look like dried up chameleons, are her sisters. Both have been unlucky with men. The three live together in a house in Barranco, they're orphans from Chancay, where they used to have a hacienda that's abandoned now. They had money once, but at this point they're nothing but a clutch of well-dressed beggars.'

Following this detailed report, Fernán paid no more attention to the bullfight. He racked his brains trying to work out how to approach Esperanza, to invite her for a stroll along Puente de Piedra, to put her off marrying that drunkard who, he told himself to gain confidence, would only make her miserable. Suddenly, below him on the sand, Gaona made another suicidal move right in front of the animal: with no more protection than his suit of lights and a gravedigger's sangfroid, he leapt like a gymnast until he was bent over in the air, his feet brushing the beast's horns, and aiming shrewdly from that dominant position, he punished the bull, burying two banderillas in its bulging neck. An impeccable, virtuosic manoeuvre. When he cut off the tail and the ear, the front row went wild. The plump Portal stuffed his cigar into his mouth to applaud. Saturnino Durand tossed his hat into the sand. The big-nosed Gastañeta flew into a frenzy.

'Bravo! That is poetry! Poetry!' he wept, gathering red poppies from the ground to shower into the ring, the audience's traditional reward for the Mexican's stoicism.

Fernán thought he sensed a message in the excited words of Gastañeta and he escaped the revelry to head straight for the offices of *La Prensa*, where he wrote a report on the bullfight he had barely watched, intending to declare his love for the young Vizquerra from his own ring, from behind the barrier of his own bullfighting column, with the only banderillas he had at his disposal: some anonymous yet lethal verses he hoped would offer a worthwhile performance.

In Acho yesterday, the sight of you
so full of Macarena's grace
kept me from even noticing the bull.
Your charms have lanced

my soul straight through.
Nobody knows, dark lady, how
I suffer not to look on you.
As only in the stadium
do you appear,
I spend my days subsumed
in dreams about the fight.
I dream I am a bull, I dream you charge
and lunge at me
and put my life at risk, my darling girl,
thrusting your horns.
If you should care to have my love,
don't be a lance,
don't settle for me loving you,
but give me, lady,
give me hope,
give me my Esperanza.

* * *

With the Christmas and New Year's celebrations past, Esperanza returned to her work and Fernán resumed his stakeout operation, following her from Monday to Friday from the window of *La Prensa*. On Saturdays he suffered, but on Sundays he found her in Acho, where he contented himself with admiring her from afar, unable to say a word to her, and dashed back from the bullring to write these columns that included further encrypted verses. To ensure that Esperanza read them, Fernán begged Gastañeta to locate the house in Barranco where she lived with her sisters and push a copy of *La Prensa* under their door every Monday.

On the clear-skied February afternoon that he finally summoned up courage to introduce himself to this young lady who would much later become my grandmother, intercepting her as she exited the Casa Welsch, it was she who spoke to him first. Loosening the clips in her hair and letting it down with the petulance she would retain until old age, Esperanza asked Fernán not to beat around the bush: she told him she knew about his childish behaviour up there in the window of *La Prensa*, about the insolent looks he sent from one end to the other of the Acho stands, and she even made fun of the old-fashioned suits that he wore to the bullfights.

'Yet I must acknowledge that I do enjoy your Monday columns, "Retazos". Is that how I should address you?'

My grandfather was left undone, unable to react.

'Your friend Gastañeta is a blabbermouth,' she clarified, with a benevolent smile, primly fanning her brand-new eyelash extensions.

Fernán's cheeks turned red as a pepper. He suddenly looked much younger. He must have seemed like a lost child far from home because Esperanza, more experienced or more determined to conceal her insecurities, proposed they take tea together to get over 'his fright'. Yet it wasn't fright that Fernán felt, but something closer to incredulity: he could hardly believe the young lady's directness, her droll scrutiny of him. He was going to have to keep his guard up from now on, he said to himself.

They went to the busy patisserie on the first floor of the former Casa Barragán, known as the Palais Concert, and stayed there talking about everything they didn't know of each other's lives until the place emptied out. When they finally looked about them, the last customers had vanished and the windows were dark.

This first outing was followed by others at which, if they didn't repeat tea, they drank chichi, or sometimes Camparis, and ate spicy Catalan sausage or mocha cream cakes; but regardless, they spent hours eagerly ranging from one topic of conversation to the other. Fernán took great care with each appointment: he walked on the outside of the pavements, made way for her, opened doors for her, pulled back her chair, took her coat, offered his hand to climb or descend a step. Esperanza acted as if she deserved this display of chivalry, but inside she appreciated each gesture, thinking each time that she might never see the man again.

If they didn't meet at the Palais Concert or in one of the department stores that were already beginning to open in Lima, they would go down to the periphery of the Santa Beatriz Racecourse, where people strolled unhurriedly; or they would wander the villas, squares and gardens of the Barrios Altos, where the sculptures seemed to watch over them from their niches; or arrange to meet by the yellow bandstands in the parks where nightly concerts took place; or they would choose one of the polished benches in the Alameda de los Descalzos and sit there, dwelling on trifles, watching time pass in the changing colours of the landscape, in the gentle ambush of the winds that got up after sundown, or in the sudden loneliness of the allée lined symmetrically with trees and statues.

On one of those occasions, Esperanza told him about the love lives of her sisters Apolonia and Rufina, tales of frustrations that perhaps explained the obstinacy with which both promoted her marriage to Tomasito Cazorla.

Apolonia, the eldest, had been unable to marry Florencio de la Piedra despite a courtship lasting forty years. He was a successful entrepreneur in the banana and cotton businesses, owner of vast lands to the south of Lima in the Mala and Cañete areas. One day he fell ill with a very high fever as a result of a chicken pox epidemic, which not only scarred his face with pockmarks but also left him impotent, an embarrassing reverse that prevented him marrying Apolonia and consummating their union.

Florencio de la Piedra subjected himself to countless treatments, even going so far as to allow a witchdoctor from his estates to make hot compresses of apricot leaves and Malayan roots that only led to scalded genitals, not to the revival of his depressed member. Given the lack of antidotes, a doctor even suggested the implantation of dog testicles, but Florencio preferred to wait for time to restore his masculine vigour rather than undergo unorthodox surgeries. The demoralised Apolonia, who knelt every night to ask San Judas Tadeo, the Christ of Maracaibo and Santa María de la Caridad to cure her fiancé's worrying flaccidity, ignored the slanders of evil tongues who maintained that Florencio was miraculously able to overcome the painful inconveniences of his mysterious illness with a dark-eyed woman of large and incendiary hips who worked at one of the Cañete haciendas, and without the need for elixirs, tonics, preparations or concoctions.

For decades Apolonia put up with defamatory whispers such as these, and waited for the young hacienda owner to recover his virility, trusting that sooner or later he would walk her to the altar. In the interim, she took pleasure in collecting gifts for her future trousseau, because every five years, when they renewed the vows of their doomed courtship, Florencio de la Piedra showered her with presents to compensate his fiancée's fortitude and patience. Some said they had seen bales of ermine and chinchilla fur at the Vizquerra sisters' house; hundreds of fans made with Chantilly lace; emerald and aquamarine rings; medieval bracelets; a score of silver vases and pitchers; glass lamps; gold cruets and bells; Ming dynasty vases; spruce wood violins; towers of sealed boxes of champagne, whisky, sherry, brandy and port; and the colourful porcelain tableware that was intended to be used at that long-awaited wedding celebration. The room's musty floor sank five centimetres under the weight of all those old gifts, among which one in particular caught the attention of prying eyes: the enormous, canopied bridal bed on whose headboard a master craftsman, Jerónimo Quintanillas, had carved a hunting scene, a bed that would never make its debut, and that ended up auctioned off and turned into a famous piece of art in a tiny London museum.

Upon Florencio's death, Apolonia declared herself a 'moral widow' and cloistered herself for four years, dedicating her hours to praying, reading the social pages of the newspapers, playing cards once a fortnight with her friends – dolled-up, scaly-skinned old women who smoked green tobacco cigarettes rolled with Indio Rosa paper – and organising lavish Christmas celebrations together with her long-time assistants, the nanny Zenaida and the butler Zenón. Little by little, she rebuilt her social life and reappeared in the Plaza de Acho and at aristocratic parties, but she would never be the same: the martyrdom of waiting and widowhood had changed her face forever. The ghost of Florencio de la Piedra, impotent even as a ghost, continued to visit her in dreams and delusions until Apolonia was ninety years old. She never got over the grief of widowhood or shared a bed with any man. And although at first she boasted of her virginity, in the end she felt an emptiness at never having experienced any form of carnal love. The same night that a heart attack carried her off, she had confided to Zenaida what would become her final wish: that no one should know she died chaste.

Rufina, the second, had fared no better. At sixteen, after her parents died, she fell pregnant to a married hacienda owner from Chancay named Serapio Orbegoso, the last descendant of conservative landowners and agrarian bourgeois, who lived with his family in an ostentatious stone house adjacent to the swamps of the valley, and whom everyone avoided or feared because of his sullen character and his rustic, tyrannical manners. Serapio had persuaded Rufina they were in love and, once he deflowered her, he began to take walks with her every afternoon in the cane fields of his hacienda. But the day Rufina told him that she was expecting a child, Serapio refused to acknowledge paternity and insolently ordered her to get rid of the child.

'The creature isn't mine! Go and blame someone else if you want, or better toss it in the river for the current to carry off!' he spat in her face.

As she told this story, Esperanza remembered her sister turned into a bundle of nerves, weeping for weeks on end, drinking foul-smelling potions to ease her suffering.

Rufina fled to Lima to stay with a maiden aunt who reluctantly helped her the day her waters broke. The child who emerged from her belly had Rufina's flat nose, the amber eyes of Serapio Orbegoso and a prematurely aged look, as if he knew how many headaches his existence had already caused. One night, her aunt announced to Rufina that they would take the child to the Lima Maternity Hospital the next morning to put him up for adoption.

'No, Auntie, please! I don't want to give up my child!' begged Rufina.

'Don't be an idiot! How are you going to feed him? Your tits are barely out yet!' her aunt rebuked her.

'Don't do this to me, Auntie. I can look after him!'

'That's what they all say. They're all stupid. First they get knocked up but later, with no husband, no money, they kick out their kids. I've seen them lining up their little bundles outside the parish churches, that is if they don't leave them in the rubbish heaps or in the cemetery by the first row of niches.'

Late that night, Rufina escaped with the baby in a basket, with no idea of where she should go. No one knew how they survived over the following days, weeks and months. Although she didn't have the child baptised, from the very first day she called him Crisaldo. But whether out of shame at not being married, or at being such a young mother, or out of simple fear of not knowing how to deal with the mess she found herself in, Rufina raised him not as her son but as her younger brother, as if he were the fourth child, the sole boy, as much an orphan as she and her sisters: Crisaldo Vizquerra.

Together in Lima, Apolonia and Esperanza became accomplices in this falsehood. Rufina told them everything only after making them promise not to tell the boy 'for anything in the world', 'however much they wish to', 'for the memory of our parents'. Both gave their word, assuring Rufina they would take the secret to their graves. Nevertheless, when Crisaldo was sixteen years old, Apolonia broke her promise in the course of a domestic row and brought him up to date with a hysterical outburst:

'Before you talk to me like that, you snotty little devil, ask who the shameless hussy was who brought you into the world and didn't want to accept you!'

Apolonia was filled with regret before she had even finished her yelling, for she looked on as her nephew Crisaldo stood up, mechanically packed his bags and walked out the door with a self-possession that hardly matched the scale of the revelation. Indeed, his decisive and pragmatic attitude suggested he had suspected as much for years. Crisaldo headed off to find out who his father was and Rufina wept torrents as she had in the days of her pregnancy in Chancay, directing her hatred as much towards her sister for having broken the pact as towards Serapio Orbegoso, the detestable man who had aged into an obese, warty curmudgeon to whom none of his five legitimate sons brought any joy, and nor did they pay him any attention. Whenever Rufina looked in the mirror, a rare occurrence, she barely recognised herself: her neck was papery, her breasts shrunken, her waist withered, dark circles around her eyes and a sinister hump emerging between her shoulders.

Hoping to make amends to her sister and drag her out of her despondency, Apolonia began to take Sunday walks with her until, little by little, Rufina regained her spirits somewhat. Although they never received proposals from any man, they were still invited to parties, soirées and shows. It was around that time that they became regulars at the Acho bullfights, where they were introduced to the young Tomás Cazorla. As soon as they met him, both allowed themselves to obsess over pairing him with Esperanza and incorporating him into the family, believing that in this way they could improve their economic prospects and, in the process, correct the misfortunes of their own past.

* * *

Esperanza and Fernán began to meet every day and, although they still addressed each other in a courteous and formal manner, they felt a great sense of closeness and trust, as if they had borne witness to the lives they lived before they met. They weren't friends, precisely, but wanted to convince themselves they could become so. She was engaged, he married, and neither was ready to take the first step towards romance. These obstacles, however, proved useless. Their glances turned ever more tender, their words more ambiguous, the omens more fervent, the desires more treacherous.

The day that the banns were published for her

marriage to Tomás Cazorla, Esperanza barely said a word to Fernán at the Palais Concert. Nor did a mouthful pass her lips. It was enough for him to ask what was wrong for her to throw herself across the tabletop, weeping uncontrollably, toppled by the imminence of this unwise marriage she felt dragged into.

'Why are you marrying, if you are not in love?' asked Fernán, delicately taking hold of her forearm.

'Because my sisters have decided it so,' she cried, her face pressed against the table.

'If you would allow me, Esperanza, perhaps I could speak with Tomás. I know him. I know he will understand the situation,' ventured Fernán, imagining to himself that this unlikely chat with Cazorla, whom he had of course never met, would finish with a punch-up if not a duel with gloves and seconds and all.

'It would do no good,' Esperanza replied, her eyes swollen, the artificial lashes spoiled. 'My sisters want me to be married. If it's not with Tomás they'll find someone else. In their eyes I can't look after myself. They don't trust me.'

She sat back up straight as she said this, sipping the last of the hot tea to calm her sobbing.

'And if I were to offer to…?'

'If you were to offer to what…?'

A wave of silence ran around the room.

'If I were to offer to love you all your life?' Fernán took hold of both her hands now.

'All my life?' sighed Esperanza, her creased brow relaxing, wiping away the last of her tears, open-mouthed not so much at the proposal itself as at the enormity of the idea.

'Yes. This I offer you,' insisted Fernán. 'To love you all your life!'

I can picture now my grandfather bewitched by

the young Esperanza, completely outside of himself, forgetting his wife and his children, or perhaps remembering them all too well and for that very reason trying to evade his responsibilities and his role if only for a moment, knowing how unhappy he was in the marriage that Hermelinda Caicedo's pregnancy had made necessary so many years earlier. Now he realised, now he understood that the experience with the Spanish dancer had not been a crude slip, but the symptom of a greater dissatisfaction that continued to haunt him.

I can picture perfectly what Fernán was thinking in that café, in that mansion house or on those benches in the Alameda de los Descalzos while listening to my future grandmother lay out her pains. He thought that no one could deny him the right to be happy with her, that he deserved a woman like the one in front of him, not like Hermelinda. He thought that Hermelinda was a past mistake that could still be corrected, and that with Esperanza he would be restored to the vitality stolen from him by his wife, that woman who was waiting for him a few blocks away, along with their five children, with dinner ready at eight o'clock. Fernán didn't want to think about them, at least not now that he was about to fall off a cliff, or perhaps had already fallen off a cliff, on an adventure that would be much more than a spontaneous romance and that would make him happy in a new way, and which at the same time would engulf him in the very sea of illegitimacy that had harried his heart since before he was born.

Esperanza broke off the engagement with Tomas Cazorla, writing him a benign letter, the last line of which read 'I courteously ask you to set me free.' By then she had been excited about Fernán for a long time. They had kissed on the afternoon of 3 March behind Casa Welsch, in what for her was the prelude to a love that would never forget its parallel and subterranean nature. Esperanza knew where her love for that man had to come from, and she accepted the inevitable setbacks without making any demands, blindly surrendering to whatever good and bad would come.

In the months and years ahead, every time she remembered the night they were finally able to love each other, Esperanza evoked not so much the dimly lit rented room, but the bright and triumphant feeling they had when they left, ready to do everything for each other after having felt their skins so close for the first time. That night, after accompanying Esperanza to the corner of her house in Barranco, Fernán took the tram back to his house. He walked slowly, counting the few stars that were visible in Lima. The skies opened suddenly and the rain forced him to take shelter under an awning. He didn't know – he had no idea – that he was repeating the same story as his father, only in reverse: he wasn't running away from an all-consuming passion in exchange for a cold marriage; he was fleeing a cold marriage in exchange for an absolute passion. And he did it without guilt. Almost proudly.

When the rain stopped, he walked on and couldn't stop reciting to himself some verses that he always used to repeat with his friend Leonidas Yerovi, and that Yerovi babbled in his ear the day he died, just a month earlier, in his last minute of life, on a stretcher at the Maison de Santé clinic, where he had bled to death after taking five bullets to the chest in a duel with a Chilean who had offended the woman in his company.

> Just like the ebbing, flowing sea,
> so did I wish to be in love,
> and leave a woman so I could return,
> rejoin another woman to begin.

And ever like an ocean's wave,
I would be bound to die on God
Himself knows what vast shores of love.

* * *

Despite his love for Esperanza and joy at her breaking off
the engagement, Fernán did not leave Hermelinda. Trying
to assuage his cowardice, he told himself that leaving her
would be 'irresponsible'. It wasn't ethical questions that
held him back – that much was clear – but a deep fear of
the inevitable domestic consequences: losing his children's
love, disappointing his siblings, unleashing the ire of his
mother, Cristina Bustamante, or causing Hermelinda to
do something dreadful. Above all, the fear of damaging
his public image as a righteous journalist who fought
the dictator of the day in the name of high ideals. These
fears together weighed upon him like an anvil or iceberg.
The gossips of Lima, Fernán thought, would condemn
his sin and banalise his drama, reducing him to a weak
and irrational caricature of a man who first committed
adultery and then abandoned the mother of his children
for his 'fancy woman'. Fernán knew all too well the
malice of the city's rumours and had no desire to expose
anyone to carping insults or sanctimonious tittle-tattle. If
his father had acted with caution, fearing that some snide
soul would confront him with his bastard origins, then
he would do the same, taking refuge in other shadows,
in a different darkness, and thus he convinced himself
he was not what he already had been for a long time: an
adulterer.

Fearing that his bigamy would become public
knowledge, he chose to live two simultaneous realities:
one with his wife Hermelinda and their five children
in that house on Plaza Bolognesi that was all neatness

and serenity; and another with Esperanza just five blocks from there, in a second-floor room, inside a ramshackle old building located at the intersection of Del Sol avenue and España avenue, where all the buildings were rooming houses with dusty and faded façades, and where the children's nocturnal entertainment was throwing stones at the rats. Over the years, this same room would acquire a reputation for upsetting its guests and would become known in street stories and urban chronicles as the haunted 'Casa Matusita'.

They were two parallel universes. Two border territories. Two lives. One real, another ghostly. But while Esperanza always knew everything about the first home, it took Hermelinda a long time to find out about the existence of this second woman, or rather of this second family, because when she did, when she finally was told her husband was with someone else, it was already May 1921 and Juvenal had just been born, my Uncle Juvenal, the first of the seven natural children of that relationship, beautiful yet impure.

CHAPTER 16

Lima, 1921

Fernán was unable to spend even two months with Esperanza and their new son because, in mid-July 1921, he was sent into exile by the dictator Leguía. That morning in Callao, from the upper deck of the steamer *Mantaro*, before the ship weighed anchor, my grandfather managed to say a few words to his colleagues from *La Prensa* who came to cheer him off, thundering solemnly in the manner of men facing tragic moments:

> *La Prensa* has established itself as a popular tribune of the citizens' conscience. In its pulsating pages, the most disinterested and patriotic campaign in history has been waged, more detached from partisanship that in all the annals of our journalistic struggles. Could we risk being unworthy of this honourable history? Never! We fight and will fight those among us who aspire to nothing beyond professional honour! As for myself, I don't know my destiny, but rest assured that today I feel more of a journalist and more Peruvian than ever.

Behind the line of bleary-eyed journalists who listened to him with a funereal air and a knot in their throats, Cristina and Hermelinda, mother and wife, held onto each other as they were supported by children, friends and relatives whose ashen faces adumbrated the uncertain hardships that exile would inflict on all of them. Some offered Hermelinda their condolences, as if instead of seeing Fernán off they were already mourning him. Further back, blending into the crowd, beneath a broad-brimmed hat that barely held its own against the sea breeze, and with a baby wrapped in a shawl pressed tight to her breast, was the young Esperanza in her shift dress, stiff-necked, observing the scene helplessly. It was all she could do not to make public the rage that rose from her belly and spread from her fingernails to the tips of her toes.

After a few months in Panama, Fernán spent a year in Ecuador trying out business ventures that he hoped would bring in enough money to allow him to settle in Argentina, where he wanted to seek employment at a newspaper. At each calling point of the *Mantaro*, my grandfather and his travelling companions were met by journalists supportive of this handful of Peruvians who had denounced the dictatorship and been exiled for their pains. Newspapers including *El Guante* of Guayaquil, Ecuador, *El Liberal* of Bolivia, *Excélsior* of Mexico and *La Nación* of Argentina reprinted Fernán's articles detailing the excesses of President Leguía and brought out editorials on current events in Peru with emphatic headlines like 'Outrages of a Tyrant' and 'Journalism in Mourning'.

In the nights spent on the boat, Fernán sat down to write to both Hermelinda and Esperanza and tell them about his travels: to the former he sent informative reports dotted with fond kisses for the children; to the second he sent despairing and febrile letters that showed his love was very much alive, projecting an unlikely optimism despite the uncertainties, privations and miseries they described.

> Here we hardly have any resources. There is no shortage of afflicted colleagues offering food and moral support, but the truth is that nobody knows what will happen to us tomorrow. I still don't have a date to leave Guayaquil, even less for my eventual arrival in Buenos Aires. From here, my love, I can only ask that you endure my absence. You will see that we will be together before you even have to teach our son to pronounce the name of the father who misses him so much.

In Guayaquil my grandfather set about importing sugar from Peru and exporting butter, cheeses, chocolates, ropes, cables, fruits and anything of Ecuadorian origin. Just like his father, who learned to survive in professions wholly alien to him in those hazy days in Le Havre, Fernán was obliged to become an expert in customs tariffs, shipping costs, exchange rates and international trade, which is how he got hold of the money he needed to set himself up in Buenos Aires.

Once he had reached the Argentinian capital he took up residence in the Hotel Royal in the centre, improvising an office in the form of a table at the Florida restaurant on Avenida de Mayo, where local journalists would come to interview him, eager to hear his story. The newspaper *La Plata* described him as 'the tenacious and tireless leader of the press battles', while *La Capital* called him 'the refined and idealistic Peruvian poet who finds himself exiled in our lands, bitterly disappointed at his country's shameful setbacks under the tyrant who governs it'.

'What is your opinion of Leguía, Don Fernán?' asked a reporter from *Mundo Argentino*.

'His dictatorship is despicable, not only because it is a dictatorship but because it is disorganised, dishonourable, without virtue.'

Little by little, my grandfather's afflictions were relieved with strokes of luck and he would soon feel less of an outsider. Dr Antonio Sagarna, vice-chancellor of the Universidad Nacional del Litoral, who had followed his odyssey through the newspapers, invited him to teach a course at the university. A few years earlier, in October 1919, when Sagarna had been ambassador of his country to Lima, he had heard Fernán deliver a homily at the burial of the writer Ricardo Palma: 'Palma, you are a compatriot who bequeathed us pride and honour; the national press mourns your death, but gives thanks for your life.' Sagarna approached him to praise his words and confessed he had enjoyed reading some of his columns in *La Prensa*, and indicated his willingness to offer any necessary assistance in the future.

> In late 1922 I arrived in Buenos Aires, where providence intervened. I was a timid, sidelined man. Within ten days of arriving I received a telegram from Antonio Sagarna expressing his interest in my patriotic misadventure, and his pleasure in my having chosen his country for my exile. He was vice-chancellor of the Litoral university and offered me a professorship. A professorship! I had never taught anything!

Sagarna encouraged my grandfather to put himself forward to teach a further four courses, and also put him in touch with the editors of the *La Nación* newspaper, where he was finally able to take up his journalistic career again. Two years later, Sagarna was designated Minister of Justice and Public Education, and on each of his official journeys by train, from Buenos Aires to Tucumán, Rosario, Mendoza, Santiago del Estero, Quilmes and Córdoba, he took Fernán – 'his favourite poet', according to the local press – with him to present lectures, visit schools and expand the horizon of his work opportunities. Years later, on the day he returned to Peru, my grandfather visited Sagarna to thank him for his invaluable protection and his countless displays of respect during the most difficult days of his exile, and to tell him that he would always be welcome at his home in Lima.

Many decades later, when my grandparents lived in a mansion on La Paz avenue in Miraflores, and even after Fernán's death, Esperanza would continue to refer to Sagarna with reverence, announcing to children, grand-children, nephews, nieces and neighbours that one day that fine man would come and visit from Argentina.

'This crockery here is for Sagarna's visit,' my grand-mother would say, opening wide the doors of the enormous wooden sideboard overrun with tattered cobwebs and dead moths and containing the forty-five pieces of her French tableware set. Only on her death would it be discovered that the key to the cupboard was jealously guarded underneath the life-size plaster effigy of St Francis that 'watched over the house' from a dark corner, at whose feet every week my grandmother placed a paten filled with tap water for the saint to bless. I don't know if the other grandchildren felt the same way, but every time I approached that inanimate saint to inspect his features, or even when I just walked past him, averting my eyes, I had the firm impression that his gaze – injected with a creepy expression, a mixture of fear, guilt and oblivion – moved in my direction, setting off the alarms of my nervous system.

Everything in that house felt suggestive and mysterious to me: the timeless, high-ceilinged rooms closed by latched doors; the mirrors tarnished with black spots that presented a flawed reflection; the armchairs and furniture surviving from centuries past that had once accommodated the men and women depicted in the oil paintings that hung on the walls; the smoked glass doors that concealed the mysterious contents of the cupboards; the bronze ornaments that looked like they'd been stolen from some museum or embassy; the mothballed trunks that we were forbidden to go near; the books that made us sneeze, from which we learned the poems we were made to recite at family reunions – the only way to learn something about our dead ancestors. Anyone who passed through that house might hear the rustling of heaped up memories, sensing in every corner the presence of hidden stories – always lurid, in my eyes – that for some reason no one dared to tell.

I can see my grandmother in that house, or more precisely in the garden: tall, white-haired, hands on her hips, always dressed in black, with dark nylon socks and wooden-soled shoes. A tall and well-rooted tree. Not even when she went blind in one eye did she lose that dignity. Her assistant, Arsenio, was a short fellow with indigenous features, who clumsily handled spades, brooms, shears and rakes, and suffered in silence my grandmother's orders and tellings off. 'It's not called *gravel*, idiot, it's *grass!*' she would cry, less didactic than conceited. 'What a mule you are, you Indian! I've had it up to here! One day you'll turn my hair white!' she'd spit whenever Arsenio answered back. They seemed to detest each other, and yet they had spent their whole lives putting up with each other. I observed them as I swang on the ancient swing, the favourite pastime of all child visitors to that house, especially those of us who lived there on the second floor and who bore witness to almost everything that went on around the place. When Arsenio was done with the toughest work, my grandmother would collect the fallen leaves and weeds from the garden, gather the fruits from the trees that she claimed to have planted (in reality Arsenio had done so), and sowed flowers with outlandish names like lady of the night, snapdragon, stepmother, narcissus, nemesias, petunias… When these had flowered she would cut them to adorn the entrance hall and lounge, ensuring the house was beautiful 'for Sagarna's visit'.

She would continue to repeat this phrase like a mantra even on her nights of sclerosis. When her eyes became riddled with cataracts, she resigned herself to organising the French dishes by touch; she would inhale the aroma from the garden she could no longer see nor plant; run her fingers over her flower stems; handle the ceramic pots; and talk to the flowers with the affection and patience that she never had for Arsenio or for the other domestic staff she hired, many of whom could not abide her senile temperament and fled the house screaming.

The very day of her death, which came at the age of eighty-six and was due to leukaemia – much to our astonishment, as she had foretold this end without ever receiving a diagnosis – in a final breath of lucidity, she ordered Imelda, the last of her maids, to comb her silvery hair, wrap her in her most elegant black dress, adorn her with the most cherished rings and bracelets she kept hidden in chests and cigar boxes, perfume her with oils of sandalwood and bergamot, dust her cheeks with cornflour, paint her withered lips red, and feed her warm milk to tonify her appearance. Once she was finished, Imelda asked her why she was going to so much effort.

'In case Sagarna visits today,' the old woman crowed, minutes before expiring.

★ ★ ★

At *La Nación* in Buenos Aires, where he became archive director, Fernán penned articles, literary essays and an international column where he wrote, among other topics, about the war in Morocco, the coup d'état by the Spanish General Miguel Primo de Rivera, and the vicissitudes of King Alfonso XIII. He also wrote about Peru, denouncing the bill designed to amend the constitution to permit the re-election of Augusto B. Leguía. The dictator, ignoring this and other criticisms, changed the rules and had himself re-elected. Fernán then wrote an article begging the intellectuals of Latin America not to indulge the satrap: this was in response to an open letter from Argentinian writer Leopoldo Lugones who, having been an official guest of Leguía, had praised him to the skies, to Fernán's disgust.

Yet my grandfather was also trying to push his rift with Peru into the background, in order to better avail of his cultural connections in Argentina: he published his single book of poems, *All Is Love*; began an affectionate epistolary friendship with Uruguayan poet Juana de Ibarborou; and shared a stage with Alfonsina Storni at the 1928 Book Fair. On that occasion, a journalist asked his opinion of President Hipólito Irigoyen, who had just returned to power. His answer: 'He is a decrepit old man who receives women with his fly open.'

★ ★ ★

Fernán sent Esperanza the money he had saved for her to travel to Argentina together with Juvenal. 'My cousin Agripina will help you,' he wrote. Without saying a word to her sisters, following Agripina Cisneros' instructions, Esperanza arranged the journey by ship and nine days later she and my Uncle Juvenal were welcomed to the port of Buenos Aires by my grandfather. Finally, the three of them would live together.

At first they rented rooms in cheap hotels and later in some rundown flats in the city centre that left lasting impressions: the one-room apartment with a brand-new elevator at Suipacha 400; the room with the balcony at Cerrito 330, where they'd have stayed if it weren't for the nest of mosquitos that buzzed around the shared bathroom; and finally the tenement at Paraguay 2200, where the quarrels and amorous moans of the neighbours carried through the gaps in the air vents.

The feeling of paradise found did not last long. Not even a year. At the instigation of her sisters, cousins and friends – and above all of her mother-in-law, my great-grandmother Cristina, who despised Esperanza with a vengeance – Hermelinda Caicedo travelled to Buenos Aires with her five children, prepared to set boundaries and to let everybody know who was the true wife, and who the legitimate children of the exiled journalist Fernán Cisneros Bustamante.

From that time on they all lived in the same city. On top of breaking his back to earn more money and meet the needs of both families, my grandfather had to arrange things so that he could live with Hermelinda, spend his nights with Esperanza and return to the former early each morning.

Since Hermelinda didn't know how to cook, Esperanza – wishing to ease Fernán's obligations – began to prepare lunch for both houses, making frugal but tasty dishes created with what little she had on hand: fried tripe, beans and vegetable stews, polenta with ricotta, barley cake, sautéed breadcrumbs. Taking care for the two women not to meet, Fernán asked his fourteen-year-old son Fortunato to go each morning to the junction of Laprida and Charcas streets and collect a pot from a woman who would be waiting for him. 'A tall, good-looking young lady,' he told him on the first day. Fortunato became accustomed to this daily encounter with the friendly woman he had no idea was his father's mistress, chatting with her and obediently collecting the hot dish each day. Sometimes his mother persuaded Fortunato to also take Esperanza a basket of dirty sheets and clothing for her to return them clean the next morning. To make her work harder, Hermelinda made sure the bundle was plunged into a trough of murky water first.

My grandmother not only took on domestic tasks that were clearly not her responsibility, but also put up with Fernán – not content with managing two relationships at once – having an affair with a student from one of the courses he taught at the university, a girl by the name of Rubita Ledesma, to whom he dedicated the same fevered poems that had once proved so effective in wooing Esperanza herself.

On one occasion, Rubita Ledesma turned up at the tenement building on Paraguay street with her hand on her belly, claiming to my grandmother that she was pregnant by Fernán. Self-sacrificing but practical, too sure of herself to be thrown off balance, Esperanza detected the lie in the eyes of the scrawny girl and chased her back on to the street with a stream of insults. The next day she found out where she lived – who knows how – and personally delivered a letter she had taken all night to write. She handed it over with such self-confidence and decency that the girl never bothered her again.

Miss Ledesma:

I have come here with the sole aim of defending

the deep love I have held for eight years, for a man who has always returned it with the greatest sacrifices. I admit this man may be impressed by your beauty today, but I dispute with you the right to love him with all my soul and all the hardships life brings. I have no doubt your love is only the cause of a momentary foolishness in him. I am the only reality in his life, and you make a grave mistake in seeking so deviously to drive me away from him. He, who is a poet and great psychologist, will realise as much.

This is my resolve. E.V.

Rubita Ledesma stopped attending Fernán's classes, and the latter never learned about the letter or his student's pregnancy claim. Esperanza decided to overlook the infidelity, but insisted my grandfather move them into a larger apartment, a request he interpreted as a veiled protest against his continuous dalliances.

Thanks to his intermittent teaching work and his frequent contributions to *La Nación*, Fernán was able to rent a less austere home for his second family: apartment number 20 at 865, Esmeralda street, a converted adobe-hued mansion house, its entrance hall lined with cold tiles and exposed pipes.

This flat saw the births over the next few years of my father, the Gaucho, and my uncles Gustavo and Roque – the one with mental difficulties who later wanted to marry the maid. Before them had come Carlota, the only daughter.

The costs of the new apartment and the new children obliged my grandparents to perform miracles to stay within their tight budget. While he taught courses here and there, she sold beetroot salad and cauliflower tortillas to the neighbours, as well as sewing and pawning her few old jewels in the hope of covering the first school fees. As money waned, the prudent Esperanza began to visit headmasters' offices at the start of each academic year to try and persuade them to accept her children free of charge.

'Sir,' she told one of the school heads, 'it would be a privilege for a school like yours to have the children of such an important man as my husband among your pupils.'

'I'm sorry, madam, but what does your husband do?'

'What? You don't know him?'

'I haven't had the pleasure. What did you say his name is?'

'Fernán Cisneros Bustamante.'

'And he is…?'

'What do you mean? He is the next president of Peru!'

Her conviction was so overwhelming and her tone so shameless that more than one fell for her scheme and agreed to waive the school fees. When she got home and told the story, laughing, my grandfather retrieved the bottle of whisky from its hiding place in a drawer and took two gulps to calm his nerves.

* * *

It was in the old mansion house on Esmeralda that Fernán learned, in August 1930, about the rebellion in Arequipa of the Lieutenant Colonel Sánchez Cerro and the overthrow of Leguía, the man who had sent him into exile. The same night the dictator fell, his brother Alfonso sent a brief cable reading simply: WE ARE FREE. Only then did Fernán understand the repercussions this turn of events would have on his life, and went out at midnight to drink a cognac alone at his favourite table in the Florida restaurant.

Days later, President Sánchez Cerro himself wrote to him to declare that the country needed 'the participation of all proscribed Peruvians'. The epic idea of finally returning to Peru had barely taken shape in his mind before Fernán rejected it out of hand. 'I can't leave now,' he reasoned, understanding that he was by then a man of fifty who had worked hard to become who he was, earn the positions he held, and win the trust of more than a few Argentinian friends. In addition, his family – or rather his families – were healthy and safe and kept at a careful distance from one another; although this distance would not last much longer.

* * *

One morning, bothered by the repeated mocking and teasing from a boy in his school who yelled at him 'at least I don't share my dad, like you do', Juvenal secretly followed his father when he set off for the newspaper office. After a leisurely forty-minute chase on foot, he turned a corner and saw, on the other side of the avenue, his father entering a house with a large door that was caught in the sunlight, where he was welcomed by a bunch of kids who hugged him excitedly and a woman who kissed him on the mouth before taking his briefcase and leading him inside by the hand. Juvenal wanted to run over and throw himself at him to check it really was his father, the same one who that very morning had left the building they purportedly lived in together, but he either held himself back or didn't have the courage. As the door closed, Juvenal felt a great weight fall on his shoulders, and deep inside he knew that he, his mother and his siblings were an obstacle to the world that had just been revealed to him, and that they belonged to another, more isolated and furtive one. As he drifted back the way he had come, trying to absorb the bitter scene he had just witnessed, Juvenal remembered a letter his grandmother Cristina Bustamante had sent years earlier to Fernán. When that day he collected the envelope from the doormat and held it up against the light, trying to decipher the contents before passing it to his father, he could only make out a few blurred words. It was precisely these words that leapt to his mind now, full of new clarity, pain and significance:

'The only thing I ask of you is that you keep them away from me.'

It can't have been easy for Juvenal to discover like this, on his own, that he was the eldest child of an illegitimate relationship, nor to confront from one day to the next the hidden tradition that he would unravel in detail over the years. To the silenced histories of his priest great-grandfather and his bastard grandfather, there could now be added that of his bigamist father.

It was with good reason, I now think, that Juvenal discreetly distanced himself from the other Cisneros as an adult, just as Juan – the eldest son of Nicolasa and Gregorio Cartagena – had done in his time, becoming a kind of hermit who never left Cerro de Pasco, and who washed his hands of the rest, only replying to a handful of letters that no one bothered to keep.

Without going to such extremes, Uncle Juvenal – the most even-minded, the one I was most fond of – was also wary of the family crowd. He preferred to meet privately with his brothers, receive in his library certain cousins or nephews he got along with, but he kept apart from the big Cisneros family reunions, or left early if he did attend, and organised his world around the university, his academic colleagues, his doctor friends, his wife Sofía, their children and grandchildren, their books, their records, always keeping a distance, just like that day in 1930 when he committed the reckless yet urgent act of pursuing his father through the labyrinth of Buenos Aires.

CHAPTER 17

Montevideo, 1933

'Mum, who is the woman beside Dad in the newspaper?' Carlota and Gustavo chorused one evening, showing Esperanza a copy of the Montevideo daily *El País*, in whose social pages they'd come across a photograph with a caption reading:

Ambassador Fernán Cisneros with his wife, the distinguished Señora Hermelinda Caicedo

Esperanza leant on the handle of the mop she had been using to clean the kitchen floor, picked up the newspaper and stared at the image for several seconds. She couldn't take her eyes from the words *distinguished Señora*.

'They've made a mistake,' she said, swallowing hard.

'So who is it then?' asked Juvenal, entering the kitchen with a toy truck in his hand. His tone was accusatory.

'That lady is the wife of Uncle Alfonso, but since she has a wild imagination and likes to show up everywhere and parade around, I let her call herself the "ambassador's wife",' Esperanza replied, making air quotes, pulling an ace from her sleeve as always. Then she filled their glasses with milk and sluiced a bucket of water over the white tiles.

Juvenal stared at her, fed up.

'And who are those children?' nine-year-old Carlota persisted, pointing to another picture of a smiling Rosaura and Magdalena, the oldest daughters of Fernán and Hermelinda Caicedo.

'They… right, yes, they are… in fact… the daughters of your Uncle Alfonso,' stuttered Esperanza, her acting less effective this time.

'I want to appear in the newspaper too, Mum!' exclaimed Carlota.

'No problem, dear, I'll speak to the owners of *El País* today and ask them for a three-page article on you, together with your ballet teacher,' promised Esperanza, focusing on her mopping.

'And can I appear together with Daddy?' the girl gasped.

'Of course! You're his only little darling!' Esperanza replied.

Juvenal couldn't contain himself and threw the toy truck against the wall before retreating, muttering under his breath. Esperanza watched him go, guessing the reason for his behaviour, while Carlota cried in fright at the noise.

Since Fernán had been named Peru's ambassador to Uruguay, the two families had moved to Montevideo and spent two years in the city without ever meeting. The legitimate family, the one that had Cristina's blessing, lived in the official diplomatic residence on Obligado street, while the illegitimate one resided four streets away at 2671 Bartolomé Mitre. They were separated by just a few walls and buildings. A few secrets and lies. Just like in Buenos Aires, my grandfather maintained his ritual of spending the day with Hermelinda, the night with Esperanza.

My grandmother knew that her daughter's demand was not jealousy but something deeper and more visceral, and she felt she had to respond. That's why one night, without telling anyone – perhaps feeling more sensitive as a result of her latest, penultimate pregnancy – she took the child to a ceremony at the Estévez Palace, the seat of government, where Fernán was to be decorated together with other diplomats by President Gabriel Terra. Esperanza knew she was risking an encounter with Hermelinda and the older children, but she didn't care. After all, the only one who might recognise her was Fortunato, who had so often received from her a pot of warm stew and a bundle of clean clothing on a street corner in Buenos Aires.

That evening she dressed Carlota in a rented outfit and braided her hair. They crossed Plaza Independencia and passed between the stout columns of the Palace, defying the security guards to stop them; with their confident step no one dared ask for their invitations or who they were. As they entered the presidential hall, with a graceful bearing and the girl clinging to her arm, tapping the floor tiles with her heels, Esperanza realised that she was motivated by the desire to see her daughter meet her father in a place like this one, in front of people like these. 'Fernán won't refuse to take her in his arms,' my grandmother thought as she looked around the sumptuous decorations in the ceremony room, silently contrasting them with the trifles that adorned her house. Carlota, for her part, couldn't take her eyes off the silver trays carried by the butlers attired, she thought, like penguins, or the enormous shields, the stained-glass windows, the flame-tongued chandeliers, or the many heroic paintings of surly-looking national heroes who she would later describe as 'a bunch of fat, ugly and sad men'.

A door opened. The diplomats receiving the honours were led to the front of the room by President Terra, to general applause. There were seven in total, and Fernán was sixth. The president made a brief speech setting out the reasons for the decorations, before approaching each in turn and placing the medal on their lapel. There were more speeches and more applause. The penguin-butlers reappeared offering glasses of champagne and sweet-meats, while a line formed for the guests to offer their congratulations. At the front of this line was Hermelinda Caicedo and her children, chatting with other guests. Esperanza grabbed Carlota's hand and found herself at the end of the line, behind a couple who looked at the girl with forced cordiality, or so it seemed to my grandmother, who only then realised that her dress and hairdo were out of place, and hesitated whether to stay or leave. But it was already too late. The line advanced swiftly and in minutes it was their turn to greet these tall men who thanked them for their presence with a few murmured words, and a stiff, repetitive expression. Before she reached Fernán, my grandmother grasped Carlota's arm and felt the parquet floor squeak beneath her. The two of them stared at him like accomplices, the way they always did when he returned each night to the house on Bartolito Mitre – but instead of following their cue, instead of reacting naturally, he felt cornered and came unhinged like a puppet with broken strings. He turned so pale the other diplomats around him thought he was going to faint. Gripped by bewilderment, fear of being unmasked and the congenital cowardice with which he fled from conflict, Fernán hid any sign of affection from Carlota and only offered her a gelatinous hand, nervously rubbing her head and patting her on the back, glancing to each side, as if he didn't know who she was, as if she were just any girl, a lost girl, or the daughter of some other man who had come to the Estévez Palace that night.

He didn't even look at my grandmother.

With her mouth clamped shut in disappointment, Esperanza took her daughter's hand and marched out in a fury before anyone could see what had happened. From afar, just as she was about to disappear around the corner, she turned her head and with a single fulminating look let Fernán know that she would never forgive his callousness.

She forgave him anyway; but not soon, and not free of charge. Tired of Montevideo, or rather of sharing the city with another family, the 'legal' one, my grandmother waited for her penultimate child to be born – Reynaldo, the only one with a Uruguayan birth certificate – and returned with all the children to Buenos Aires, to 3104 Avellaneda, where they spent two years without Fernán.

From Avellaneda they moved to 611 Boyacá, a damp flat with salt-stained walls and no ceiling lamps but two great skylights that, when they weren't obscured by dew or drizzle, let in plenty of light and a view of the wind shaking the trees in the mornings.

Once he had reconciled with Esperanza, in his comings and goings between Argentina and Uruguay Fernán acquired the habit of staying with her on Monday and Wednesday nights. When he returned to Montevideo, his other family awaited him in a climate of discretion and conjugal formality.

By this stage, one clan's assumptions about the other's existence had become so palpable and ordinary that Fernán resigned himself to answering the frequent questions his children asked him, on both sides of the Río de la Plata. Each time he took the ferry across the river he would stand at the rail contemplating the oblique course of the waters, showering them with contrite thoughts, inventing persuasive replies. For years he wove benevolent lies with such a meticulous shamelessness that he never made a slip or contradicted himself and in this way kept in check, as far as possible, the demands of both parties; though in the end things got so mixed up that no one knew whose child they were or which branch of the family they belonged to.

Around about that time nervous trouble began to afflict Hermelinda Caicedo. One day, at an embassy reception, she remarked quite naturally that she had been visited by her daughter Bernarda, and that they had taken a walk along Parra del Riego, where the neighbours approached to congratulate the girl on how healthy she seemed, considering she had been dead for months.

The first time, Fernán didn't pay much attention, writing it off as a grief-inflicted softening of the brain, but when a few days later Hermelinda insisted that Bernarda kept appearing to her every afternoon dressed in ermine and that her voice, childish but pitiful, echoed through the house like the bleating of a lamb, he began to worry.

Whenever he returned to Montevideo from Buenos Aires he would ask his older children about the state of their mother, and received ever more alarming reports. They said that Hermelinda uttered random phrases in front of the mirror; that she had developed a mania for hiding cups of curdled milk in wardrobes and pantries; that she sang or rather whined supplications in strange languages; that she would not bathe for days on end but scratched her arms until they bled; that she would sometimes wander the corridors at night, out of herself, dressed in mourning clothes, grinding her teeth, and when she awoke from her somnambulism she would weep inconsolably and invoke her grandparents, dead forty years earlier, with contempt.

When Fernán tried to persuade her to see a doctor, Hermelinda just yelled at him: 'Go to hell, you bastard!' She repeated it over and over. Only then did Fernán really get scared, and placed his wife in the hands of a doctor who took one look at her bedraggled, violent state, spitting obscenities, before he committed her to the Vilarderbó Hospital, the city asylum, better known as 'the cemetery of the living' or 'the purgatory of the demented'.

The voluble Hermelinda Caicedo remained there for two and a half months, tied to a bed, surrounded by medicines and catheters, treated with electroshocks, cold baths and daily injections until one day, just when she seemed to be emerging from this poorly diagnosed state, she contracted a runaway pneumonia that within a week led to severe respiratory failure. The tranquilisers stopped working and so the migraines, swearing and visions of Bernarda returned, now mixed with fevers and a constant sensation of asphyxia. Within days a spectral aura took hold, reducing her to a cadaverous appearance.

The Cisneros Caicedo children never spoke about their mother's madness. They held a vigil for twenty-four hours, and sent a single telegram to Peru informing relatives that she had died 'of a heart attack'. She was embalmed and her body wrapped in a kind of shroud to prevent it decomposing, but at the last minute they decided she would be cremated at the Cementerio del Norte. Hours later, they scattered Hermelinda's ashes in the little square of Parra del Riego, before packing their bags and heading for the port to take the next boat to Callao. Reappearing in Lima after so many years, it took them some time to get used to the city, but once they did so, they adopted ordinary routines and kept their pain and shame to themselves forever.

★ ★ ★

Soon afterwards, Cristina died too, and only then did Fernán, without a wife or mother, feel free to propose marriage to Esperanza.

'Why should I marry a widower?' she challenged him.

'I owe you a marriage,' Fernán said.

'Are you sure? We are so old that the marriage will last less than the courtship,' she observed.

Giving in to Fernán's supplications, my grandmother chose to be married in the Divina Providencia church in Buenos Aires, on Traful street.

That morning Juvenal and Carlota performed the role of altar servers, carrying the cross, swinging the incense, passing the offering plate along the pews, passing the priest the missal, placing the pyx and chalice with the host on the altar and the offerings taken from the tabernacle, all without taking their eyes off their mother who, kneeling on her hassock, approved their every gesture.

On leaving the church, as they received in the atrium the effusive embraces of acquaintances who came to congratulate them, Esperanza whispered in Fernán's ear: 'Look at these sanctimonious hypocrites, greeting me now after a lifetime of calling me your concubine.'

The only relative who travelled from Peru to attend the wedding was Agripina Cisneros, Aunt Agripina, my grandfather's cousin: the same one who had helped Esperanza find a boat to Argentina so many years earlier and who would later take Uncle Gustavo to the Présbitero Maestro cemetery to show him 'the lovers' graves'. The day of the wedding, Agripina – a very pious woman who loved to travel the world collecting Christian relics – appeared at the church in Buenos Aires to gift the newlyweds a chest that, she claimed, contained

286

soil from the very spot of the Assumption of the Virgin Mary, fragments of the True Cross, shards of one of the six stone jugs that Christ filled with wine in Cana, and even remnants of one of St Peter's sandals.

My grandmother kept that chest until the end of her days in the highest drawer of a gloomy dresser, but with age she forgot its contents or no longer wanted to share them. When I visited her bedroom she – accompanied by other old women, cousins or aunts of hers, all lying on the bedspread playing cards or gossiping and drinking herbal teas – would tease me saying: 'Up there I've got your grandfather's teeth. Do you want to see?'

CHAPTER 18

Buenos Aires, 1940

The years after the marriage were marked by a greater closeness between Fernán and his second family. At last he could accompany, day by day, his younger children growing up. He learned to distinguish their laughter, their silences, their tears and their different ways of sleeping; he would think out loud to expand their education; and he composed instructive household verses to teach them to wash their hands, teeth and ears under his supervision: apparently banal activities that would become etched in some of the children – including my father – who as adults would be moved to tears undertaking the operation with their own little ones.

One night, Fernán returned home to the house on Boyacá street with a shortwave radio he had bought at a flea market to listen to the news from Peru. The apparatus – a varnished Addison with original grille and knobs that became known as 'the miniature Palace of Justice' – also brought my grandfather the first news of the Spanish Civil War and the rumblings of the upcoming Second World War. In those years, in the late Buenos Aires evenings, my father and his siblings would gather under the bed to hear the delirious speeches of Hitler and Mussolini broadcast by the news bulletins. They didn't understand any German or Italian, but there was something in their yelling that both intimidated and fascinated them. Instead of explaining who those men were, Fernán moved the heavy dial searching for music stations and took advantage to teach them all kind of songs, from 'Cara al Sol' – the Francoist hymn they learned by heart and would still sing as adults at the culmination of those reunions where I watched from the corner – to 'It's a Long Way to Tipperary', the song the British troops popularised in the First World War as they marched for France, by way of the 'Lambeth Walk', the hit song from a famous British musical that referenced the London neighbourhood of ragged beggars where Luis Benjamín and Cristina had once walked, which was danced with a choreography that Fernán performed comically whenever his children asked him to.

With these gestures, Fernán sought to compensate for the bittersweet years he had spent far away, or present only for brief periods, more a man who came and went from the house than a proper father. Even Juvenal, who at first had refused to behave normally in his presence, ended up accepting his affection and encouragement, despite a deep conviction that he would never wholly forgive his lies nor his hurtful shamelessness.

One evening Fernán and my grandmother sat the kids down in the living room of the apartment on Suipacha to put on a little show for them. While she pretended to descend the stairs of an airplane, wrapped in ruffs and boas, he recited a recent poem entitled 'Parce que je viens de Paris', written in the voice of a sophisticated woman who, recently arrived in Lima, dazzled all and sundry boasting about her life in the city of lights.

Just look at all this elegance,
this chic, this arrogance,
and tell me that it doesn't seem
as if I hail, from head to toe,
from Paris, France.
Do tell me if there is a wealth of waists
like this one on the city streets;
confess with all solemnity
that I remind you of Versailles
back in the empire's golden days.
And tell me if my life here isn't fine:
mornings in Madeleine,
noon on the Seine,
and twilight in the Bois.
For when this enterprise should end
and I return to my country
and land in Lima with the naughty gaze
that marks a French dame's eyes,
the men shall flock to me.
And I will tell them straight away:
Do you know why
I am so elegant, so fair?
Parce que je viens de Paris.
And when some fellow…
I can see him…
dares to whisper in my ear
some words I do not understand,
I'll tell him with my hand:
no, no, no, forgive me, brother,
I'll never tell you oui,
and never speak to me in Spanish,
parce que je viens de Paris.

Fernán's diction was so clear and Esperanza's gesticulations so convincing and amusing that the children would never forget these verses, especially Carlota, the only girl, the third of the seven children, who learned it by heart and over the years made it her star turn at family get-togethers.

* * *

Only as an adult did I learn about the many rebellions and protests that had punctuated Aunt Carlota's life. Baptised as Luisa Fernanda, one day she decided to call herself Carlota, changing her name legally as soon as she was old enough to do so. A decade later, guided by a guru from Indonesia who assured her that the prophet Elías had 'chosen' her, she renamed herself Elia Carlota, though no one ever called her that.

Earlier, at the age of fourteen, she had renounced the Catholic church when a priest gave her a strict telling off for claiming in confession that religion was 'a consolation invented to avoid the fear of death'. While the horrified confessor was recriminating her, she heard a voice in her conscience repeating incessantly 'you have faith, the priest does not; you have faith, the priest does not'.

My grandmother Esperanza couldn't help associating her only daughter's combative spirit with what had happened that night in the Estévez Palace, when Fernán feigned not to know her before a crowd of dignitaries. So she was not surprised when, as she grew older, Carlota would retaliate by taking the greatest interest in precisely the suitors her father least approved of.

The first of these was Julián del Campo, a friend of her brothers, whose surname happened to coincide with a famous soap brand. 'Are you here to sell me some soap?' Fernán scoffed when my future aunt introduced him at a diplomatic event in Buenos Aires. The only thing my grandfather achieved with this joke was to ensure that Carlota danced with Julián all night. 'They danced "Frenesí" fifteen times!' Fernán exclaimed to Esperanza before going to bed, still scandalised.

Another boyfriend was Juan Ernesto Wiener, a tall moustachioed German lad who one day in 1943 turned up at 2363 Serrano street, the family's final residence in Argentina. The young man was a paper plane fanatic and visited Carlota with his hands full of model planes that she hung from the bedroom ceiling. He didn't take long to ask for her hand, nor my aunt to accept. At that time Fernán was Peru's ambassador to Mexico. Alarmed by the sudden marriage plans, Esperanza contacted him, and he took the first flight from Mexico City to Buenos Aires with the express purpose of bringing Carlota back with him. He did so, but not without first tearing up all of Juan Ernesto Wiener's paper aeroplanes in front of her.

My grandfather knew it was only a matter of time before his twenty-year-old daughter – who was pretty, educated, spoke French and played waltzes on the guitar – fell in love again, but he was determined to put this off as long as possible.

He managed to do so until 1947, when he became ambassador to Brazil. His headaches resumed. Esperanza moved to Rio de Janeiro to help him run the embassy, and Carlota went with them, intending to study and socialise with the diplomatic circles. That is how she met Roberto Calzadillas, secretary to the Bolivian embassy, with whom she had a romance that lasted the summer of 1948. Fernán was furious when he found out, and since he could not directly oppose it – after all, Calzadillas was part of his circle – he began a campaign against him, writing in letters to his children that he was nothing but 'a hopeless piss-ass: in Bolivia they name you a diplomat in one revolution and sack you in the next'.

The same year another man appeared at the embassy who declared he was in love with Carlota: Paco Moncada, the son of a close friend of my grandfather. Fernán knew him as an idle social climber, a layabout who was a bullfighting fanatic, a small-time left-wing agitator who, to top it all, had been engaged years earlier to a Venezuelan woman, so without hesitation, to scotch the matter once and for all, he sent Carlota to continue her studies in Lima.

When the following year, now aged twenty-four, she came home saying she had fallen in love with a divorced man, my grandfather had exhausted his resources and said nothing. 'His name is David Ruzo and he's an archae-ologist, poet, photographer, humanist and interpreter of Nostradamus.' Fernán didn't sleep a wink that night. The next day, he asked around his press contacts and learned this was the very same Daniel Ruzo he had once garlanded with a prize for 'Young Poet of Peru', almost half a century earlier. He was now a man of seventy-two, father of five children by four different women. Carlota had met him at a country house in Chosica and been dazzled by his knowledge, his sophisticated discourse, his fine manner, his spiritual air. She talked with him for hours and knew she couldn't resist him from the moment she heard him say: 'No one understands people like us, but don't worry: you and I are going to under-stand each other.'

Although he was a consummate womaniser, Fernán accepted Ruzo because he was an intellectual. He was known for having discovered Marcahuasi, 'the most sacred mountain on earth', a monumental grouping of manmade caves and natural sculptures to the east of Lima that was supposed to have been a holy fortress for the ancient inhabitants of this region. Although the international scientific community had expressed reservations about the claims, for the most part Daniel Ruzo was considered a well-respected scholar.

Trying to behave reasonably, Fernán allowed Carlota to receive him in the La Paz house in Miraflores once a week, for a maximum of one hour, chaperoned by one of her older brothers.

But my future aunt had other plans. She began to take off at weekends to hole up with Daniel at his Chosica house, and despite the threats Fernán made when he found out, she continued escaping until he gave up.

Carlota and Ruzo lived together for several years, spent between Peru, Brazil – where they married in 1960 at the Nossa Senhora da Gloria church in Rio de Janeiro, with Víctor Raúl Haya de la Torre, founder of Peru's socialist Aprista party, as one of their witnesses – and Mexico, where they later divorced only to marry again.

I knew none of this when I met her in the early 1980s, but it was enough to see the excitement and murmurs that greeted her arrival, or to hear her talk about anything at all or just observe her in action for a while to intuit something of her adventurous life.

* * *

My grandfather's work as a journalist, his failed political exploits, his divergences with communist thought and open quarrels with the early leaders of the Aprista party are already well-documented in dusty volumes and have little place in this book. Less has been written about his itinerant diplomatic work, but perhaps there is less to say. In eighteen years of missions, Fernán moved from Uruguay to Mexico and from there to Brazil, where he held exhausting meetings, organised select parties on the anniversary of Peruvian independence where he sang waltzes, rancheras, tangos and cuplés, attended performances, parades and cultural soirées where he made speeches that overused words like 'hope', 'united', 'the Americas', 'faith', 'fraternity' and 'motherland'. He gave and received decorations. He visited radio stations to read his own and his father's poems and to offer his opinions on the disastrous consequences of the Second World War. He befriended presidents, ambassadors, monsignors, artists and writers, and eminent, eccentric, mundane and sinister figures of all kinds, later attending their birthdays, weddings and funerals. One night in Mexico in 1940 at the Belmont cantina in the Juárez district, a favourite of politicians and journalists alike, Fernán met a Catalan man by the name of Jacques Mornard, son of a Belgian diplomat. They clicked immediately and for two weeks they met there every night to speak about politics and literature, amid the hubbub of people devouring blue corn tortillas, drinking cold beer and listening to the Mexican corridos sung by ancient blind troubadours. They were just becoming firm friends when the Catalan abruptly stopped showing up at the Belmont. The next time my grandfather saw him was on the front page of the newspapers. His face turned ash-grey when he read that Jacques Mornard was in fact Ramón Mercader and was not the son of a diplomat but a spy and the previous evening, just as he was waiting for him to show up at the Belmont, he had murdered Leon Trotsky in Coyoacán with an ice axe.

* * *

In 1951, Fernán returned to Peru definitively.

Thirty years had passed since the morning he had boarded the ship that carried him into exile. Over the decades he had only once – in 1937 – been able to make a brief visit to Lima, on the occasion of the centenary of his father Luis Benjamín's birth. After countless bureaucratic complications, the government allowed him to arrange the celebrations together with a special commission, and he dedicated himself to this matter as soon as he arrived. Over those busy days, his siblings received anonymous calls demanding to know 'Why so much racket about the illegitimate son of a priest?' A century later, the ghost of Gregorio Cartagena was still finding ways to trouble the Cisneros, reviving ill-fated pages in the family's past that they believed forgotten, and reminding them that the paternal surname they bore was a placeholder, not a legacy.

While Fernán was ambassador to Mexico, living in the luxuriant hills of the Lomas de Chapultepec neighbourhood, he received a lengthy visit from his elder daughters, Rosaura and Magdalena. The Cisneros Caicedo brothers, meanwhile – Fortunato, Sarino and Benito – never left Lima, where they worked. Esperanza remained in Buenos Aires, living now in Serrano street, cooking for the neighbours, resorting to barter when she was left without a cent for the newspaper, sowing clover, lilies and begonias in clay pots and waiting for her youngest children to finish school.

Until then, contact between the two halves of the family had been limited to a tempestuous nocturnal visit by Sarino to the house on Boyacá, while he was working as Fernán's secretary. That night, he persuaded his father to let him come up the stairs to the house 'where the others lived' for a few minutes. That is how he met Esperanza – whom he always referred to as 'Dad's mistress' – and his younger half-siblings, who stared at him as if he were a stranger, never imagining he shared their blood.

Much time passed before the two sides met again. One day in May 1942, Benito, the younger of the Cisneros Caicedo, felt a pressing – almost biological – need to build a bridge towards that misty island represented by his younger siblings there in Argentina and, without consulting his father or older brothers, wrote a letter to Juvenal, the one closest to him in age. He had heard that he would soon travel to Peru and wanted to win his friendship before the feelings between the families – still genuine due to the mediation of Fernán – hardened into artifice.

Lima, 20 May 1942

My dear Juvenal:

You at the age of twenty-two and I at twenty-six are soon to embrace for the first time. I hope it is a warm embrace, so that we may remain united in the future.

I am Benito, your brother, and I seek with an open heart, unbidden, to inveigle my way into your affections. I'm sure we've sensed each other's presence without daring to meet.

Today I am resolved to seek your friendship and I hope it shall be everlasting.

I know that you are a good person. That you fill our father's heart with hope and that your studious efforts shall soon earn you a status that will be a source of great joy for him. He deserved that at least one of us should bring him this satisfaction and I am glad that it fell to you. This alone is enough to make me fond of you.

Write to me. Help me to bring together these lives that for so long have been kept apart, and tell me about Carlota, Gaucho, Gustavo, Roque, Reynaldo and Adrián. Give them all a silent kiss in my name.

My fraternal affection awaits your words and your sentiments.

With warmest regards,
Your brother Benito

When he finished the letter, Juvenal recalled the morning he followed his father across Buenos Aires and turned a corner to discover him entering another house and greeting other children – 'Was Benito one of the ones I saw?' he wondered now – and he understood that, at the age of twenty-two, his mission was none other than to facilitate contact between the two clans. It was thanks to this one letter that my grandfather's older and younger sets of children began to build a relationship where the previous generation had failed.

The Cisneros Caicedo and the Cisneros Vizquerra were children of the same man, though not the same father. The older ones had known a young and elusive Fernán, up to his neck in busy offices, bars, cafés and whatever bohemian goings-on there were at the time in Lima, a fellow without much money who was always ready to fight, risking his neck and soon discovering the inside of prison cells, and the hell of exile. These first children had no chance to study or flourish and they ended up working in temporary jobs or practising professions they were not trained for. Sarino and Benito were the most hard-working and achieved a certain level of prosperity that allowed them to secure their future. Fortunato was less fortunate. He was tiresome, narrow-minded, party-loving and irresponsible and ended up unemployed, his wife leaving him for the same reason, a cause of shame to his parents.

With this record, it was only natural that Benito should be impressed that Juvenal had completed his studies. What he didn't know was that his perseverance had more to do with a desire to overcome and defeat his father than with pleasing him.

Unlike the older set, the Cisneros Vizquerra were children of a Fernán defined by the poverty and strictures of exile, who later became ambassador and gradually acquired a lifestyle more fitting to his position. His salary was never enough but did allow him to cover countless costs and ease the final years of his exile. This Fernán, who also relied on a hardened accomplice in Esperanza, was able to shape with greater care his younger children, marking and defining their personalities. No one could say, however, that the father of those children was a better man, since he availed so extensively of lies and pretence.

The younger Fernán, dressed in his single suit and pair of good shoes, the passionate reporter who earned his thirty or fifty pounds a month to pay off his myriad debts, perhaps precisely because he was poor and insecure was also a real and present father of flesh and blood. By contrast the older Fernán, a much more judicious, refined and regarded man, who had learned not to suffer shortages, who travelled the world in boats, who appeared in newspapers, who had a car and driver in Uruguay, Mexico and Brazil, this settled and uninhibited man who rubbed shoulders with leading literary lights, was also an absent father, smart but elusive, and who cared above all about returning to Peru and that his double family life would not damage his reputation as a decent and sober-minded intellectual.

This is how the older and the younger Cisneros children ended up sharing Fernán. They knew they were siblings but they also felt they were the children of a two-faced father who, hard as he tried, was unable to present a consistent self to any of them. Each child had a different father, each constructed a father out of different spiritual materials to all the rest, and the epistolary efforts of Benito and Juvenal to bring them together were at the same time attempts to unite the scattered pieces of this broken jigsaw that was my grandfather.

I say jigsaw and think immediately of that strange and revealing photograph he had taken in March 1949 when he attended a UN General Assembly in New York. In this picture with its black backdrop, Fernán appears multiplied around an oval table – a mirror trick very popular at the time. The image suggests five Fernán Cisneros at a kind of executive meeting. Five individuals with the same face, seated, meditative, gazing at each other as if business partners or fellow guests. Five extensions of the same being. Each one seems to embody a facet of my grandfather: the journalist, the diplomat, the ambassador, the poet, the bigamist. What decisions are they negotiating? I look at this photograph now and imagine that perhaps something similar takes place in our minds: a group of individuals sits down each day to debate which of them will usurp or direct, for the next twenty-four hours or for an even briefer time, the personality of the person whose head they live in. Is that what we are, in the end? A succession of creatures with the same façade? A cluster of characters, each one forged in its own compartment? The sum or rather the intersection of an indeterminate number of alter egos? How confusing yet hypnotic I found this photograph each time I saw it in a credenza in the mysterious house on La Paz.

My grandfather copied and repeated.

They were all the same. Identical, yet different.

To this day I don't know which of the five was the original model.

★ ★ ★

Fernán died of a heart attack on 17 March 1954.

He was at the home of the director of *La Prensa* planning his return to the newspaper with a column, the details of which were yet to be determined, accompanied by another executive.

Suddenly, in the middle of the negotiations, Fernán felt a burning sensation in his chest followed by difficulty breathing and a growing paralysis in his right arm. The director asked him twice what was wrong and saw his face was so distorted he laid him out on the floor while the other man present ran to get a nearby cardiologist by the name of Ferradas. Their quick response was not enough.

By the time the doctor arrived, my grandfather's heart, rattled, I imagine, by the accumulated years of persecutions, extenuating episodes and the many secrets it had never confessed, had already burst.

CHAPTER 19

Lima, 2014

When I was young and ignorant I used to boast about my paternal surname. Although as an adolescent I strove to criticise my father's side of the family in silence, once I had grown fond of their roistering idiosyncrasies and their Miraflores politesse, I set aside these early signs, forgot (or tried to forget) the many enigmas and abandoned myself to the charm of their traditions and stories until I became their most enthusiastic broadcaster.

At the Cisneros family gatherings I was the one who encouraged us all to sing the childhood songs of my aunts and uncles, the tangos and zarzuelas from their youth, the military songs, our grandfather's verses that they had put to music, the boleros in Portuguese they intoned with their eyes closed, as if longing for a previous life.

I believed I knew the history of my surname and clung to it like an umbilical cord. This boasting, I now realise, was a way of hiding my insecurity, but at the time I found it very comfortable to stay on the side of those who defended the advantages and the nobility of what we called our 'lineage'.

Unlike my second, maternal surname – which never aroused my investigative curiosity – I saw the paternal name as an emblem. My forefathers had paraded it through the world's great cities, endowing it with prestige, distinction, intellectual standing and patriotism. And then there was the Buenos Aires factor: all that my grandfather, my father and my uncles and aunts had experienced there made me believe that I too, by some arbitrary extension, had an Argentinian tenor of some kind, which at the age of twenty I stupidly exhibited as an air of superiority.

I remember the trip I made to Spain with the sole desire of reaching the village of Cisneros, in Palencia, some 300 kilometres from Madrid, a place I had assessed as the epicentre of my surname; prior to the Colombian municipality that also bore the name, once inhabited by the Tahami people; and to Villa Cisneros, a city in Western Sahara founded under Spanish sovereignty but now under the control of Morocco.

Still fixed in my memory are the yellowed grasslands around the road into the village, the semi-deserted narrow streets of the centre and the fountain in its plaza, attended by two stone swans – *cisnes* in Spanish. How often had I heard that the toponymy of our surname was based on the name of these birds: *Cisneros*, a place where *cisnes* live. And that this was how friends of my great-grandfather had referred to his quiet, dapper, affected manner: 'You, oh immortal swan, you shall sing forever more', someone declaimed at his funeral.

Entering the village of Cisneros, an elderly couple, Maruja and Manolo, eagerly greeted me as if they hadn't seen a tourist in years. They took me on a tour to show me the dome and gloomy interiors of the Church of San Facundo and San Primitivo, the patron saints of the village. It was they (the old couple, not the saints) who told me the traumatic story of a woman who had died in the middle of a procession when the clapper from the church bell fell on her; and then they told me in great detail about the famous Cardinal Cisneros who had been born right here, in one of these houses, a theory gainsaid a few minutes later by the sacristan when he appeared from nowhere and put an end to these tales.

I recall this journey and I see myself walking down De la Cruz street, entering a café – the only café in the village – filled with tables occupied by octogenarians eating lentils and dealing cards to play a game the barman tells me is called Tute. I see myself contending with a grotesque drunk – the only drunk in the village – outside the Las Acacias bar; following a bullfight on the TV screen in the butcher's shop; and returning with a gentle kick the runaway ball of some children – the only children in the village – playing at penalty shootouts against the grimy wall of a mansion house.

* * *

I returned from that excursion feeling very deeply a Cisneros, and from that point on I held aloft my surname not only as an emblem, but as an honorific legacy, a legacy that in a country like Peru – a country for centuries divided by caste, hierarchy and clan, riven by social discrimination, where surnames can be letters of safe passage or guarantees, or indeed curses and sentences that determine the fate and destiny of individuals in advance – a legacy that I felt sure would sooner or later offer me certain prerogatives. A surname like mine, I thought then, associated with a set of social, academic, literary and political virtues – even when so many of its supposed beneficiaries had fallen into economic hardship, moral decline and other forms of decadence – would continue to be an advantage. A crude, shameful, pathetic, unjust advantage, but an effective one.

I felt that I had an undying bond of blood with my family. An alliance like that among soldiers. An indestructibly welded joint. And I felt that way until the day I learned that we were only 'Cisneros' out of error, negligence and cowardice, and that we should have been called 'Cartagena', like Gregorio my great-great-grandfather, the man who whispered our lineage into being together with Nicolasa Cisneros, and who was later roundly denied by his children, and by the children of his children, and by their children until he was erased, as if he had never existed, as if he were not the seed, the womb, the backbone.

When I discovered that my paternal surname was another, I felt dislocated, as if by an earth tremor. As if over all the previous years I had venerated the wrong patriarch and acted on the basis of mistaken premises. The upright and irreproachable men I had admired for as long as I could remember, the flesh of my flesh, abruptly became blurred, reduced to timid, vulgar and inconsequential individuals. My former clarity became turbid. Clay became crust. The tight weave became unstitched, revealing its threads.

However, something flourished amid that confusion. At first, I was surprised that these discoveries had gone unperceived or simply seemed unimportant to everyone else. Then it stopped mattering. It was enough to know that my surname was an imposition to reassess my own notions of 'family' and 'identity' and cast a new look at my past. Those were days of questions that came in droves. What other things might be false? What other lies had we internalised? Who were we really? Where did we come from? Who was this Cartagena fellow anyway? What did he do? Why didn't he allow his surname to be passed on? Why was no one proud to be his descendant?

I was so eager to dismantle the hidden history of my ancestors that I set about identifying the source of the 'error' without any further delay. I felt that I was acting, not on a whim or wilfully, but out of a kind of preordained mandate. And just as I had previously exhumed my father to write a novel about him or about my relationship with him, I obliged myself to repeat the operation with the men who came before my father, trying to stage something like a posthumous confrontation between them, to see if they could come to agreement on anything.

I rummaged around above and below what was permitted, delving into holes and cracks with no real idea where my inquiries would lead. Only after removing the rustiest of cogs did I discover what previous generations had considered a 'stain', an 'ignominy' that undermined the family's prestige: the fact we all descended from a priest.

A priest, no less.

The evidence, ironically, survives thanks to the oversights and whispers of those who sought to correct the ancestral root by tearing it up.

By that point I no longer cared if my quest was viewed as indiscretion, disobedience or sabotage. Nor if the most conservative family members saw me as unruly, a cretin or a traitor. The discord and reproaches were the least of it. To me it felt more despicable to have the facts and do nothing with them. My indignation might be as erratic and deplorable as they liked, but it was aimed at a legitimate goal, at least for me: to determine my origins as precisely as possible, and thereby refute the incomplete stories we all held to be true – stories that had been passed down to me and that I myself had repeated time and again – so that I could tell them the way I wanted to in the future, but in the full knowledge of what I was doing.

On top of that, how much could my research really trouble them when so little of the former family mystique was left, when we weren't the same as we'd once been. All the traditions that defined us and that had seemed eternal or immortal had faded with the gradual disappearance of the older generation, the forebears who knew by heart the stories, songs, poems, anecdotes and truths. Grandma Esperanza. Aunt Agripina. Uncle Juvenal. Uncle Adrián. My father, the Gaucho. Those who hadn't died were close to it, or fed up with life, or too weak to remember. The big house in La Paz wasn't even available to host us all like before. That kingdom had become a limbo. Now everyone got together in their own little groupings, in rented flats or rundown residences, to gossip about the others. Or perhaps not even that.

What is certain is that those fondly remembered clan gatherings had suddenly dissolved, like a great building that collapses and disappears from the landscape in a matter of seconds, leaving a hole in the ground. So how much could it really bother them that I should come and rake through the rubble?

I'm not sure of the exact day that I learned of the existence of the controversial Gregorio Cartagena and the phantasmal Roberto Benjamín, but I know that this day never ended and instead stayed with me. There are days like that, decisive days, that don't go away, don't become a memory. However much time passes, their impact never fades. They are days that alter our experience of the world. Days that adhere to our very fibre and character. That endure not as shards, as resonance or echo, but like a piece of glass in the heart.

I don't feel like I was disappointed when I learned about Gregorio, but rather fascinated by the revelation about his forbidden love for Nicolasa Cisneros, and by all that it meant for my own life story and innate emotional constitution. It became impossible, for example, not to relate these discoveries to the vivid interest I had had in the priesthood in the final years of high school, an interest that over the years I dismissed as insignificant, but that now, with the news that I had a priest for a forefather, seemed less a juvenile confusion than a true atavistic remnant, an inner pulse of the vocation my great-great-grandfather Gregorio had pursued.

Nor could I stop thinking about the great sense of guilt I had always felt about sins, including the most venal and trivial, which caused me to maintain for years, before any kind of authority figure, an endless spiral of blatant lies, half-confessions and false repentance. Such was my weakness that every time I attended mass, when it came to saying the Confiteor prayer of penitence, I closed my eyes and asked for salvation with a fear and sense of necessity that, I now understood, came from far back.

Today I know that Cartagena is my genetic and hereditary surname. The surname that was concealed and replaced. I am a Cartagena from the beginning of this story, though others have told me and I have persuaded myself that I should bear another name. A name that I feel to be my own, though it is not.

* * *

One morning I read on a front page at a newspaper stand two pieces of information that seemed to have come straight from my family pre-history. One, from Huánuco, reported the collapse of a bridge connecting it with Huacaybamba that had left this remote town in a state of isolation not unlike that of 1828, when the story of my great-great-grandmother Nicolasa and the priest began. The other piece, even harder to believe, reported that in a province of Arequipa, a parish priest by the name of Cartagena had been photographed leaving a hotel in the company of a young woman. Reading one after the other, in large letters on a single page, the words 'Huacaybamba', 'priest', 'Cartagena' and 'woman' made my head spin. A simple coincidence, but for a moment I felt certain that events I had only recently disinterred had transferred themselves to the present day. It was as if a part of this book had extended into real life, taking place in parallel to its writing.

At that moment, I was struck by the need to seek out my great-great-grandfather once more; his remains, that is. I didn't want to see his bones at the Presbítero Maestro, but a portrait of him. I felt that somewhere there must exist a proper likeness of Gregorio, and that I wouldn't be at peace until I saw it. Uncle Gustavo and I had searched the many floors of the National Library, the rooms of the Independence Society, and the halls of the Archbishopric; we'd rummaged in the oldest photograph archives and even in the backrooms of Huánuco's churches; but something told me that if I were only to insist at the school in Huácar that bears his name, I would find a new clue.

I travelled there alone and on exiting the airport took a bus that left me at the edge of the province of Ambo. I walked to the lethargic district of Huácar and once there I crossed the bustling central market. Each Monday the local farmers gather on the outskirts of this market to sell their produce. It was a Monday, so a barrage of motorcycle taxis let out a never-ending roar, while in the distance a Ferris wheel rose, lonely, incongruous, among dozens of stalls and carts where the residents – most of them women between forty and sixty years old, dressed in sweaters and skirts – exhibited their wares: pulses, tubers, corn, toasted corn, fruits, citrus juices, pumpkins, guinea pigs, partridges and woolly rams tied by the legs, ready for slaughter. In the background, loudspeakers blasted out mournful huayno songs of rootlessness and heartbreak.

I walked for five dusty blocks until I reached the secondary school on Comercio street, close to the central plaza: the school named after Gregorio Cartagena with its three pavilions, 200 students and shabby but proud classrooms. From there I could still hear the flutes and guitars of the music in the market.

There were more people around on my second visit. This time, I did find the school director behind a crooked desk. He had a name impossible to forget: Silverio Serrano. An aging, ailing man, stuffed into an unironed suit jacket with sleeves that retreated up his arms whenever he waved them around as he spoke. Beside his office, an iron bell hung from a beam that, I was told, was used to call to assemblies or to mass, warn of earthquakes, and mark the beginning and end of recess.

Don Silverio asked me to come in, and when he heard the story of the priest who gave his name to the school that he had directed for twenty years, he turned pale. He was so eager to learn more and also to keep the conversation confidential that he got up, closed the door and slid the latch closed, leaving a cluster of teachers with urgent queries waiting outside. Only then did he confess to me that the matter of Cartagena's children was completely new to him.

'So, there were seven bastards?' he asked, both incredulous and amused, running a hand through his tinted hair. To satisfy his curiosity, I recounted some details of the priest's youth, the complaints made against him during his years as sub-deacon, and how his surname had been frozen in time, becoming a kind of onerous shadow or fetters for my great-grandfather and his brothers, and those of us who came after.

'Sadly,' I told him, 'I have not found a single painting of him, that would allow me to learn he looked like.'

Something lit up in the smiling eyes of this taciturn man.

'You're in luck,' he replied. 'Here I have a small oil painting hidden away. You've no idea what I had to do to get hold of it.'

Don Silverio explained that he had discovered it buried in some gloomy chests and had to beg the director on his knees to let him have the painting, which would otherwise have been lost forever.

Listening not so much to his words as to their echo I felt my stomach turn over. The director stood up and, hunchbacked as he was, headed over to a cabinet set into the long wall of the room. He dragged his feet so much that it seemed to take an eternity. I wondered if this was really happening. Eight years after having disturbed the foundations of the family secret, I was finally going to meet my great-great-grandfather. Don Silverio turned around, holding up the image. A painting of some thirty by twenty centimetres, with the following legend at the bottom:

Dr Gregorio Cartagena
Parish Priest of Huácar, Deputy of Huánuco.
Founder of the College of Sciences and its first rector in 1829.

There he was, looking at me, in his black frock coat, the eternally elusive Cartagena. Finally he was showing his face. It was oval and pale. Sullen features. A timeless expression. The forehead as vast as a bay. The ears and lips so similar to those of my grandfather, my father, and my uncles, all Cisneros. If the painting was from 1829, I deduced that Cartagena would have been forty-one at the time it was painted. Five years after he met Nicolasa and just one since he became father to Juan. I grasped the frame firmly and saw or believed I saw in the likeness of Gregorio some trace of his many setbacks suffered in silence. I paused on the shadows around his eyes, his prominent cheekbones, the arc of his mouth, his smooth chin, the early signs of baldness not inherited by his children, but by his grandchildren.

'It all started with him,' I thought and suddenly I felt sure that liberating it from this hiding place would be a way of mending things.

Don Silverio seemed to read my mind because he right away uttered, without hesitation, exactly the words I wanted to hear: 'Take it. It's no good to me any longer.'

A few hours later I boarded the plane with the portrait in a bag that I placed at my feet before take-off. During the flight, from time to time I would glance inside to check that the priest was still there, and I smiled imagining the shock Uncle Gustavo would have when he saw it.

'The mystery is over,' I murmured to no one in particular.

I finally had in my hands the longed-for foundation stone of a building now in ruins, and now – precisely because of its ruinous state – restored. I could at last take in the shape of this stone and assess its value: it was no longer out of reach nor unknown to me.

I was filled then with a feeling of barrenness. Of triumph and defeat at one and the same time. I thought about the people of Huácar, the stories of Cartagena, the inventions of Nicolasa, the adjacent graves in the cemetery, the anger of Pedro Cisneros when he learned the truth. I thought about the poverty of Luis Benjamín, the double life of Fernán, the silences of my father; and I asked myself why all of this still fascinated and pained me.

And when later I looked out the window and spied the city of Lima on the edge of the ocean, and saw the murky sea contained by the coast, and the houses and buildings haphazardly scattered along the grey line of the cliffs, I felt or I knew that this would be the last frontier I would have to cross in a very long time.

ACKNOWLEDGEMENTS

I could not have written this novel without the testimony, guidance and advice of Gonzalo Cisneros Vizquerra. Equally invaluable was the support of Renato Cisneros Vizquerra, Carola Cisneros Vizquerra, Luis Fernán Cisneros Ferreyros, as well as that of my friends Laura Gutiérrez Arbulú, Rodolfo Tello Carranza, Jerónimo Pimentel Prieto and Eugenio Calmet Bohme.

To all of them, my most sincere thanks.

TRANSLATOR'S

ACKNOWLEDGEMENTS

My warmest thanks – once again – to Robin Myers, not only for her countless editing improvements, but also for bringing her talent as a translator of verse to the poems quoted in the novel.

Fionn Petch
Berlin, August 2022

CHARCO PRESS

Director & Editor: Carolina Orloff
Director: Samuel McDowell

www.charcopress.com

You Shall Leave Your Land was published on
80gsm Munken Premium Cream paper.

The text was designed using Bembo 11.5 and ITC Galliard.

Printed in August 2022 by TJ Books
Padstow, Cornwall, PL28 8RW using responsibly
sourced paper and environmentally-friendly adhesive.